"Deeply moving depictions of family life and the progression of alcoholism and its effects—as well as a fascinating take on the afterlife we all will face."
—*G. Miki Hayden*, New York Times-*plauded Edgar winner*

"Excellent handling of a dysfunctional family actually coming full circle. The topic of life after death puts an intriguing spin on this story. Captivating!"
—*Victoria Christopher-Murray, author of* Truth Be Told, *and* Sinners & Saints, *plus many other titles*

*"Roni Teson is a gifted storyteller who brings to life a hardened alcoholic with the same grace and honesty she employs in writing about an angel. Her timing is flawless—*Heaven or Hell *is a page-turner. I didn't want it to end!"*
—*Karen Coccioli, Author of* The Yellow Braid

"This was absolutely phenomenal! I did cry and figured the end would be heartbreaking, but I ended up smiling as I read it. Wonderful story!"
—Diana Cox, www.novelproofreading.com

HEAVEN

OR

HELL

A Novel by

RONI TESON

BALBOA.
PRESS
A DIVISION OF HAY HOUSE

ISBN: 978-1-4525-5498-3 (sc)
ISBN: 978-1-4525-5499-0 (hc)
ISBN: 978-1-4525-5497-6 (e)
Library of Congress Control Number: 2012911858

Balboa Press books may be ordered through booksellers or by contacting:
Balboa Press
A Division of Hay House
1663 Liberty Drive
Bloomington, IN 47403
www.balboapress.com
1-(877) 407-4847

Because of the dynamic nature of the Internet, any web addresses or links contained in
this book may have changed since publication and may no longer be valid. The views
expressed in this work are solely those of the author and do not necessarily reflect the
views of the publisher, and the publisher hereby disclaims any responsibility for them.

The author of this book does not dispense medical advice or prescribe the use
of any technique as a form of treatment for physical, emotional, or medical
problems without the advice of a physician, either directly or indirectly. The
intent of the author is only to offer information of a general nature to help you
in your quest for emotional and spiritual well-being. In the event you use any
of the information in this book for yourself, which is your constitutional right,
the author and the publisher assume no responsibility for your actions.

Any people depicted in stock imagery provided by Thinkstock are models,
and such images are being used for illustrative purposes only.
Certain stock imagery © Thinkstock.

Printed in the United States of America

Balboa Press rev. date: 7/31/2012

For Katie and Izabella

Acknowledgements:

The endeavor of writing a book can be quite overwhelming, as I learned. Much more than the creative thought process is involved in pulling together the pages of a novel. It is with much gratitude that I acknowledge the following people: G. Miki Hayden, my editor and mentor. Victoria Christopher, my dear friend and coach. Karen Coccioli, my best cheerleader, and a most talented author. Diana Cox, for her detailed proofreading. Shauna Gerber, my first reader, and the many other readers who provided much brilliant feedback. And the myriad of other folks who've touched my life during this writing process. I thank you all.

CHAPTER 1

JOE OBSERVED HIS BODY FROM ABOVE. He was totally confused because only moments earlier he and Father Benjamin had entered Skid Row in search of the General. They were walking side by side, Joe with his cane and the father chatting endlessly at him. Then suddenly Joe seemed to be disembodied, somehow floating over the top of his body watching the drama unfold.

The priest held his cell phone up to his ear, and Joe heard the other end of the call as if it were he who was on the phone, and not Father Benjamin.

"Nine-one-one, what's your emergency?"

"This is Father Benjamin," the man blurted out. Then the next few sentences rolled off his tongue as one complete word with several syllables. "He's not breathing. We're out at Washington and Fourteenth, close to the parish where we work."

"Okay, sir ... Take a deep breath, please." The phone crackled in Joe's ear. "What's the address? Are you outside?" a woman asked.

"Yes, at the base of Skid Row. There isn't an address. Send an ambulance." Father Benjamin dropped the phone and began pumping Joe's chest.

"Sir, sir ... Are you there?" Joe heard the miniature voice yell up from the gutter where the phone lay.

He watched in disbelief as Father Benjamin breathed air into his mouth, pumped on his chest, and scooped up the cell phone in one swift sweep. The muck from the street splattered on the priest's cheek as he put the phone to his ear. "Yes, yes, I'm sorry. He's not breathing and please know that this is not a normal call from this area. I'm a priest and he's an addiction counselor. Please send somebody now—Washington and Fourteenth." Beads of sweat covered the father's brow.

The priest knelt over Joe's body while the homeless in the area went about their business as usual, paying no mind to the man and his patient. One old guy stepped over Joe's legs without a glance, another man eyed Joe's cane, and a woman lit a cigarette stub from the wrong side while she sat down on the curb to the right of Joe's feet.

Father Benjamin, in turn, ignored the folks on the street while he worked persistently on the body—Joe's body. And to Joe's amazement, from somewhere above his body, he continued to watch his own chest move with the air his friend, the priest, provided.

The man pounded on Joe's chest. "Breathe, damn it."

Father Benjamin then wiped his forehead with the back of his hand while he quickly viewed the surrounding area. He seemed to be searching for help, and Joe felt sorry for him as he couldn't see a single capable person in the vicinity.

After the priest swung his head back down to breathe again—once, twice—for his friend, finally Joe coughed and gasped for air. And at that moment, the floating feeling came to an end.

Joe somehow landed flat on his back, startled at his new vantage point. He was now in the scene he'd been viewing from a distance seconds earlier, and he was looking up into the face of Father Benjamin—strange.

Did that just happen? Joe thought to himself. *Did I just die?*

"Oh, thank God you're breathing." The priest slumped down on the sidewalk.

"You better have breasts or at the very least a good reason to be kissing me." Joe gagged and spit, and somehow managed to lift his left eyebrow while he chuckled a little.

"Sorry, just a collar." Father Benjamin motioned toward his neck.

"What's that crap on your cheek. Don't put that near me." Joe coughed and laughed a little again, all the while leaving one eye open. While he struggled to breathe, the salty taste of blood entered his mouth.

The priest ignored Joe's comments. He wiped his phone on his pants and quickly punched in some numbers.

"Aaay, you're not so immaculate now, are you, Father." Joe motioned with his head toward the father's now dirty pants and shirt. Oh, how he enjoyed teasing the priest about his manicured hands and perfectly pressed pants.

But Father Benjamin frowned at Joe and focused on the call he was making. This time, Joe only heard one side of the conversation, and the seriousness of the incident finally occurred to him.

"Yes, this is Father Benjamin, again. I've got the same emergency at Fourteenth and Washington. One of our counselors is down, and I called you over five minutes ago. Where's the ambulance?" he demanded.

Joe closed his eyes. He was so tired now ... If he could just sleep for a second ...

"Where are they? I've got him breathing, but it's shallow." The priest raised his voice to a volume loud enough to rouse Joe from his lethargy.

"No. No." Joe tried to sit up and immediately fell back to the sidewalk.

"Stay down, please." With the phone held to his own chest, the priest put his hand on Joe and held him down, then spoke to Joe as he would to a child. "You're going to the hospital this time. You're not going to joke your way out of this."

"We've gotta find the General," Joe slurred. His head was heavy, and his body refused to follow his commands.

The father turned away from Joe and talked into the phone. "He's slurring now, and not too coherent. No! The man hasn't been drinking. He's an alcoholism counselor. As I said before, this isn't a normal call from around here."

Joe on some level understood the priest's motive for being so pushy. His friend normally wasn't so rude. But over the years Skid Row had become one of the most unpleasant areas in Los Angeles for police and emergency personnel to work. Unfortunately, things had become even worse lately, and it could take up to an hour or more to get help into the area.

When Joe coughed up blood, Father Benjamin rolled him on his side. "Come on, come on. What's taking so long? He's coughing up blood now."

Joe's head pounded, and his lungs burned as he gulped for air and watched Father Benjamin snap his phone shut and stuff it in his pocket.

The priest ran toward the street when the sound of a distant siren began to grow stronger. "Here, here," Joe heard the priest yell from the middle of the road where he stood waving his arms frantically at the ambulance. Then Joe must've dozed off or something because instantly it seemed as if two men jumped out of the vehicle.

A scruffy old bag man walked off with Joe's cane, the same man who'd been eyeing the cane previously.

"Unbelievable." The priest ran to Joe's side yelling, "Hey, you with the cane."

"Leave it." Joe grabbed Father Benjamin's pant leg. "He's going to use it more than I will. We both know what's next for me." Joe closed his eyes and released his friend's leg.

"Okay. As you wish." The priest turned to the emergency crew and spoke in an efficient, professional manner. "This is Juan Joseph Torres. He's a counselor at the parish. We were only here for a few minutes when he passed out. He has advanced stage cirrhosis of the liver. He's been sober over five years, and up until a few minutes ago, he used a cane to get around. I gave him mouth-to-mouth because he wasn't breathing. It took a few minutes to resuscitate him."

"Okay, Father. Thank you." The emergency worker looked so young—as if he were still in high school.

He turned to Joe and spoke loudly while enunciating every syllable. "Mr. Torres, can you answer a few questions?"

The bigger, quiet one put an oxygen mask on Joe and set up a monitor. He kept busy working on Joe while the young one spoke.

"Sure," Joe answered through the oxygen mask.

"My name is Nick. How old are you, Mr. Torres?" The young one held his pen poised on his clipboard.

"Sixty-six."

"What's the date, today?" he continued in a loud voice.

"I'm not deaf, Nick. I can hear you," Joe snapped. "It's Tuesday, September 10."

"Who's the president?"

"Lee something or other." Joe's eyes fluttered.

"Are you with me, Mr. Torres?" Joe felt someone push on his cheeks.

"Yes, yes." His eyes flicked open in response to the pressure. "Easy, please."

Nick whispered something to his big co-worker and turned back to Joe, who had just shut his eyes again. "Okay, I prefer it when you're sassy with me. But I can work with this in-and-out stuff. We're taking you to Memorial."

Joe opened his eyes and scowled. "Again, kid, you don't need to yell. I can hear you."

"The toxins in your body are causing some of this, but we need a doctor to look at you."

Joe was quickly moved into the ambulance. Father Benjamin jumped in beside him, and with sirens blaring, they drove to the closest hospital. Joe was aware of the fact that both emergency workers, the young one and the big one, thought he was about to die. He felt as though he *was* dying, in reality. He knew he even looked dead already—a skinny shrunken body with a puffed out stomach and yellow skin.

He sensed the two paramedics wanted off this duty as soon as possible.

After only minutes they arrived at Memorial Hospital and he was whisked into the emergency room, where a second round of technicians stabilized him.

Tubes, lines, and monitors were attached all over his body. He was admitted into the hospital with discussions of a hospice if necessary. Simply put, if he made it through the week, they were going to move him out of the hospital and into an extended care facility to await his demise.

"Father, I have a favor to ask of you." Joe lay perfectly still in his hospital bed and stared up at the ceiling when he spoke.

"Anything, anything at all," answered the priest.

"I want to see my daughter before I die."

The priest stood in silence and gaped at Joe with his mouth partially dropped.

"What the heck are you staring at?" Joe raised his voice as loud as he could, which seemed to be just above a whisper. "I would have said the F word there if you weren't a priest," he then mumbled.

"Well, they said you were going to hallucinate ... and I ... well, a daughter?" The priest hesitated.

"No, I'm not making this up. I have a daughter," Joe croaked.

"What are you talking about? I've known you for years. You don't have a daughter." Father Benjamin shook his head and seemed to snicker.

"Well, there are some things, my friend, that you just don't know." Joe raised his brow. "I'm sorry."

The nurse entered the room. "Is it time now, Mr. Torres?"

"No, Willa. Thank you, though. I need an hour here."

"An hour's a long time to go with that pain," she said.

"I know. I need to be clear minded for my friend." Joe motioned his head to the right. The nurse's eyes followed, and she jumped when she saw the priest.

"Oh, my. I'm sorry, Father. I didn't know you were here." She held her hand up to her necklace and spun back around to Joe as she backed out of the room. "I'll check on you in a bit."

"What was that?" the priest asked.

"I asked her to wait on the pain medicine. I want to talk to you and I need to be clear—because I need your help."

The priest walked to the foot of Joe's bed and stood there with a bewildered look on his face. "What's going on, Juan?"

"My daughter has a son, and he's about fifteen. I've never met the boy." Joe's breathing became labored.

"Juan, you're like a brother to me. Why wouldn't I know this?" the priest pleaded.

"Well, for one, Father, it never came up. Think about what we do all day long ..." A tear fell down Joe's cheek.

"I'm sorry. I don't understand." Father Benjamin shook his head again. "I think I don't know you."

"Well, unfortunately, this isn't about you," Joe snapped at the priest. A rush of blood pounded through his head. He hadn't meant to jump all over the man. In fact, the rush of energy he'd had at that moment seemed to be depleted now. His vision blurred and his eyes grew heavy.

Father Benjamin frowned. "Okay, Juan. I'm sorry. You're right. I'm listening."

Joe's voice cracked and he somehow managed to hold his eyes open. "I didn't handle things so well, back then." Tears streamed down his face.

The room was silent for a while except for the sounds of the medical apparatus.

"I didn't hide this from you. We never talked about my younger years much. Think about it ..." muttered Joe.

Father Benjamin adjusted his collar. "Okay, I'm listening."

"I just want to talk to her, if nothing else to at least give her closure. I've been wanting to do this for the last five years. I've got to talk to her." Joe held back the details of why he needed to see his daughter. Some things weren't meant to be known by everyone. Besides, he was fully aware the priest wouldn't believe his story or the important business he had to complete with Teresa. No, this matter was best left within the family.

"Will you at least help my daughter?" Joe whispered.

The whirs and beeps of the hospital echoed in Joe's ears as he waited for what seemed like hours for the priest to answer.

Father Benjamin appeared to be having some type of an internal struggle. The man took a long time to finally exhale and then respond. "Yes. I will help your daughter."

The priest then frowned and focused on a spot at the foot of the bed just in front of where he stood. "I'm thinking your family doesn't know you go by the name Juan, now, correct?"

"No, but it shouldn't matter in the long run. My name is Juan. I still think of myself as Joe, anyway." The space between his ears felt like mush. He was so tired now, he couldn't think straight. He didn't understand why the priest was fighting him on this topic, and seemingly focused on all the wrong things.

What did his name matter, anyway? His life was over. He'd never thought of himself as Juan—that was just fiction. Now, Joe—well, that guy was brutal reality. Thinking back to the time he'd decided to change his name to Juan Torres and completely drop his middle name "Joe"—the name he'd used his entire life— he really couldn't remember why. He did know if people called him Juan they'd probably only seen his—later in life—saintly side, the part of him that felt like pure fiction. If they thought of him as Joe most likely what they thought was bad. Maybe that was the reason.

"Father, all I'm asking is that I see my daughter before I die. If you can't get through to her, contact my sister, Jessie," Joe whispered with his last bit of energy. His eyelids weighed heavily on his face as he gave in to his exhaustion.

The priest was trying to tell him something, but he didn't understand. His mind turned off as his body went to sleep.

CHAPTER 2

TERESA'S HEART FLUTTERED. WHO'D HAVE THOUGHT the smell of soap mixed with a tad bit of bleach could make someone so happy? Her nostrils tingled a little as she inhaled through her nose and enjoyed the moment. Something about the whole process of cleaning soothed her soul to its very core. Last night she'd scrubbed her entire bathroom well into the morning hours leaving no area untouched.

With her body braced against the edge of the bathroom counter and her hip pushed into the tile, Teresa moved her face up to within inches of the mirror—then she frowned. Her forefinger pulled at the newest wrinkle around her left eye, but she decided to ignore the aging process or half-hoped she could simply cover it up since it would never go away. So she dipped her brush into the pale mineral powder and moved the bristles slowly across her cheek, then around the corner of her eye.

Fog covered the mirror as she exhaled and thought about her real age. She felt as if last week weren't her real fortieth birthday because parts of her life seemed to be missing.

Where did my twenties go? Teresa wondered. *And then my thirties ... I must've cleaned them away.* She chuckled nervously.

It was true that in years gone by Teresa had spent too many hours trying to wash away her tears with a scrub brush in one hand and a bucket of sudsy water in the other. Probably not normal activity for a young, healthy woman, but a habit she'd developed over time.

Odd that she'd think of all that today. It'd been years since she'd let herself dwell on the nightmare of her past. Especially reaching so close to the dark time, a period when she'd lost ... everyone. A shiver of remembrance shot up her spine. Teresa closed her eyes and very deliberately pushed back those thoughts, down into the hidden recesses of her mind. For years she'd managed to keep those heartbreaking times away from her life of today, far from the world she'd created for herself and her son.

She stepped away from the mirror and took a deep breath, but didn't notice the brush slip from her hand until she heard the clanking sound when it landed on the bathroom floor. Her head spun as she bent over to pick up the brush. She stood up too fast. Dizzy, she grabbed the counter to regain her balance.

"No more," Teresa scolded her reflection. And soon, as she'd done so many times before, she forced a happy face and focused on the present, leaving the past where it belonged, in the past.

"Mom, what are you doing?" JJ shouted from the hallway. "We're going to be late."

She had to hand it to him—the kid had excellent timing, and this certainly was a welcome interruption.

She smiled at the thought of her son, JJ, a typical teenager. Nothing abnormal happening with him. In fact, he'd informed Teresa on more than one occasion that when he had his own place he was going to throw his clothes around and sit on the living room furniture. "I just don't get having a room we can't use," JJ had told her over and over again.

Teresa thought about her pretty, nearly perfect room and for a single second she even considered lifting the boundary, but then—no.

"I'll be there in a second," Teresa yelled to her son.

She flipped her wrist around to look at her watch. God, if they didn't leave in the next few minutes they'd be hung up in Los Angeles traffic, and late for both school and work. What had gotten into her? Nostalgia wasn't usually a part of her life. Hurrying now, her hands seemed to lose all coordination as she fumbled through her jewelry box trying to find earrings. She finally settled on a pair of silver hoop dazzlers.

"Moooooommmmm ..." A loud singing, whining sound came from JJ's mouth and carried throughout the house all the way into Teresa's bathroom.

"Okay, hold on," she yelled toward her son.

She brushed the final touches of powder across her cheek, dropped her makeup bag in the drawer, and slammed it shut. Her earrings snapped into place easily as she trotted to the front door where she found JJ with his backpack slung over his left shoulder, his right hand busy text messaging.

"Let's go, JJ." Teresa in a panic grabbed JJ's shoulders and spun him around. She pushed him out the front door toward the car. "Move it. The longer we take, the longer the drive will take."

"Hey, I've been waiting for you." JJ stumbled down the sidewalk balancing his backpack while he continued to send out a greeting to whatever friend.

"When you start driving in a few months, you'll understand." Teresa closed and locked the front door, jogged to the driver's side, pressed the *open* button on her car key, and within a second was in the driver's seat ready to go. JJ was still standing outside the car, with the door open, focused on a text message.

"Get in. We need to go, now," Teresa snapped.

"Okay, okay." JJ landed in the passenger seat.

Aunt Jessie's words came immediately to mind—"That boy is a true product of his generation, helpless without a remote control, a calculator, and a mom to drive him to school." Teresa dismissed her aunt's voice, checked the mirrors, started the car, and moved through the neighborhood.

Her heart pounded rapidly over the last-minute rush. "Cross your fingers and say a prayer to the traffic gods," she requested.

She pulled her seatbelt across her lap while she drove.

"Jeez, Mom, you're supposed to do that before you step on it." JJ talked while he tapped out another text message on his phone.

"That's rude to be constantly on the phone texting." Teresa pointed at JJ and his phone. "Why don't you put it away for a while, JJ? You don't do that in class, do you?"

"Mom, both hands, please. I want to live to my sixteenth birthday," JJ said. "Everybody texts in class."

"John Joseph Reynolds—the teachers let you?" Teresa demanded.

"They don't know." JJ laughed. "I'm good at hiding it—most of the kids are."

Teresa made a mental note to deal with JJ's texting later; she shook her head and focused on the road.

She was relieved to find only the first bell ringing when they arrived at Grant High School. A fast commute on the freeway in the morning was rare in Southern California, and she felt as if the world had magically opened up to aid in this on-time arrival. Teresa sighed and relaxed a bit.

"It's a good sign." Teresa's voice rose a pitch as she clapped her hands. "We made it, and now it's going to be a good day."

"It's always a good day, Mom." JJ leaned over and kissed Teresa on the cheek, a practice he had never been ashamed of. "I'll try and find a ride home after school. See you later, alligator."

Teresa watched her son, amazed at how like an adult JJ appeared, yet how like a child he behaved. In a moment, JJ jumped into the middle of a group of teens, many of whom he'd been friends with since kindergarten. He slapped knuckles and giggled like an overgrown infant. As Teresa watched, JJ's long legs lost all of the athletic agility she'd witnessed only seconds before. "Goofy" appeared to have taken over his body.

He swatted at the dark curly locks that covered his eyes and rested slightly above his shoulders. *Time for a haircut,* Teresa thought. She pulled away from the curb and felt a sense of calm roll over her body. In this aspect of her life, at least, she knew she'd done well.

Teresa thought about work while she maneuvered through traffic. It'd been almost a decade since she'd opened The Soap Store and had become her own boss. Soap, of all things. An appropriate product for a clean lifestyle. "Natural cleaning products for the body, the house, and industry." What a thrill for her, owning soap products and selling cleanliness. Uncle Joe, her friend Rita, and a few others thought she was insane for taking on such a huge risk. "So specialized ..." Rita had said. Teresa hadn't talked to Rita since. Not one of them understood Teresa's passion for cleanliness. But her Aunt Jessie, full of endless faith, had loaned Teresa the seed money for the store. She'd always been Teresa's biggest fan.

It was a disappointment to Teresa that The Soap Store didn't take off as she'd anticipated, but she'd managed to make it work anyway. She didn't want Rita coming back around and saying, "I told you so."

14

When Teresa allowed herself to think about it, she didn't understand how she'd managed to stay in business for so long. She had even paid back her aunt, in full and with interest. Thank goodness for the Internet, which had been the best thing for her store, and lately produced more than enough revenue to make up for the loss of foot traffic at the mall. She might not be driving a Mercedes Benz, but Teresa had been a good provider for her son. Certainly better than her ex-husband with his never-seen child support checks.

Deep in thought, Teresa almost drove past the entrance to the mall where the soap store was located. She frowned when she turned her car into the parking lot and spotted a beat-up old sedan parked over the line, invading her favorite spot. Her hands squeezed the steering wheel until her knuckles turned white, and she drove past that vehicle toward the back of the lot, where she chose a corner space and parked diagonally to avoid door dings. Teresa's car might be slightly aged but it was in excellent condition and she intended to keep it that way.

After she pulled her bag out of the back seat, Teresa wiped the door handle clean and dabbed at a spot on the side of her car. Clean as clean could be, it left her with a feeling of satisfaction until she looked around the lot. The asphalt was lined with pieces of trash—again. She'd have to call the landlord and get him out here to straighten up this mess. Barney's Pub must've had another busy weekend. The bar was located on the other side of the parking lot, not attached to the neighborhood strip mall where Teresa's soap store was located, but close enough to create disorder for the entire retail area.

A typical Monday.

Teresa walked the distance to the back door of her store with her keys in hand. She moved into the building quickly and heard the alarm beep as she ran to the keypad and punched in the code.

Inside, she felt for the light switch along the wall in the dark back room and flipped the light on. Her heart fell to her toes.

Clutter everywhere. Shipping labels, boxes, and orders unfilled. The place looked as if it'd been ransacked. Her part-time help must've been in a hurry over the weekend.

A light blinked on the answering machine that sat on the desk in the corner of her makeshift office. For the moment, she ignored the chaos and walked through the room toward the machine, where she hit the play button on the antiquated device. The mechanical voice said, "You have three messages."

Beep. "I'm looking for Teresa. It's Sunday evening. My name is Father Benjamin. Please call me back at (310) 548-1100."

Beep. "Hello, Teresa, are you there?" Teresa laughed at the sound of Aunt Jessie's voice. For someone seemingly so young at sixty-two, the woman sure had a hard time with technology.

Beep. "Teresa, call me. These darn machines. Why isn't your cell phone on?"

Teresa pulled her cell phone out of her pocket and pushed the call log button—three missed calls. It was unusual for her aunt to call her on all her phones. She picked up the landline and dialed her Aunt Jessie's number.

"Hello." Her Aunt Jessie had refused to get caller ID or call waiting on her phone service. If Teresa hadn't insisted, she'd still be using a rotary dial.

"Aunt Jessie?" Teresa spoke. "It's me, Teresa. What's going on?"

"Teresita. My baby, hello." Teresa's aunt had a habit of yelling at the phone. "I want to talk to you. I need to see you."

A rush of blood fell to the bottom of Teresa's feet. The woman was like a mother to her. If anything happened to her aunt, Teresa didn't know what she'd do.

"What's going on, Aunt Jessie?" Teresa's heart pounded in her ears.

"It's about your father. Why don't you step out for a while and come over to my house? I'll explain," she responded.

"My father?" Teresa's head began to ache. She squeezed her jaw shut and felt her cheek muscles flex—her breathing sped up. "What's going on? It's been years ..."

"Please, come over. I tried to catch you on your way to work so you wouldn't have to backtrack. But you didn't answer your phone."

"Is that bastard finally dead?" The words flew from Teresa's mouth.

"No, he's not dead." Her aunt sighed. "I need to explain."

"Okay, Auntie." Teresa put her hand on her forehead and exhaled. "Let me tie up some loose ends here, and I'll be right over."

"I'll put on the coffee and see you in a little while, then," her Aunt Jessie said. "Oh, and Teresa ... mind your potty mouth."

The sound of dial tone filled Teresa's ear. She set the phone back in its cradle, walked to the front of the store, and stared out the window. She hadn't seen her dad in over twenty years. Her last remembrances of him were awful and framed by that period of time she'd like to leave forgotten altogether.

The worst moment in her life was when her dad disappeared during her mother's final days, a memory she hadn't allowed herself to think about in ages. Oh, how she missed her mom. Her body constricted as she squeezed her hands shut and let the weight of her fists dangle at her side. Teresa closed her eyes, allowing a single tear to fall while her thoughts carried her back to the place she'd avoided for so many years.

She'd sat with her mom hour after hour, holding the cool washcloth on her mother's forehead while the cancer and the chemo wreaked havoc on the poor woman's frail body. Her mother remained continually awash with sweat, and hallucinating. Without an okay from the hospice nurse—who was gone for the night—the doctors wouldn't prescribe any more pain medicine.

Teresa, at eighteen years of age and having recently buried her only sister, sat alone comforting her dying mother. She'd kept back the tears for her mother's sake, and she'd repeatedly lied about her father hurrying on his way home.

She left her mom's side for a quick second to make a frantic call to her Aunt Jessie. Teresa told Jessie her dad had gone to work as usual that morning but hadn't shown up at the factory where she'd been trying to reach him all day long. Her aunt said Teresa shouldn't call the police, that Jessie would look for him at the bars he frequented. Teresa's aunt knew exactly where she would find her older brother.

A few hours later, Aunt Jessie arrived at the house with puffy red eyes and a ripped sleeve. She'd said Teresa's dad was okay, and that he'd be home soon, but she refused to discuss the matter further. After that, Teresa and her Aunt Jessie had sat together with her mother until they both had fallen asleep sitting upright in the chairs next to her mother's bed.

Then the following morning, Teresa found her dad in the front yard. He lay in a pile of vomit and smelled like a latrine. God only knew how he'd gotten home since the driveway was empty, and his car wasn't parked on the street. Teresa had forgotten what was so important that morning that her aunt had to leave, but she remembered her aunt's anger toward Teresa's father. Teresa was given strict instructions to leave him in the yard.

"He's alive. Let him wake up in his own filth." And as her Aunt Jessie spoke, she stepped around her brother's limp body and spat on him. "And don't help him into the house. He needs to find himself in this mess. Maybe he'll snap out of it."

Now, thinking of that day so many years later, Teresa felt wetness run across her cheeks. She went to the mirror on the back wall of her store and examined her red eyes. Then she pulled the window cleaner from under the counter, put on her rubber gloves, and scrubbed the mirror. The energy he took ... Just thinking about her father brought heaviness into her world along with the old feelings that she hated.

After a few minutes, she put down the cleaning fluid and pulled off her gloves. Teresa looked at her teeth in the mirror. Her investment in braces years before had paid off. She touched up her hair and wiped the streaks off her face.

What could be happening with her father now?

Shaking away thoughts of the past, Teresa moved to the cupboard in the front of the store and pulled out the Rolodex. Her fingers found the Ks for Kelly's number (she never used last names because she couldn't remember them). Kelly, her best part-timer, picked up after a single ring. Yes, she'd gladly open, clean up, and handle the day, "... no problem."

As Teresa walked to her car, she stared down the dirty sedan in her parking place, as if it were a live human being who had kidnapped her firstborn. She snapped out of it when she realized how silly she was being. It was just a car. Teresa shook her head and chuckled to herself. "Stop it," she whispered. The owner of that sedan was probably a patron of Barney's Pub. The vehicle had most likely spent a night or two in the lot. It was better parked here than driven, though, if its owner had been drinking.

While Teresa drove toward Sepulveda Boulevard, her past continued to flood through her mind—more of the darkness. The accident that had taken her sister's life came back like a tidal wave. Teresa's grip tightened on the steering wheel.

She bent over her dash and looked up toward the sky. "What is this?" she asked, half expecting the sky to open up and swallow the car, with her in it.

She rubbed her left leg—remnants from the accident so many years ago. But she couldn't be too ungrateful because the physical damage Teresa had sustained was minimal compared to Angela's fate. A hit and run that the police, her mother, her aunt, her uncle, and, annoyingly enough—considering his own fate—her father, agreed had been caused by a drunk driver.

Witnesses claimed the car weaved in and out of traffic about two minutes before the accident. A dark sedan was the only description the police had to go on, and they never found the person who had run down Teresa and Angela.

Her entire body trembled while she thought about the past, and she forced herself back into the present. She loosened her grip on the steering wheel as she drove into the small community where her aunt lived. The neighborhood wasn't as safe as it used to be, or as pleasantly middle class.

When the homes were built way back in the sixties, the small, three-bedroom bungalows must've looked identical or showed some type of continuity. Now, the styles and colors of the homes presented quite a mixed bag. Teresa thought that many of these folks either couldn't afford the upkeep on their homes, or simply didn't care. On one side of the street, in front of a house in need of painting, a yellow lawn was overrun with weeds. Next to that home sat a perfectly manicured yard surrounded by a white picket fence—the house displaying a recent addition of bars on the windows.

At her aunt's usually perfectly tended place, surprisingly, gardening gloves and tools lay scattered across the well-clipped grass. Teresa parked her car in the driveway and moved quickly up the front steps where Aunt Jessie yanked the door open at Teresa's first knock.

"Teresita, honey, come in." Her aunt had aged well over the years. She power-walked every day and went to the gym a few times a week and it showed.

"Auntie Jessie, have you been in the garden this morning?" Teresa pointed toward the tools.

"Oh my. I forgot to bring those in last night. The phone rang and I ... Teresa, I'm getting too old to deal with this crap." She seemed almost on the verge of tears.

"What's going on, Auntie?"

Teresa's Aunt Jessie marched out to the front yard, her large, blue housecoat floating around her skinny body. She picked up the tools and the gloves and dropped the items in a storage box that posed as a tree stump. Then she gestured to Teresa to follow her back into the house. "Come inside. Let's have some coffee and talk."

Teresa loved the smell of the home's interior, a cleaning-fluid scent mixed with coffee that her aunt still made in an ancient percolator—a mechanism Teresa's great-grandmother had passed down. Her aunt often reminded Teresa that one day she'd be the proud owner of this wonderful machine.

"One day, Teresita, this fine machine will be yours." Aunt Jessie now rubbed the side of the percolator and winked.

Teresa laughed. "I was just thinking you'd say that. It smells so good, Auntie. But I'd rather have you in my life."

Her aunt set the coffee cups on the table. "Come and sit down. We need to talk."

"Okay, what's so important you called me away from work today? I'm a big girl already, so tell it like it is." Teresa sat at the familiar round table with the chipped Formica top. She chose the same chair she used to sit in for hours studying for finals and writing papers. Teresa was lucky. Her aunt let her move in after her mother died. All through college and for a while after, they shared the house.

"That's right. My mija is in her forties now. I can't believe it."

"What's going on with Joe Torres, Auntie?" Teresa reached across the table and put her hand on her aunt's.

"I got this call last night from a man, a priest. I thought to myself, I don't know a Father Benjamin." Aunt Jessie paused and took a sip of her coffee.

"I had a message from him as well," Teresa said, surprised.

"Oh, he's trying to reach you all right. But I'm glad he didn't. I'd like to be the one to tell you instead. I'll just cut to the chase. Your father is dying, and he wants to see you."

Teresa swallowed and resisted the urge to jump up and clean the sink.

"I thought he was dead. In fact, I hoped he was dead after what he did." A wave of emotions welled up in her throat. "How does a grown man leave his teenage daughter twice, and then disappear forever? First at Angela's funeral and then mom's …" She pulled a tissue out of her bag and dabbed at her eyes, shocked at how affected she was by the thought of her father.

"What about what I want? What about what I needed years ago? What about what you needed?" Teresa's voice rippled as she tried to maintain control.

She stared at the coat closet across the living room where the vacuum was stored, fighting her desire to pull out the machine and vacuum the house.

"Mija, I'm here." Her aunt put her hand on Teresa's chin and turned the younger woman's face toward her—seemingly for the purpose of eye contact. "Take a deep breath," her aunt advised.

And then Aunt Jessie stood up and moved to Teresa's side putting her arm across Teresa's shoulders and sliding down beside her. Her aunt then squeezed Teresa's torso and rocked with her gently to the ticking of the clock.

"You know, my father, your granddad, had the same problem. He drank himself to death," Aunt Jessie said a minute later.

"What's Joe dying of?" Teresa asked, returning to the moment.

"That's another thing, Mija, he's using his first name now, Juan. The priest told me it was symbolic to Joe, your dad—well, I guess, Juan, now. He believes it's the only way he can stay sober, by using a different name. Sort of like a new identity." Teresa's aunt rolled her eyes.

"Auntie, wasn't he wonderful before my mom got sick? Or is my memory messed up?" Teresa asked.

"No, you've got it partially right. He was wonderful at times, but Joe had his moments. I guess you could say he was haunted, like his father." Her aunt moved back to her place at the table, across from Teresa.

"What?" Teresa sat up straight. "He had a problem before Mom got sick?"

"Oh, yes. I thought you knew. Your mother and he had split up for a short while when you and Angela were little. She was a strong woman, your mom." Aunt Jessie took a deep breath. "Your mom's ultimatum worked, until your dad blew up over the stress of the tragedies."

Teresa tried to recall those years, memories she'd worked so hard for so long to erase completely. "Oh God, he must've been going to meetings a few times a week. I remember that now." She put her hand up to her mouth. "He seemed to be so strong back then."

"Your mother was the strength behind the man, and he openly admitted it too. His honesty was a part of his charm. Oh, your father had charisma." Her aunt smiled.

"Remember the Torres family reunion, when I was twelve or so? Dad had put up streamers in the back yard and flags in the front yard. He manned the grill out in the back of our house. The men and the women, all of them wanted to be around him there. His jokes, his smile." Teresa felt her jaw loosen as she recalled the earlier days with her father.

He hadn't always been a drunk. For years her dad had been a good family man. When Teresa and her sister, Angela, were little, they waited on the front porch for their dad to get home from work. How they both loved their wonderful daddy.

At one point in her childhood, she did the math with her friends—Teresa's parents were married the longest and seemed the happiest of all the couples around them. Many of her friends were growing up in single-parent homes, and most of those girls wanted to be at Teresa's house on weekends. Her dad was the life of the party, and her beautiful mother knew how to cook and always took care of any guest. Teresa's memories were of a home filled with love, until her mother's cancer diagnosis. Their lives seemed to unravel from that point forward.

"Well, his liver's shot," Aunt Jessie blurted out, interrupting Teresa's short stroll down memory lane. "The priest said your father's years of alcohol abuse have caught up with him.

"I tried so hard, Auntie, to create a family like the one I thought I had as a child. My version was parents who loved each other, and I wanted a house full of children ..." Teresa tore at the tissue in her hand. "I failed miserably, didn't I?"

"No, no. Never say that." Her aunt took her hands. "You've raised a wonderful son, who adores you. Mija, look at your store as well. You're a big success. I don't want to hear you speak like that anymore."

"I swore I'd never let him hurt me, ever again. I'm not sure how to handle this. Did you say five years? He's been sober ..."

Teresa's head pounded. She pushed down the emotions that tried to engulf her, memories of the bleak, lonely time—such a heavy feeling of despair. Teresa squeezed both of her eyes shut. "Yes. He's been living in the maintenance quarters at St. Augustine's on Third Street for almost the last five years. He's like a saint to the people there. In fact, the priest had no idea your dad had a family until Joe went into the hospital."

Her Aunt Jessie stared in her coffee cup for a couple of seconds and then continued. "The father wants both of us to come by the church first. Before we see your dad ... if we see your dad. Though, I don't know how I'm going to call Joe, Juan."

They sat in silence, Teresa's energy already depleted, yet another sign that Juan Joseph Torres was around if only in spirit. But the past was the past, Teresa reminded herself as she rocked her body back and forth. She looked at the floor and thought about the bucket her aunt kept under the sink, and then she dismissed her irrational desire to mop.

"Well, Auntie, I'm not sure I want to see my selfish dad. He couldn't pull it together at the worst possible time when Mama and Angela died. And now that he's dying he wants his family around him?" Teresa's cheeks filled with heat.

"Yes, I know, Mija." Her aunt touched Teresa's arm and spoke in a soothing voice. "It doesn't have to be about him. It could be about you. We're all hurt over what happened during that time."

With no warning or reason, Teresa's insides suddenly filled with warmth, and her anger fell away. It was a feeling she'd had before, and always at the oddest moments in her life, but never close enough to the surface for her to quite retain the memory. A sensation of overwhelming softness which began in the core of her being and then spread slowly like a glow-light throughout her body.

It was odd to feel such delight during what seemed to be the most distressing periods of her life. She hoped the sensation was a sign from her mother, but as always, as quickly as the feeling arose, it disappeared. She touched her stomach for a moment, almost forgetting why, and dismissed the warm impression from seconds ago as just her imagination.

CHAPTER 3

ANGEL PUT AN ARM AROUND TERESA while she sat with the two women. She hadn't known Teresa'd had a sister or that her father was still alive. All of these years and no mention of either in the presence of Angel.

"Sometimes I think Mom is around," Teresa said.

"I have to believe she is," Teresa's aunt answered.

"I can feel something, though I can't really explain it."

"I have an idea, Teresita. Why don't you go with me to see Father Benjamin? No commitment to anything else." Teresa's aunt looked hopeful.

Angel nodded at this idea and wished Teresa could see her sitting right here. She'd encourage Teresa to deal with this unfinished business, which she'd always sensed around the woman. How Angel wanted to be heard by these two women who had no knowledge of her existence.

"For some odd reason I'm open to that," answered Teresa. "It's like something Mom and Angela would've wanted. At least test the waters, so to speak. I'll go with you."

Teresa's aunt jumped up. "I'll get ready now, and call Father Benjamin."

Angel sat with Teresa as she pulled a cell phone out of her pocket and dialed the store. "Kelly? Good. I'm glad you made it in. Thank you."

Teresa smoothed out her left eyebrow while she spoke. "I might be gone the rest of the day. Call me if you need me. I'm not sure what happened in that back room but I know you'll take care of it." Teresa paused for a moment, "All right, we'll talk later. Thank you, again."

Angel had little understanding of her purpose in the living, breathing lives of Teresa and her son, or Teresa's Aunt Jessie. What she did know was that she'd been watching Teresa and her family for many years. At first, she tried to speak to Teresa and anyone who'd listen. Why she continually came back to see Teresa, with no interaction, day after day, was a mystery she hadn't resolved. Of course, she'd simply been drawn to do what she did.

Not a single one of them heard Angel or responded to her. Still, Angel did feel some comfort from being around Teresa, and for a while, she'd prepared to be born into this family. Teresa went through the pregnancy by herself, after Greg had left. Angel believed she'd been sent early to be around her new mother, and she was looking forward to being in the flesh again. Then, JJ arrived.

After his birth, Angel had no explanation for her way of life. She thought she was some type of ghost or something else non-worldly, since occasionally, when she wasn't watching over Teresa, but staying up in the clouds, some folks could actually see her. She preferred to keep to herself though, and her only means of back and forth communication continued to be her two pups.

The pups were a godsend, and perhaps literally. Belle came first. If they'd been alive and breathing, and not the doggie ghosts Angel thought they were, Belle would weigh in at about three pounds and Kail would be about five pounds, tops. Neither looked real, yet both seemed more real than all of Angel's other surroundings.

The talking part of her pups' existence had at first seemed difficult for Angel to accept. The day she met Belle she'd stopped at the park to enjoy the grass. Angel was flat on her back, basking in the sun, when she heard someone speak. Because rarely did anyone talk to her, she ignored the voice. Angel understood at this point she was 'see through'; she didn't exist in the world, although some part of her knew that she used to be a part of it all. The longer she remained in this 'limbo' state, she realized, the more she forgot about what it was like to be in the flesh. Angel hadn't determined yet if this was heaven or hell, though she hoped it was neither.

"Why do you think they make the dogs stay on leashes?" Angel saw Belle and saw her mouth move, but she dismissed it because she thought the words weren't meant for her ears.

"I said, why do you think they make the dogs wear leashes?" Angel heard the question again and looked up. A cream colored, petite Pomeranian, with short hair and an overbite was standing within two inches of her face. Looking her straight in the eye, in fact.

"Can you see me?" Angel whispered.

"Yes, I'm talking to you." The little thing responded.

"About the leashes?" Angel asked.

"Yes, I want to know."

"So they won't bite each other, or scare the people in the park. Can you see me?" Angel asked again.

"Yes. I said I could see you. My name is Belle."

"Belle, that's a nice name. My name is Angel. How are you able to talk?" Angel wasn't sure why, but this didn't seem right.

"Probably for the same reason I can see you," Belle answered.

"Where did you come from?" Angel asked.

"I was following my family until they got another pet. They seem okay now."

"Did you die? Are we ghosts?"

"Well, aren't you an angel?" Belle asked.

"I don't think so," answered Angel. She thought about it for a while and had considered all the ins and outs. "I have no special powers and I've never been to heaven, at least I hope not. I don't even know who I was when I was on earth. Although, I think I was somebody. The only thing I can figure is that I'm stuck."

"I think I am too." The small dog's eyebrows lifted in some show of emotion.

"It's like I'm in between places," Angel said. "And I really can't remember how long I've been here. My life now is real, but not really real."

"Yes." Belle nodded.

From that day forward Angel shared her cloud with pretty little Belle. As soft as a bed, and peacefully away from the world below, the cloud served as their escape.

The two spent their days apart, out in the world, but when they tired, usually at night, they met on that special cloud, to rest. Wherever the cloud may have floated to in the meantime, Angel and Belle always found their way back.

Then one day Belle brought home Kail, and they became a family of three. Angel loved her girls, and for some reason it was easy for her to trust the pups. Angel's trust issues were with the few unknown people who somehow managed to see her when nobody else could. It didn't happen often, but when it did, Angel moved her little family as far away as possible.

Belle and Kail would be interested in this newest twist to Teresa's life, though Angel couldn't leave quite yet to catch the girls up on these thought-provoking happenings. She wanted to be around for the upcoming visit. For years she'd watched Teresa simply exist. If what the women now were talking about had actually happened—the accident, the cancer, and all the rest—it explained a lot of the emptiness in Teresa's life. And probably why Teresa, like Angel, avoided people, or relationships.

A while back, Angel told Teresa to get a dog—her life would be a lot less lonely; at least that was what Angel had discovered for herself. Since Teresa never heard her, Angel had tried to visit Teresa's dreams, and in waking moments she whispered in Teresa's ear. Eventually, Angel had managed to guide Teresa toward a pet store where Teresa looked for a while at the puppies. But Angel's plans hadn't worked out, because in the end, Teresa left the store empty handed.

Now, Angel decided to stay close to Teresa and be with her when she met the priest. She also intended to visit Teresa's dad, regardless of whatever decision Teresa made. Angel was curious about this man and wanted to learn more.

CHAPTER 4

THE WAITING AREA AT THE CHURCH office smelled musty. A graffiti laden, three-legged desk had been balanced in the corner, and Jessie sat on one of four plastic, wobbly chairs scattered randomly about the room. Next to the second, double door entry, a bulletin board was propped up against the wall on the cheap laminate floor. The words 'Sober Living Program' were posted across the top.

It took Jessie a moment to recognize her brother's face. A picture of Joe had been pinned to the middle of the board. A few more wrinkles and some gray hair, but she knew it was Joe. And from where she sat, it appeared he'd aged well. The alcohol must've preserved his skin.

Remaining seated, Jessie stifled her desire to walk over and see the picture close-up, for fear of Teresa also seeing the photo. Jessie believed it was too much, too soon. The poor girl needed a moment or so to catch her breath. It'd been less than an hour since she'd learned of her father's being alive and his request to see her.

Jessie watched Teresa scan the small lobby from the entryway and quietly sighed as her niece's eyes lit up in recognition of the man in the picture. Because Teresa rarely missed a thing, she'd tuned into that photo within seconds. And without pause, she went directly to the board and knelt down to look. Her voice echoed in the room as she read out loud, "Juan Torres, founder of the Sober Living Program."

Jessie walked over and placed her hand on her niece's shoulder as she squatted down next to her.

"He looks the same, only older," Jessie said, and they both studied the photo. Behind them, a clock ticked on the wall.

"It's like a time warp," her niece said as she stared at the photo.

"I really didn't want you to see it," Jessie told Teresa. "I thought you'd need more time."

"Oh, Tia, I'm not so sure I want to be here. My dad makes me so angry."

"I know." Jessie stood and returned to her chair. She patted the chair next to her. "Sit down, Teresita."

"I always thought he'd died and that is why we never heard from him. I made up my mind he was dead. It hurt less that way, or at least that's what I thought." Teresa stared at the floor as she sat down. "I don't know what to think, now."

"We take it a step at a time." Jessie took her niece's hand in her own as she thought back to the night, long ago, when she tried to bring Joe home.

Jessie went to Joe's favorite bar on Lexington Street, because she knew he'd be there. She shook her head now, trying not to think about the horrible incident in the parking lot. The bar was in a rough neighborhood. She wouldn't have gone to the bar or been in that part of town, had it not been for her brother's indiscretions.

The son of a bitch had refused to return with her. He'd called her every name imaginable, including the "C" word.

Jessie had told him about what the men in the parking lot did to her, and Joe laughed at her. He'd told her to go home. "This is a man's place. You have no business being here," Joe went on and on ... And what was she doing in this part of town anyway? Women didn't belong here. He'd said she'd gotten what she deserved, and then physically pushed her out the door.

Up until the moment that had happened, she'd never seen her brother behave in that manner. Jessie wouldn't have believed it, had it not happened to her. Afterward, when they found him passed out in the front yard, she'd hoped and prayed he'd snap out of it. Jessie thought he'd hit rock bottom then. In retrospect, she didn't know if she'd been naïve, or simply stupid. Her father—Joe's father—had drunk himself to death. It was in their blood, a part of their history. Why hadn't she done more to stop her brother?

Jessie's stomach went into spasms at the sound of approaching footsteps. The double doors flung wide open, and she immediately sat upright and at attention. Posture had been her biggest issue with the nuns in grade school, and her head began playing those terrible old tapes. She straightened her shirt with her hands and checked her niece with a quick sideways glance.

Teresa always looked like perfection. She wore tailored suits and the finest silk blouses. Jessie was very proud of her niece, in fact. The girl, well ... the forty-year-old woman, had been through more in her years of life than most people would ever have to go through in several lifetimes, and she'd handled it all with remarkable courage.

"Father Benjamin?" Jessie's knees cracked as she stood and moved toward the man. She felt like a child being sent to the principal's office. The many years she attended a Catholic school had instilled a fear in her of religious authority.

The priest went directly over to Jessie. "I'm sorry I'm late." He revealed a set of flawless white teeth and piercing blue eyes as he reached out to shake Jessie's hand. "I'm Father Benjamin."

"Hello Father, I'm Jessie and this is my niece, Teresa." Jessie heard a stranger's high-pitched voice come out of her mouth. Her left hand fluttered at her thigh while she stretched out her right hand to accept the priest's handshake.

Father Benjamin took her hand in both of his and looked at her. When he finally turned to address Teresa, Jessie let out a silent sigh of relief. She felt as if the priest's eyes had penetrated her soul and somehow learned more about her then she knew of herself.

"Come with me into my office, please." He motioned with his arm and led them back through the doors into a long stretch of hallway. Jessie's throat tightened. Perspiration broke out across her upper lip, and her limbs began to shake. In this brief second the walls seemed to close in around her.

She moved double-time to keep up with Father Benjamin, and thank goodness for this distraction. The closed-in feeling was quickly forgotten with her efforts to stay right behind him. The building was much larger than it appeared, but the priest obviously knew all of its ins and outs intimately. He moved quickly down the hall making several turns without hesitation. Jessie hoped she and Teresa wouldn't have to find their way out on their own.

"This office, right here." He pushed open the final door within a long maze of stark white halls. A large wooden desk filled one side of the office, and with a mismatch of colors a visitor seating area filled the other half of the space. Jessie was touched by the lack of decor rather than dismayed by it. The father seemed to truly have a calling here.

As he sat in an overstuffed chair across from the couch the women had settled on, the priest spoke again. "I'm sorry we meet under these unhappy circumstances." With manicured hands, polished patent leather shoes, and his priest collar rising from a black, freshly dry-cleaned shirt, the priest looked impeccable.

"I think we're a little unclear about the circumstances," snapped Teresa.

"Well, unfortunately, the outlook isn't good. Your dad, Juan, was admitted to Memorial Hospital. His liver isn't functioning," explained the priest. "It's one of the reasons he cleaned up five years ago. They discovered the cirrhosis when he'd had a gallstone attack."

Jessie swallowed and quietly asked, "Does he know you called us?"

"He requested it." Father Benjamin rested his arms on his legs and tilted his body toward the women, while he continued in a soft tone. "I'm sure this is hard. From what I've been told, you haven't seen or heard from him in many years."

Jessie reached for a tissue from a box on a table to her right. "Oh, Mija, I'm sorry. I was going to be strong for you," she said as the tears started in earnest.

Teresa put her hand out and grabbed Jessie's other hand. "It's okay, Auntie. His behavior was bad to all of us." She took a deep breath and turned toward the priest in indignation. "If he's been clean for over five years, why no attempt to contact us during all that time?"

"I think he wanted to contact you. I hope he has an opportunity to explain to you personally. He told me days turned into months, and months turned into years. He'd had bouts of staying clean and working over the last twenty years." The priest sat upright as he spoke in a more formal voice, "I'm not sure how this will sound, but in his mind he had one more chance to be around his family and not disappoint. He claims every time he got near the point of reentering your lives, he broke under the pressure."

They all sat quietly for a few minutes, then Jessie stood and deposited her wet tissue into the wastebasket. Heat filled her cheeks as rage took over. "Father, what do we make of this? He abandoned his wife during her darkest hour and left his daughter to fend for herself after she was in a car accident that killed her sister, his other daughter. He refused to accept help. We spent the first several years after his disappearance trying to find him."

Jessie's heart pounded. She licked her lips and continued, "Every birthday, graduation, wedding, and holiday were excruciating to live through the eyes of his beautiful daughter he'd abandoned."

Jessie paused and looked at her niece. "She didn't say it, but I know she silently waited for him to reappear. And then one day, all of us quietly accepted his death. We'd heard the house had been foreclosed, and we all grew tired of worrying about Joe. His cousins, uncles, aunts, and his daughter—all of us—we were done."

Father Benjamin raised his hand and shook his head left to right, "I understand." He looked at Teresa.

"How can you understand? Did your father leave you?" Teresa made no attempt to hide the fury in her voice. "And I'm not sure what I want to do now. I may opt to go back to my life untouched and treat my dad as he was to me yesterday, dead."

The priest nodded and continued to maintain eye contact with Teresa.

"You know, Father, my dad has a specialty of bringing drama with him everywhere he goes. I can't help but think ..." Teresa looked down and swallowed. She then lifted her head and met the priest's eyes. With her cheeks red and the vein across her forehead bulging, she continued as Jessie, trying to control her sobs, reached for yet another several tissues from the box. She'd always wanted to shield Teresa from this precise pain.

"Where was he when his wife lay dying asking for him, over and over again?" Teresa demanded. "Why should we be there for him now that he is dying? Selfish, selfish man."

Father Benjamin stood and paced back and forth for a few seconds. He stopped in front of the women and nervously rubbed his chin as he spoke. "I can tell you about Juan's most recent five years. Juan has lived in the maintenance quarters. He's been employed as the church's maintenance man the entire time. Over the last few decades, however, he'd somehow managed to take some college course work."

The priest cleared his throat. "This put him in a position to finish a college degree when he first arrived at our center. Juan then became a licensed counselor. He's been one of our most successful addiction counselors. He also founded the Sober Living Program, which has helped so many souls."

Then the father knelt down to the eye level of the seated women. "I know Juan isn't any saint. But, the man also continued to work as the church maintenance person while acting as a counselor. His time has been spent with the outreach programs, with his groups, on skid Row finding missing sober lifers and always, always reaching out to others."

Father Benjamin stood up, turned around, and slightly above a whisper he said, "I had a better understanding of why he seemed so selfless, when he finally told me his family story."

"As a part of the Twelve Step Program, don't most people make amends to those they've hurt?" Teresa asked. Jessie noticed the moisture beneath her niece's eyes.

"Yes, it's considered a critical element to maintaining a clean lifestyle." Father Benjamin sighed.

"How could he counsel people when his own house wasn't in order?" Teresa asked.

"A question to ask your dad, if you decide to see him." The priest rubbed the back of his hand across his forehead and frowned. He then looked up, and to Jessie it appeared he forced a smile.

With a deep breath, the priest continued, "I'd like to show you his living quarters and where he has worked for the last five years. Would you like to see it?"

"I'm not so sure I want to spend any more time here," Teresa answered. "What about you, Aunt Jessie?" she appealed.

For whatever reason, Jessie had a need to know more about her brother's life, and she felt that maybe Teresa should come and see as well. "Well, we're here, so let's take a quick peek," Jessie suggested. Then she turned to Father Benjamin, "How long will it take?"

"Just a few minutes, his office is down the hall and his living quarters are in the next building," Father Benjamin answered.

Chapter 5

Father Benjamin stood up and moved toward the door, grabbing the set of keys he'd placed on his desk earlier that morning. The priest's motions were so swift he didn't noticed both women remained seated on the couch until he finally turned to escort them out. They'd been whispering intensely back and forth and continued to speak softly as he waited by the door to show them Juan's office.

Who could blame the daughter for not wanting to be near anything her father had touched? Who would blame either of these women if they chose to walk away, forever? Father Benjamin had to deal with his feelings of betrayal by Juan, the level of which landed much lower on the Richter Scale than a sibling's loss, or a daughter's broken heart.

Had it been less than a week? It seemed like a lifetime ago when the turmoil of Juan's life exploded into his own. Only last week he and Juan had still worked side by side. They had scoured the streets of Skid Row looking for the General.

"Father, this is not a mission for the timid," Juan had warned the priest a few years before when he'd enlisted Father Benjamin to help find some other lost soul out in the streets of LA.

"Come on, Juan."

"I'm not making this up. I know you think I kid a lot, but this is ugly business."

At the time, Juan had a smile on his face, and his eyes were filled with an unexplainable spark. So the priest thought he was joking, though eventually, Father Benjamin recognized this "look" on Juan's face as the "look" that could make Lucifer kneel down and pray. Juan had a knack of persuading anyone to do anything, and it began with this particular "look."

"Marcus." Father Benjamin was silenced by the sound of his first name. Juan's smile had disappeared; he held the priest's eyes. "I can't describe the odor in these streets. It's a stench beyond all description. You might feel the need to vomit. You might vomit."

"I'll be okay."

Father Benjamin laughed now at the thought of it. He'd been so sure the street odors and liveliness wouldn't faze him. He'd spent hours in the shelter and in the church kitchen with homeless men and women. He'd been aware of body, alcohol, and puke odors involved in this work.

Yet nothing had prepared him for the level of stench on Skid Row itself. It was far more intense then he'd expected, or had ever encountered in his life. Juan was right; Father Benjamin didn't handle that first excursion very well. As he recalled it now, he'd been little help to his helper.

He'd returned home after a short search and an apology to Juan. At least Father Benjamin had refrained from getting sick in front of the other man.

Since that first incident, Father Benjamin had completed many searches on Skid Row with Juan. He'd learned how to handle the stench, and now, Father Benjamin realized, last week when the General disappeared, he and Juan attempted their final search together.

"Okay, let's get this done quickly." Teresa stood in front of him. He'd been so engrossed in his own thoughts he'd forgotten the task at hand.

"Oh, sure," the priest answered.

Earlier, Father Benjamin hadn't noticed the seriousness in Teresa's face. But as she stood a few feet away, he saw the deep lines across her forehead and the cold distance of her eyes. Her expression indicated a bitter annoyance.

"Would you rather do this another time?" Father Benjamin asked Teresa.

"Father," Teresa looked down at her cell phone while she spoke, "I'd rather not do it all. But I promised my Aunt Jessie I'd go with her to see where her brother worked." Teresa stepped through the office door with Jessie only a few steps behind.

As the aunt approached Father Benjamin, she hesitated right in front of him. At that moment, he thought he saw her wink, an action that reminded him of Juan. He was almost certain, Jessie's left eyebrow lifted as she winked her right eye. Or was that a twitch? He had to admit, he already missed Juan. His anger toward Juan would only hold out for so long, and that's how it worked with his friend. The priest knew this one was going to hurt and maybe that's why he was so angry. He followed the women into the hall and shut the office door.

"Right this way, ladies." Father Benjamin led the women to Juan's office while he thought about that search for the General.

The General had been a fixture at the shelter, and Juan believed they could find him and bring him home. Or more importantly, he believed they needed to find him and bring him home. The General, whose nickname was given to him because of his bossy demeanor and the stripes on his jacket, was too old and too sick to stay outside all night. Years ago they'd tried to find his true identity, but to no avail. On this topic, the General had refused to help, or, perhaps, as he'd claimed, he didn't remember who he was.

When they'd started out on the second day of their mission to find the General, Father Benjamin had told Juan he didn't look good.

"Thanks, Father, I appreciate that." Juan smiled.

"Hey, this business isn't for the timid," Father Benjamin said.

"Yeah, it seems I've heard that, once or twice before. I'll be okay."

Juan had been using a cane to get around for the previous few months. On this day, he'd seemed to lean on it somewhat more than usual. His face was pale and he appeared to have lost some weight, yet he looked swollen.

"Have you been to your doctor?" the priest asked.

"Father, we need to find the General." Juan ignored Father Benjamin's question.

They'd made it down Washington Street, when Juan had doubled over and collapsed. Knowing this wasn't a favorite area of emergency services, Father Benjamin had shamefully taken great care in telling the 911 operator this was not a typical call from Skid Row. He'd called back twice, and through it all the priest had managed to wake Juan and keep his friend alive. Thank goodness he'd gotten the ambulance there in less than thirty minutes. They'd saved Juan's life—or for the moment at least.

After Juan was hospitalized, Father Benjamin learned of Juan's family and his abandonment of them. Before Juan's disclosure, Father Benjamin had thought Juan was the closest thing to a brother he'd ever had. Together, they'd seen their share of deaths and tragedies at the center, and they'd bonded through the commonality of their work.

Father Benjamin had been proud of Juan. He'd been under the impression that Juan had defied all odds to become a man fully recovered from his addiction. He'd been through the program, sobered up, stayed clean, and became a leader. A feat that the priest had rarely seen.

Now, Juan's recovery seemed like a deception to him. He'd felt personally betrayed and used. Indeed, Father Benjamin had helped Juan change his identity from Joe to Juan. Had he enabled this man to hide from his family and not be accountable for his own actions? Had he made up his own version of their brotherly love, too? His friendship with Juan now appeared false. It reminded Father Benjamin of the many one sided, couple relationships he'd personally counseled.

He'd returned to Juan's hospital room the day after the man was admitted. The day after he promised he'd help him with his daughter. "Why don't I know this already?" he'd selfishly asked Juan, after Juan had spent a few hours describing the incidents, and the history surrounding the accident, the illness, and his final abandonment of his family.

"How does one go about telling this story, Father? It's not pleasant. I'm ashamed."

"Oh, come on, Juan," Father Benjamin said. "How many Al-anon meetings have you led? How could ... Why have we not done this years ago?"

"Father, I'm exhausted." Juan had a tube in his nose, an IV in his arm, and machines beeping around him. His skin was a yellowish tint, and the priest could see that Juan had trouble keeping his eyes open. "I'm dying. I'd like my daughter to have closure. I've never asked you for anything for myself. Just do this, please?"

"Yes, yes. I will," Father Benjamin answered.

The priest had no choice and yet he worked hard at finding a resolution that didn't involve him personally. Father Benjamin had developed a list of possible candidates, people whom both he and Juan had worked with, who could bring Juan together with his family. When he'd returned to the hospital, later that day, he'd provided several choices of counselors to Juan who could contact his family, every one of which Juan had declined.

"Father, you agreed to help my daughter. I don't want anyone else contacting her." Juan had closed his eyes and swallowed, his voice became a whisper. "This is delicate, please."

"I'm way too close to this situation," he'd told Juan.

"Which is exactly the reason I asked you." Juan had turned toward the window. "The phone numbers and addresses are in my office. I keep them in the notebook, on my shelf, with the word "family" on it ... We're running out of time."

As it stood now, Father Benjamin believed he could leave the rest of this mission in the hands of Jessie. It was evident she would be at Juan's side, and she'd do everything within her power to get Teresa to be there too.

"Father, how long have you known my brother, Joe?" Jessie walked at his heels in double time to keep up with his long legs.

"For quite some time." Father Benjamin stopped in front of Juan's office.

"So you knew him as Joe?"

"Yes."

"What did my brother tell you about our family?" Jessie stood by his side at the door to Juan's office.

"He hasn't shared much."

CHAPTER 6

ANGEL HAD REMAINED BY TERESA'S SIDE throughout the meeting with the priest. She wanted details on Juan's abandonment of his family. The entire situation felt familiar, a bit like a movie she'd seen before.

The priest spoke to Teresa and her aunt as they entered Juan's office. "Your dad spent little time in this room. As you can see, he's not a paperwork person."

A desk, a shelf, and a few chairs filled the dimly lit office. Stacks of folders sat on both corners of the desk and the shelf held a pile of white three-ring notebooks.

"We were looking for the General the day Juan was admitted into the hospital." The priest sat down in the chair farthest from the wall, opposite the desk, and Teresa stood in front of the shelving unit.

Angel immediately focused on two framed photographs near the top of the bookcase. She pointed at the pictures just as Teresa looked up. Teresa's aunt was oblivious.

"The General?" Jessie asked Father Benjamin.

"Yes, he's an older gentleman who's been living in the shelter near Washington Street. When he didn't check in last week Juan was worried. The General was too old for the night air."

"Was?" Jessie responded.

"I hope not. We're still trying to find him," the father whispered.

Angel's insides were about to explode over the unseen photos until Teresa finally recognized the pictures and pulled them both down from the shelf. "Look at this!" Teresa turned one frame toward her aunt. "This is me, and that's Angela. I don't remember this photo."

Angel saw the picture and felt the most unusual sensation in her being. So warm and complete, like a soft flutter that grew from a few to a million butterflies floating inside her core and tickling her insides.

"We were young. I think this was right before the accident," Teresa said to her aunt. "Look. Angela had those silly boots on." Both women laughed.

"She loved those boots. My goodness, that was taken more than twenty years ago." Jessie flipped the picture over and read the written words out loud. "Angel and Teresa ... That's right, Joe called Angela his angel, and more often than not he referred to her as Angel."

"Look at my mother." Teresa held the other framed photo in her right hand. "I've never seen this picture before. I only have that real old one."

Angel felt a tear—or what would've been a tear if she could cry in her world—as she looked at the second photo. She knew this woman. An impression from deep down in her being bubbled to the surface of her consciousness as the words flew out of her mouth. "I know that woman."

"Did you hear that?" Teresa asked.

47

"What?"

Angel's thoughts came to the surface again, and another word flew out of her mouth. "Mother?"

"Again, did you hear that?" Teresa asked.

"Can you hear me?" Angel asked.

"It's like a low level hum or a ringing, but I swear I heard the word 'mother.' Do you think my mother's trying to talk to me?"

"I don't hear anything," the priest interrupted.

Angel had forgotten Father Benjamin was with the women in the cramped office. She stood with Teresa looking down at the pictures and wished the priest would've kept his mouth shut. He'd broken the deepest connection she'd ever made with Teresa.

Could Angel's link to this family be that simple? Was she Angela, also known as Angel? The idea seemed right, but so had the belief that she was going to enter the world as Teresa's child. Angel had prepared for such a long time to be born to this family, and she had to deal with a lot of heartbreak when it didn't happened. The day JJ was born should've been a beautiful day, but for Angel despair and loneliness had filled her heart as she remained clueless about her suspended state.

Teresa's face relaxed, and her entire body seemed to loosen up. She pulled down the book with the word "family" written on its spine.

"May I?" Teresa lifted the notebook toward Father Benjamin.

"Absolutely."

Angel stood right next to Teresa. Her insides felt like a slot machine hitting a jackpot. She wanted to find Belle and Kail to tell them her newest theory, but that conversation would have to wait. She'd need to ride this out and learn as many details about Angela as possible.

Teresa flipped through the notebook and held up a page that contained a chart. "Auntie, look at this. A family tree. What is this called?" Teresa ran her hand over the page. "Uncle Joe ... Who's Hermeania Manuel? I don't recognize the name."

Teresa's Aunt Jessie closed her eyes and smiled. She whispered to herself, "Oh, Joe. You didn't leave, you fool ..."

"What?"

"She's my great, great aunt. Let me see that." Jessie took the notebook away from Teresa.

"I hadn't known until recently, but Juan had spent quite a bit of time on your family history. He'd developed an interest in genealogy," Father Benjamin said.

"Yes, that's the word, genealogy," Teresa responded.

"You know, there are some people here I don't know, either." Jessie flipped the pages of the notebook. Angel could see that each page had been placed in a clear, plastic sleeve. It was evident that a great deal of time and care had been put into the creation of this notebook.

"Teresita, it looks like your dad was keeping tabs on you, too." Teresa's Aunt Jessie pointed at the place where Teresa's name was listed on the top of the second sheet. A typed address and phone number had been inked out, and penciled in the margin was Teresa's current address and phone number.

"How'd he get my number? It's unlisted." Angel saw the surprised look on Teresa's face.

The priest stood up. "Why don't you just take the notebook? You'll find more information in the pages, and I think he'd like you to have it."

Immediately, Angel resented her position as unnoticeable. She'd wanted to grab the book and devour its contents. Had she thought they'd respond, she would've questioned all of them about Angela. What had Angela looked like? Could she, Angel, be

Angela? Could she take the pictures and show them to her girls, Belle and Kail? Angel's frustration grew as the others headed toward the door.

"I don't believe there's much more to this tiny office," added Father Benjamin. "Let's take a walk across the grounds, and I'll show you where Juan has stayed for the last few years." The priest led them quickly through the stark maze back to the waiting area.

"I recently learned that Juan also maintains a storage unit. I believe it holds some of the contents of your family's home." The father spoke as the three of them walked along a cracked sidewalk that outlined a well-manicured patch of grass next to the church.

"Our home on White Ridge Street? I thought he lost everything?" Teresa asked.

"Well, I'm not sure what he salvaged. But he wants you to have the contents in the storage area."

"Oh God, now I have to dispose of his junk and probably his body." Teresa spoke in a low, calm voice with only the slightest hint of a quaver.

"Teresa, what if some of your mother's things are there?" Teresa's Aunt Jessie asked.

"Oh, I hadn't thought about Mom's things." Teresa exhaled and continued, "Wow, I just haven't dealt with any of this in years."

Angel walked next to Teresa and inspected her face. She'd examined her own reflection enough times through the eyes of Belle and Kail that she now wondered why she hadn't noticed the resemblance earlier on. She and Teresa could be related; both had unusual light brown eyes and a petite stature. Although Teresa's face was rounder than her own, they could easily be sisters if Angel were in the flesh. Why hadn't she thought of this possible connection before? Had she heard anything previously about Angela's existence? Angel couldn't remember.

They followed behind the priest as he entered a dormitory type building with a long narrow hallway that housed several apartments. Father Benjamin put a key in the first door and pushed it open.

"I think it's weird that he wanted us to see his place. Why are we doing this?" Teresa mumbled.

"Juan wanted you to know that he's a man who has lived in a simple way," the priest answered. "And, we're going to get the storage unit key."

Teresa's aunt stepped through the door first, followed by Teresa and the priest. Angel drifted along beside them. Sparse furnishings and an ugly rust-colored shag carpet lay wall to wall in the small one-bedroom apartment. The space was so confined that the bathroom, bedroom, and kitchen were all completely viewable from the living room.

"It's stuffy in here." Jessie waved her hand in front of her nose and then opened the window over the kitchen sink.

"The place has been locked up for a few days." The priest moved to the desk in the corner of the living room next to the couch. He pulled an envelope from the top drawer.

"This is the storage unit address and key." The priest handed the envelope to Teresa.

Angel moved into the bedroom and was surprised to see the closet, with no door on its frame, wide open to the room and the world. Only a few pairs of pants and shirts hung from the bar and a single pair of shoes sat on the floor. The room, the whole place was practically empty.

The bedroom contained a single bed, a nightstand, a broken chair, and a weatherworn table. Angel spun around to leave when she noticed a notebook sitting on the top shelf of the closet next

51

to a motorcycle helmet, in a spot that would be difficult to see from standing position.

Teresa entered the bedroom with her aunt. "Okay, I've seen enough," she said.

"It looks like nobody lives here," Teresa's aunt said.

"Juan slept here. His life was back in the center," Father Benjamin responded.

Angel frantically pointed toward the closet and said, "No, not yet. Teresa. We need to look at that notebook."

"What?" Teresa asked.

"I said, it looks like nobody lives here," Teresa's Aunt Jessie answered.

"No, Auntie. You said something about a notebook," Teresa said.

"No, not me. You're hearing things again."

"No, no. You said my name and something else," Teresa said.

Angel spoke again. "Up here, look up here."

Teresa wandered over to the closet and poked her head in through the doorway. "Up, up, up," Angel whispered in her ear.

Teresa brushed her right ear with her hand. "What's this, Father?"

"Yes, yes, yes! It might be nothing, but let's look," Angel said.

"What?" Teresa asked.

"I didn't say anything." The priest turned toward Jessie with a quizzical look on his face. "I don't know what that is. Your dad said you're welcome to anything you want."

"Auntie, you can have this." Teresa flipped through the book and disregarded it as trash. "I think he kept a journal."

Angel tried to peek at the book but Teresa snapped it shut and handed it over to her aunt. The entire group headed out of the apartment in silence. Teresa and her Aunt Jessie followed Father Benjamin across the grounds while Angel trailed along in thought.

Teresa held the "family" notebook and her Aunt Jessie straggled behind, flipping through the pages of the journal. They stopped on the sidewalk outside the church, near the parking lot.

"Well, thank you, Father. I'm sure you have a lot to do," Teresa said.

"You know, I'd like you to ..."

As soon as Father Benjamin spoke, a woman walking toward them from the parking lot interrupted him.

"Father?" The heavyset Hispanic woman held a slow cooker in her hands while a plastic grocery bag dangled from her fingers. "I'm sorry to interrupt. But have you heard any more news about Juan?"

"Oh, Anna. No, nothing new yet. But this is his family." The priest waved his hand.

"Jessie?" Anna asked. "It's been years ..."

Teresa's eyes looked tired, although she kept her face expressionless in what Angel recognized as her "I'm done" look. Angel sensed Teresa was still here merely to please her aunt.

Anna moved toward Teresa. "And you must be Teresa. I've known your father for such a long time. In fact, I remember you when you were a little girl."

The woman placed the slow cooker and the bag on the sidewalk. She then grabbed Teresa in a bear hug. Angel noticed Teresa's body stiffen at the moment of impact. But Anna ignored Teresa's standoffishness and squeezed even tighter.

When Teresa eventually managed to step out of the woman's grasp, she asked, "Do you know me?"

"Oh, yes. I knew your mother, too." Anna looked toward Teresa's aunt. "Hello, Jessie. Do you remember me?"

"I do. How are you, Anna? I'm surprised to see you again. It's been years." Jessie turned toward Teresa and said, "Anna was a friend of our family. Years ago she was at one of our first family reunions. She helped your mother in the kitchen."

"I looked a lot slimmer back then." Anna looked away as she continued, "I'm so sorry about Juan."

"Thank you," Jessie responded.

"Were you in the kitchen when that lady caught her hair on fire? She was trying to light a cigarette on the stove," Teresa asked.

"I was that woman." Anna laughed and continued, "But I've put some weight on since then."

"Did you know my family well?" Teresa questioned.

"Not so much, dear. I'd met Juan at some meetings and he took me under his wing. Back then I had some issues with staying sober. That's probably why I caught my hair on fire."

"Why didn't my dad contact me before? You must've known I was out here."

"I didn't know he hadn't until Father Benjamin told me yesterday. I assumed he was in contact with you." Anna exhaled. "We spend so much time working with other people. It's hard to explain. I asked about you often, and your dad knew all the answers. He told me about your son, JJ, and your store. He said you had a rough patch with your husband and your divorce. He was so proud of you for raising JJ on your own and building a successful business. I thought you and your son were fully in his life. I really had no idea."

Anna swallowed. "He gave me all the answers for you too, Jessie. He said you lived in the same house and had really stepped up for Teresa when Marion had passed away." Anna appeared apologetic. "In thinking about it now, he never mentioned being around either of you. Juan just knew what was going on in your lives."

Angel felt her heart race. Perspiration sprang out on her upper lip—though of course both were impossible. In reality, she'd completely tuned into this new woman's feelings and physical reaction. Anna pulled a handkerchief out of her bag and wiped her upper lip.

An uncomfortable silence continued for what seemed like several minutes until Father Benjamin spoke. "Well I guess it's time to say our good-byes, at least for now."

Angel went to the car; she needed to get away from the emotions that had begun to cling to her. She didn't like this type of somber energy. A few minutes away from the others and she'd be fine. She situated herself in the back seat and waited for Teresa and Jessie. Angel wanted to know the outcome of Father Benjamin's attempt to persuade Teresa to visit her dad.

As both women approached, it sounded as if they were arguing. "I'm just saying, we should see him. If only for a minute to tell him how we feel," insisted Jessie.

"Well, I'm sorry, Aunt Jessie, I'm really mad. If I hadn't known better, I'd say the man that priest described was no relation of mine. I want to do this on my own terms, if at all."

"You know your mother paid Anna to help out. She was looking for work, and Joe had tried to give the woman a hand. I forgot about her hair catching on fire until you brought it up." Jessie chuckled.

"Auntie, you're so sweet. You said she was a family friend." Teresa softened.

"Well, she sort of was. She was around for a while. I think Anna even babysat for you and Angela. Something happened and we never saw her again."

Angel somehow could see inside Teresa, saw her going through a load of inner conflict that spun around and around like laundry running through a "heavily soiled" cycle.

Regret and confusion immediately poured out of Teresa's mouth. "What about the storage unit? How'd he manage to do these things without our finding out? He has counselor credentials. He somehow saved stuff from the house and he lives like a pauper."

"Yes, I saw that."

"Auntie, I'm exhausted." Teresa rubbed her left leg. "I can tell my dad's around because he's so draining, and I haven't even seen him yet."

"What about JJ? What are you going to tell your son?"

"I'll pick him up from school and talk to him."

Angel had heard enough for one day. As much as she wanted to stay around for the journal and see what was in the "family" notebook, she needed a break. She left Teresa, and the woman who was possibly her own aunt, somewhere in Los Angeles. Her entire being cried out for a rest, and she needed the comfort of someone to talk to. Hopefully the girls were back "home" early today.

Angel moved quickly to their current resting place. With merely a thought of the clouds they'd slept in last night, she was somehow transported right to the spot. Thank goodness, since the winds had moved the clouds pretty far south today. It had taken her weeks to find this particular set of clouds, two in all, with a special curve at the base. This set was perfect, at least for the time being—but eventually all clouds evaporate.

Angel lay back in the middle of the formation, at the softest peak. She took a single scoop off of the far edge of the cloud and ran it through her long brown hair imagining the shine it would make. Longing for an ice cream, she closed her eyes and licked the side of her vanilla cloud. No taste, no feeling, all was the same.

She curled up in a fetal position and closed her eyes. The need to sleep was a trait that had transferred with her into this existence. After the day's events, Angel was physically drained—another memory but maybe not an impossibility, she thought as she fell into a deep, dreamless sleep.

"Wake up, my Angel, wake up." Angel's body shook from a gentle push on her shoulder and a voice that didn't sound like Belle, or Kail. She stretched her arms out and turned on her side.

"Angel. Wake up," the male voice said.

A male voice?! Angel bolted straight up into a sitting position on the cloud. "Who's there?"

"It's me. Your dad," the man answered.

He sat on the far edge of the cloud dressed in blue-stripped pajama bottoms and a sleeveless T-shirt. His right leg hung over the side of the cloud. He smiled and his bright white teeth glowed against his warm-brown skin. The man was older. Though he had a full head of wavy dark hair, it was speckled with an occasional gray hair, and the thin mustache on his upper lip had gone almost completely gray. Although he frightened Angel at the suddenness of his appearance, he also captivated her with his beauty.

"It's been a long, long time, Angela," the man said.

Angel squinted and rubbed her eyes; maybe she was dreaming.

"No, I'm really here. And, I'm there, too." The man pointed down. "By the way, this is a fantastic view."

"Who are you?" Angel's heart-memory pounded down to her toes. "Where are my pups?"

"I didn't see any pups, although you've always had a thing for dogs. Do you remember? The neighbor's dog ... well, any dog. They all loved you." Her strange visitor took a deep breath. "Your mother had some dogs before she met me ... Wow, it feels good to feel good." He held his arms up to the sky and closed his eyes.

"How'd you get here? Who are you?" Angel was amazingly calm about this invasion of her cloud. She sensed no danger from this man. And though he could be her father, yes, she had no memory of him.

"I'm not sure how I got here," he said. He smiled and continued, "As I told you, I'm your father. I came to take you home, where you belong."

"Who am I?" Angel asked.

"After today you know who you are, and I'm going to help you remember the rest." He stood up and the white, pillowy formation shifted.

"Be careful with moving too fast," Angel warned him. "We don't weigh anything right now, but these vapors somehow sense our beings. We might fall out if you don't relax."

He laughed. "My Angel, always following the rules. You're a good kid."

His eyes sparkled as he looked at Angel. "I'm so happy to see you."

She felt uncomfortable with his intense inspection, as if he were soaking up every detail of her being, from her face to her inner soul.

"What are you looking at?" Angel's voice sounded strange, as if a bratty child had taken over her vocal cords.

"Okay, I'm sorry. I want to remember you forever. Something I forgot to do when we were down there. I love you, Angela. And I've missed you." The man blinked his eyes.

"My name is Angel," she whispered. "Tell me how you found me. How'd you get here?"

"Technically, I'm not dead. My body's hooked up to a lot of machines. The term for my current state of being is 'comatose.'"

"If I'm this person you say I am, then why don't I remember me?" Angel asked.

"Spending time up here eats away at your memory. Many people lose themselves this way. You've been here a long time."

"Who's my mom?" Angel thought of the photo she'd seen earlier that day.

"Marion is your mom and my wife. You were right, you saw her in the picture."

"How do you know that?" Angel folded her arms in disbelief. What type of trickery was this man up to?

"I communicate with your mom," he answered.

"What? How?" Angel had been trying for years to break the barrier with Teresa.

"You'd be amazed at what obstacles a determined woman like your mother can overcome. Not to mention she's pissed at me." He smiled sadly.

Angel cringed at the sound of the "p" word. Perhaps this was a reaction from her time in a physical body. She didn't like cursing, and certainly she hadn't developed the habit in the flesh.

"How can you be in two places at once?" Angel asked.

"I don't know. I think my body is in that hospital bed and my spirit is here." He ran his hand through his hair. "It happened so fast."

He turned into the cloud and moved closer to Angel as he spoke again. "I use to call you Angel, Angel. Because you're my angel. I like that you kept that name."

He placed his hands on Angel's arms. "Your sister, Teresa, was driving since she'd promised you a trip to the mall. The two of you loved doing things together. I know the radio was playing because the ambulance driver told me the music was still on when he got there."

He hesitated for a moment. "It was a hit and run, by a suspected drunk driver. You were thrown from the car—either your seatbelt wasn't fastened, or it didn't work. You didn't make it to the hospital. Teresa survived, but she was hurt. I'm sure you've seen the scar on her left leg."

Angel pulled away from his grasp and sat down. "How'd I end up like this? I want to remember!"

"You were supposed to wait here for your mother and go with her." The man perched across from Angel. "I messed up. I tried to drink myself to death, with a complete disregard for my life and my family."

"When am I going to remember what happened?" Angel pounded her fists down on her thighs and could almost feel the impact of the blows.

"I know it'll take some time for the memories to come back. You're experiencing a sort of amnesia."

Angel sighed, deflated by the realization she wasn't going to get what she wanted right now. "Tell me about the woman who sent you to me, the one you say is my mother. Or tell me what she said, or how you learned these things."

The cloud adjusted to each movement as Angel stood up and put her hands on her hips.

The man pursed his lips. "Your mother told me you stayed behind because you didn't want to leave Teresa alone. You have free will. She couldn't force you to go along with her." His eyes smiled at Angel as he whispered, "You're a brave young lady, my Angela."

He reached out to her but she turned aside to avoid his touch—a touch she wouldn't have felt anyway. "I should've been the one to take care of Teresa," he said. "If I'd handled it better perhaps you'd have felt good about going with your mother and leaving Teresa with me."

Her jaw dropped as the whole thing began to make sense. She'd been with Teresa all these years. Why else would she have felt a connection with no reciprocation from Teresa?

The man who claimed to be her father leaned in and continued, "I'm sorry. I've learned a lot in this life, and most of it the hard way. I've hurt many people, but until recently I didn't recognize how far this ripple of pain had run."

Angel had to acknowledge he might be her father. So she sat quietly and listened to what possibly explained this existence of hers.

"And if you think about it, here I am sitting with you, my baby girl. Had I known this day would come, I might not have stepped off the wagon all those years ago," he said.

Angel nodded.

"Life is a big circle. It does come back around." He gazed at her with an emotion she couldn't fathom.

"Were you religious—or if it's true, were we a religious family?" Angel asked.

"No, we never did the church thing together. Your Aunt Jessie and I had to go to Catholic school, and that was enough for both of us."

"Tell me about the woman you say is my mom." Angel relaxed and propped herself up on her side.

The man smiled at her. "You use to lie like that in front of the TV. I've missed my girls ... Your mother is, and has always been, the strength behind this man." He tapped his chest. "She saved my life twice, and now she's helping to resurrect my soul."

"Resurrect?"

"Okay, that's a bit dramatic. She's reluctantly helping me so that I can help you."

"Oh," Angel responded. The thought of her mother wanting to help her in some way gave her a warm feeling, though she didn't really know who her mother was.

"Quite some time ago, I'd wake up and have a vague recollection of your mother yelling at me. I realized it was part of a dream, but then over time the images fully invaded my dreams. Your mother had worked hard and learned how to communicate with me from, I guess, the other side. After all, she is deceased."

The man—her father?—took a deep breath. "She was so angry. She'd waited for you to follow her. She spoke to you and tried to get you to go with her when she passed, but though you promised to be there soon, you're still not with her. Your mom has been trying to get your attention ever since.

"For a long time after, she sent me visions of you here in the clouds. As these dreams occurred and grew steadily stronger, I only drank more. I thought I was being haunted, and so I tried to escape."

The man touched his stomach and his arms, and then he looked down at his hands and flexed his fingers. "I feel as if I need a drink of water. Or, no, I think my time with you here is running out ..."

"Don't leave me hanging, please keep talking," Angel begged him. She believed she was very close to learning what had happened to her.

"According to Marion, your mom, it was all my fault and she'd had every intention of making my life a living hell until I fixed it. Who could blame her?" He glanced around as if unsure that he was still with Angel.

"How'd she tell you that?"

"Oh, I'm jumping ahead ..."

Angel turned away from the man for a second to look at the sunset and see if she could locate the girls. Belle and Kail were usually back by now, but maybe the sight of a stranger in their cloud had kept them away.

As soon as she took her eyes off of him, she knew it was a mistake; the cloud tipped up and she felt the space behind her go empty. The man she'd been speaking to was gone.

CHAPTER 7

TERESA RESISTED THE TEMPTATION TO TAKE the journal she'd found in her father's house and burn it later. Instead, when she'd dropped off her aunt, Teresa gave her the book and told her to throw it away if she didn't want it. Teresa's shoulders were tight and her brain had gone numb.

She'd headed toward JJ's school and let her mind go empty. A few minutes later, she looked up to see the familiar flag in front of the building, but didn't remember a single image from the drive.

She sent JJ a text to let him know she was waiting out front. Teresa smiled as she reread her message to JJ, every word spelled out. He'd teased her about her texting skills because she always spelled each of the words.

His response came through with a rattle and a beep. It appeared he'd be out in about fifteen minutes; at least she wasn't completely clueless about reading his text code.

Teresa leaned her head back and closed her eyes. Memories she'd spent a lifetime repressing were beginning to come to the surface. She recalled her father and mother whispering late at night—or what a little girl might have thought was late. Her entire being wanted to believe they loved each other, but in the hushed tones after she and Angela went to bed she'd sensed something was amiss. This had been years ago, and now she suspected it was around the period Aunt Jessie had said her father and mother'd split for a short time. Try as Teresa might, other details didn't come to her.

Although, she did remember clearly that she was her mama's girl and Angela was her daddy's child. The fact wasn't a secret, and it was also evident daily.

As far as the affairs of the family were concerned, her mother was in charge. Her dad did everything and anything her mother asked—not begrudgingly either, since he was madly in love with her.

A rap on the driver's side window startled her. JJ stood beside the car, his hair a mess and his backpack slung on one side.

"Mom, can we take Seth home? Dude needs a ride."

"Dude?"

"Yeah, open up." JJ bent over, his lanky frame having shot up so high this year he appeared about six feet tall. Her son grabbed at the door handle, and it flicked out of his hand. He grabbed again at the handle making the car shake.

"Slow down! Watch smudges." Teresa unlocked the car, exhaling as she let the outside world in.

"Hi, Seth. How are you?" Teresa turned toward the back seat where Seth had entered the car.

"Excellent, and you?" JJ's long-time pal responded.

The atmosphere Teresa had created seemed to leave the car as the boys entered with a teenage testosterone energy that only a refrigerator full of food could fuel—a force Teresa didn't want to deal with today. But Seth had always been a good friend to JJ.

"I'm good. How's your mother?" A wrench seemed to tighten around her skull as she strained to smile at the boys.

"Great." JJ reached over and slapped Seth hard on the head. Seth immediately returned the blow.

"All right, okay ... Stop it, please. It's library time."

"Sorry, Mrs. Reynolds." Seth folded his arms and subtly gestured to JJ. Both boys laughed.

"Okay, come on now, or it's going to be nappy time for both of you." Teresa placed her fingers on her temple and rubbed.

"Nappy time?" JJ held back his laughter with a snort. He then proceeded to discuss a lunchroom incident with Seth jumping in during the milliseconds when JJ stopped to breathe.

The drive to Seth's house felt to Teresa like a month of Sundays, but after they all had said their good-byes, JJ dropped the facade of his cool 'dude lingo' and became serious.

"Okay, Mom, what's going on?"

"Wow, what's going on with you? Who are you? And what did you do with my son?" Teresa was finally able to let out a small laugh.

"Come on, you rarely pick me up and you seem ... preoccupied."

"Yeah, well, I want to talk to you." They drove in silence for a few moments as she maneuvered through side streets. "Did I ever talk to you about my dad?"

"Yeah, a little."

"What do you know?"

"Well, he drank too much, and he disappeared when you were eighteen. Right?"

"Close to being right, yes," Teresa answered. "Are you ready for this? He's back and he wants to see me. He's dying."

JJ exhaled a slight whistle.

"I know, it's heavy."

"You should see him. We should see him."

"Why?"

65

"Because, once he's gone this time, he'll be gone for good."

Teresa let the quiet fill her veins. It was nice to just focus on the road and not think about anything else for a second.

JJ was so sensible sometimes. A solution such as this, put in such simple terms, made sense. Teresa had been arguing with Aunt Jessie all day. Fighting in her mind with the 'do-gooders' at the church. Her time spent with the priest had been uncomfortable and truly unnecessary. Teresa snickered, and slowly the snickers became a roaring laughter.

"What's so funny?" JJ asked.

And without either of them really knowing why, she supposed, the contagious laughter simply caught on. Both mother and son laughed themselves silly, all the way home.

CHAPTER 8

SITTING DOWN AT HER KITCHEN TABLE, Jessie examined the black and white essay notebook Teresa had left with her, the same kind that both she and Joe had carried back and forth to Catholic school so many years before. The sheets contained large spaces between the lines, perhaps to allow room for juvenile ranting, or for the nun's criticisms.

God, she hadn't thought about grammar school for years, and she hadn't realized those days still bothered her so much. Jessie shook off the memory and focused on the present.

She flipped open the cover of the notebook and fanned the pages, not at all recognizing her brother's penmanship. From the first sheet to the last, the pages were filled with doodles and writing. No date, no headers, no indication of when the journal had been written. Jessie took a deep breath and read.

My wife, Marion, is angry. She's been mad at me almost as many years as she's been dead. We raised our daughters together. We built a life together. Our world came apart when she was diagnosed with pancreatic cancer.

I've learned, over time, if something is meant to happen it will happen. But I was not prepared for the death of our youngest daughter, Angela, during Marion's chemo treatments. Teresa, our oldest daughter, was driving the car, and a hit and run driver left them both for dead, a tragedy that hastened the passing of my wife.

Within months of one another, both my soul mate and my baby were gone. So I lost it. I gave Teresa no support, no care while I drank myself into a living hell.

I met Marion when we were kids. Well, I say kids, but legally we were adults. She was hanging out with Patricia, the girlfriend of some guy who spent time around us when we were in high school. I can't remember the guy's name anymore. Oh, well, neither of them was a part of our lives after Marion and I met. At the time, I was a dog toward the ladies. At twenty, I had plenty of girls lined up and didn't mind adding more. Until I met Marion.

When I saw Marion, there went my heart, although she didn't seem to be interested in me at all. Oh yeah, she was still young, at seventeen. Small frame, long black shiny hair, petite nose, and a beautiful white smile that sparkled next to her tan skin. I was going to add her to the list of ladies that I loved, but Marion was smart. She knew I was a player, so she treated me like shit, and this made me want her even more. I'm smiling right now thinking about it.

Me and the boys hung out regularly at Hermosa Park. We'd juice up our crappy little cars and loiter around the parking lot there. I always had with me a big can of Schlitz. Just a bunch of punks thinking we were badass. I laughed out loud when I wrote that.

I must say my Marion kept me on the straight and narrow most of the time ... that is, after I finally convinced her she wanted to date me. Eventually, we became inseparable. Something the boys thought would never happen, and they told me I was whipped! Then before I knew it, I had a job at the Post Office and was married to the love of my life. Yep, I was a changed man, or at least I thought I was.

By the time Teresa was born, I was working for Gordy's Auto shop. Yep, I moved around from job to job, but I was always employed. What a dreamer. I could do it better than anyone and wanted the world for my family. I wanted to own my own business, or I wanted to help people. I just couldn't decide what to do. So, I went to night school when Teresa was a baby. And, oh heaven forbid I let my wife work.

I was the man of the family—she was to be taken care of by me. And we did well in that respect for quite some time. This element of our lives was a product of my culture. The more subtle part of my Hispanic blood was the fact that at home my wife was the boss. I know, most of the men of a Latino persuasion won't admit the power of their woman. But Marion was my world, and she was in charge. Except when it came to her getting a job. I still had my pride. Besides, I don't think she minded staying at home and raising the girls.

Teresa and her mother were close, real close. And what a beautiful baby she was. Gosh, about four years later Daddy's Girl surprised us with her arrival. Angela looked very much like me, and from the beginning, as a baby, she remained calm in my arms. No mistaking she was my little girl, but they both were. And Marion felt exactly the same way. It just happened that I was Angela's closest parent and Marion was Teresa's.

When we were kids, my little sister, Jessie, and I were close, and then when we grew up, she liked to hang around the family's house; her life seemed to revolve around my girls. Jessie was an extension of my family—well, she is my family. I hope one day we get to say our good-byes.

As I ramble, with pen in hand, that's the purpose of this crazy ranting. I might not make it to see my family again and I'd like to leave something behind for Teresa, Jessie, and my namesake—Uncle Joe—as well as my grandson JJ to explain my behavior and what has happened over the years.

Right now, my body is angry. Decades of binge drinking and drugging has caught up with me. About five years ago I had a gallstone attack that focused the hospital on my liver, and that was when the cirrhosis was detected and I sobered up.

Unfortunately, the damage is irreversible. But I've lived longer than they thought, and I'm still able to manage my work right now. I use a cane sometimes, occasionally a wheel chair. I can't say when the last time I—my body, my physical being—felt good to be alive. I hurt all over and I must say, occasionally I do have some serious bouts of self-pity. But I'm not a martyr. I don't believe anyone deserves this type of pain.

The ringing of the telephone interrupted Jessie's reading. "Shoot," Jessie whispered as she picked up the phone.

"Hello."

"Aunt Jessie?"

"Yes, Teresita."

"JJ makes the best argument for seeing Dad. We'd like you to come with us."

"Yep, yep. Okay, let's go now before you change your mind." As intrigued as she was by the notebook, it'd have to wait because Jessie didn't intend to let her niece change her mind.

"Meet us at the hospital then. We'll wait in the lobby," Teresa said.

CHAPTER 9

THE ABSENCE OF JUAN SEEMED TO create a stillness in the center that disturbed Father Benjamin. The priest had expected a lot from his friend, and he realized this now as he sat in his office and contemplated his own next move. What business was it of his if Juan had made mistakes in his life?

Father Benjamin wasn't proud of his behavior toward Juan throughout these last weeks of the man's life. The priest had been quite disappointed and hurt over the whole situation, and now he believed he'd handled himself horribly. At least Juan was trying to make up for his own bad decisions, and when all is said and done the family might reunite with him. The priest decided to go to the hospital and update Juan. It was a reason to see his friend, for what might even be a final time.

When Father Benjamin arrived at the hospital a few minutes later, he somehow managed to make it through the waiting room where the kitchen gals and folks from the shelter had been holding a vigil. He slipped directly into Juan's room unnoticed. Once there, reality slapped the father in the face as soon as he heard the monitors and machines whirring and beeping around Juan's sleeping body. The priest sat down in the chair next to Juan's bed and leaned his head against the wall, shutting his eyes for a moment.

"Oh, Father. I didn't know you were here." The nurse's voice woke him.

"I must've dosed off waiting for Juan to wake up." The priest looked at his watch and noticed that he'd probably been asleep for a half an hour.

"The doctor didn't tell you? He's in a coma," the nurse said.

"Oh, no. I didn't know that." The priest stood up and leaned in to get a closer look at Juan. "He's so peaceful. I thought he was asleep."

"He might wake up. It happens sometimes." The nurse checked the IV, the monitors, and then spoke as she left. "I'll see you later, Father."

"Juan, I did it." The priest bent down and whispered to the oblivious man, "I met your daughter and your sister. I don't know if they'll be visiting, but there's a strong chance of it."

Father Benjamin touched Juan's forehead and with every ounce of his being prayed for his friend—ending the prayer with a single wish, "... and may you return from this state to spend some time with your family. God bless your soul."

The priest stood and turned to leave then he paused for a moment. Oh how he hoped Juan would wake up again, but he felt this was the last time he'd see the man alive. "Good-bye, my friend. I'm sorry I was so hard on you. I know you were doing the best you could."

He exited the room and walked through the halls of the hospital where the typical chemical smell of the medical center assailed his nostrils. The place seemed crowded tonight with what appeared to be relatives and friends of patients, most of whom displayed worried looks on their faces. Father Benjamin walked by a few kids out of control and heard a nurse snap at someone. Unfortunately, there was not much good news to be shared in this facility.

As he rounded the corner on his way to the exit, he noticed three women and a man at the end of the hallway. The priest was unsure why he was drawn to these people, but he acknowledged the shorter woman looked familiar. He walked directly toward the little huddle, and as he got closer, he recognized Jessie and Teresa with a young man who was probably Juan's grandson.

"Well, hello," said Father Benjamin. "I thought I saw another young lady standing next to you."

"Hello, Father. This is my nephew, JJ," Jessie said with a forced smile.

The priest noticed the older woman's demeanor change entirely as she spoke, just as earlier today she'd seemed uncomfortable inside the church.

"I could have sworn I saw another young lady standing with you. I must be tired." The priest reached out to Jessie in an attempt to reassure her, but she jumped back, startled.

"No, it's only the three of us. We were just about to head over to Joe's room." Teresa's voice tightened and her mouth appeared pinched. "You know, Father, my son convinced me to say my good-byes and make my peace."

A warm sensation flowed through the priest's heart. He was glad for them. "I'm sure that your dad will be pleased to see you. His room is down the hall. Just keep going—it'll seem like a football field away." The priest waved his arm toward the room. "Somehow I managed to get past Anna and some of the other folks a little while back. They may still be lurking about, but I'll see if I can make sure your visit is uninterrupted."

"How's my brother doing, Father?" Jessie asked.

"I didn't talk to the doctor, so I'm not sure of the complete diagnosis. But the nurse informed me his peaceful rest is more than a nap. She said he slipped into a coma earlier today. I'm sorry to be the one to share this with you, and now that I think about it, he probably won't be able to talk to you. But I'm sure he'll know you're there."

"Oh, my ..." Jessie's voice trailed off, "I hope we're not too late."

"Aunt Jessie, it'll be okay." As Teresa turned and spoke to the priest, her tone shifted from the gentleness aimed at her aunt to the same type of indifference she'd shown earlier that afternoon. "Father, I take it that Joe has no knowledge of our meeting today, then?"

"Funny you should mention that. I had a short conversation with him a few moments ago because I've heard patients in a coma remain aware of what people around them say. I've got to believe there's some form of understanding. I did tell him you might be stopping in."

JJ leaned in and whispered loudly to his mom, "Mom, lighten up on the padre. He's only trying to help."

Teresa put a hand on her son's shoulder and responded in such a low tone the father was unable to recognize what was said. But both mother and son laughed.

"Well, I'll let you folks get on with your visit. If I can do anything for you, please let me know." The priest sighed as he moved quickly through the exit to make his way to the rectory. He hoped he'd done his best for Juan's family.

CHAPTER 10

ANGEL STOOD THERE, IN HER CLOUD, disappointed. The man who claimed to be her father had been here and then was gone—right at the moment of revealing the mystery of her life. Her pups would be okay on their own. She had to go see him at the hospital.

She hesitated for a moment. Hospitals were full of lost beings, and most of them were in an ugly spiritual condition. Unlike beings in bodies who saw right through Angel, these disincarnate hospital dwellers could see her, and they were needy. The hospital was a busy place for her and one of her least favorite places to visit. She couldn't remember why she'd been to hospitals in the past, this was just something she knew, just as she now knew she had to go and see him. Regardless of her feelings, she needed verification that the man in her cloud had been Joe, and that Joe was her father.

Within seconds, Angel stood in front of the medical center where Teresa and JJ had just entered the facility. Her timing was impeccable, so she followed close behind her possible sister and nephew.

"What's the plan, Mom?" JJ asked.

"We'll wait for Aunt Jessie to get here, and then we'll go to Joe's room and say our good-byes." Teresa looked at her phone.

"Are you working?" JJ asked, sounding a bit cross with his mother.

"Nope. Checking e-mails and seeing if Aunt Jessie called, and it's all in one device. Gotta love technology." Teresa smiled at her son and then added, "You need a haircut."

"Yes, what's with this deprivation? I need new shoes, too."

"Now you're pushing it." Teresa led JJ past the reception area into the corridor. "Let's wait over here, out of the way. I don't want to run into the 'do-gooders.' I'm sure they're here somewhere. They all love my dad."

"Who?" JJ looked around as he followed Teresa quickly through the waiting area, almost unable to keep up. "What's your hurry?"

"Shhh, I don't want to talk to the church folks." Teresa tried to move JJ to a spot between her and the lounge, but he fidgeted away from her tugs. "Hold still."

"What'd you call them?"

"The 'do-gooders.' That type drives me crazy because they're always into everyone's business."

Angel stood next to Teresa and closely examined her facial expressions and her demeanor. She didn't really pay attention to JJ until he spoke again.

"Don't hold back, Mom. Tell me how you really feel."

"It's crazy, I know. I guess maybe being a 'do-gooder' is someone's job, because God knows there are folks who could use the help. But keep them away from me. Many of those people seem to be busybodies too." Teresa's voice rose.

"Shhh. You're about to give away our location." JJ laughed. "This is a covert operation, remember?"

"Okay, laugh all you want. But, you'll see—it's annoying. They're annoying."

"Who's annoying?" Feistiness filled the air with the arrival of Aunt Jessie. The short, powerful woman more than held her own when away from the church and the priests. Angel saw Jessie through different eyes than she had previously. She admired this woman—her possible relative. Angel would definitely talk to Teresa's Aunt Jessie—her Aunt Jessie?—if she believed she would be heard.

"Oh, hello, Auntie. How long have you been here?"

"I just arrived and walked right over to you. Why?"

"So much for hiding out of the way, Mom." JJ Laughed.

"All right, Dude. Let's go find Joe."

Angel saw the priest approach Teresa and knew they'd be held up, so she moved quickly through the halls, ahead of the group. She wanted some alone time with Joe, and oh how she hoped he'd be able to see her again. Either way, she'd still speak out loud to him—maybe he had the ability now to see her, either in or out of his coma.

She rounded the hallway in the direction the father had just come from, and with such speed she almost felt her hair flowing behind her in the breeze. Angel even imagined the wind on her cheeks as she raced to the room where she believed her the man who claimed to be her dad was resting peacefully in a coma. She had to see him.

As Angel approached the door to her supposed father's hospital room, she saw a set of bare feet at the entrance—the feet of a man whose body lay on the floor. Sometimes it was difficult for her to know what was in the living world and what was not. Maybe her clue was the fact that this man was lying on the hospital floor, but somehow she knew he wasn't in the physical world.

"Hello. Can you hear me? Where am I?" the stranger asked. His hands reached upward as if they were claws and his mouth bent grotesquely toward the left side of his face.

Angel ignored the man, and stepped over him into her father's hospital room. She hated to be so rude, but she feared he'd keep her for hours while she tried to explain what happened to him and where he was.

Joe was in the bed farthest from the door, so she moved through the curtain and was at his side in no time.

"Hey, you didn't finish explaining things to me." Angel sniffled a bit, but she knew her tears weren't real. The emotions clung to her from other people, a side effect from staying close to this place where beings were housed in physical shells.

"I'm right here." She jumped at the voice from behind her and turned to see Joe sitting in the chair across from his body. "It's that dual thing we talked about earlier, because I'm not dead yet."

He pointed at his body and continued, "The priest, my friend Father Benjamin, said a powerful prayer and made a nice apology. Well, it's what pulled me out of the cloud a little while ago. And as you know, I've got some business to attend to in that body—so I had to come back anyway."

"I know you do. They're on their way down here, Jessie, Teresa, and JJ. All of them. But, you and I aren't done yet. I want to remember ... I want to know how you talk to the woman you say is my mom."

"Remember the ouija board when you were a kid?"

"The what?" Angel asked.

"Oh, never mind. It was a bad joke." Her dad stood up. "Let's take a walk and we'll discuss it—okay?"

"You might want to stay in here ..." Angel was about to warn him, but her dad was already at the door and looking down at the barefooted man lying in the hallway.

"Hey, man." Joe leaned closer to the man as he spoke. "I think you're not alive anymore, and you need to stay near your body for the prayers and such." He turned back to Angel. "Is that how this works?"

"Sort of. It's not a bad idea, actually. It'll help him get his bearings." Angel wished she'd thought of that—Joe had good instincts.

Joe reached his hand out for her as he stepped into the hallway, and Angel made the gesture of holding his hand. She smiled. She wanted to believe her time in limbo would be over soon.

"What's the story? Tell me about my mother," Angel demanded.

"The most extraordinary woman I know." Joe's smile brightened. "You'll be seeing her again, real soon."

"How'd she tell you about me and stuff? Please finish what you were telling me."

"Oh, well, it's nothing special, Angela." Her father guided her toward the exit door. "I want to walk outside. Is that okay?"

Angel nodded.

"My communication with her has been entirely through my dreams and more recently by way of my prayers, or what I call meditation. Weird, isn't it? We're all so close together, both the dead and the living, yet we're all so far apart. Some dimensional-science crap I'll never understand. It has a lot to do with vibrations and the speed of the atoms, things I don't know much about. Start with the idea that even the objects here on earth aren't as material as they seem to be. A lot of busy particles in motion make up the physicality of our existence. They speed around so fast we can't tell that nothing is actually solid."

"So you haven't seen her or spent time with her like you and I are doing now?" Angel asked.

"Oh, no. I'm afraid she'd wallop me if we met in person." He laughed. "I'm joking. We'll be together again one day. But for now, our speeds of vibrations are way too different. It's not easy for me to be in this state today, so somehow I know she's behind this—all of it. I don't know how, but she's helped arrange this whole thing that's taking place right now and what's about to take place."

"How do I get my confirmation? I want to remember something from my life before. Will I ever?" The questions flew out of Angel's mouth.

"Yes, my dear, you will. I promise. Have some faith for now. Go with your gut feelings, because you know this is all true."

He stopped and bent down to Angel to look into her eyes. "And your sister is starting to hear you a little." He smiled shyly. "I'm going to need your help with Teresa because she's a tough one. My actions caused her to deal with more than any young girl should ever have to face, and still she has a long time to live. I want her life to be better. She's not really living now—have you noticed?"

Angel felt overwhelmed by all this information. "How do you know this?"

"Your mother tells me, that's how. You know ... like I just explained, when I meditate or sleep."

Angel put her hand near Joe's, and as they walked around the hospital grounds she wondered if anyone in their physical bodies going here and there could see them. "What have you done for all these years, and why did it take you so long to come and find me? I've been so alone ..."

"Angel, I really screwed up." He stopped and knelt before her. "Can you forgive me? I will somehow make this up to you." Joe wiped his eyes with the back of his hand.

"You can't cry in this realm, you know. As much as you want them to, the tears will never come." Angel stood in front of Joe and touched his forehead. She whispered, "I hope this works."

"It has to work." He bolted straight up into a standing position and continued, "We have to get back to my hospital room. Will you help me to help your sister? Whisper to her, stay with her ... I know your sister is starting to hear you."

Angel nodded and the two of them walked together, hand-in-hand to where Joe's body lay in a coma.

CHAPTER 11

TERESA LED HER FAMILY DOWN THE hall while she held her insides together. Almost numb, she was fully aware that her confident walk and talk was all make-believe while a mushiness of raw nerves sat directly underneath the surface. JJ was such a blessing to her, especially through this recent event with her father. Her son made everything seem so simple that sometimes she forgot he was a teenager, until he'd remind her of it with his behavior.

"JJ, stop it. Will you please calm down?" she reprimanded him as he bounced of the walls and peeked in every room they walked past.

"Okay, okay."

"Did you have too much soda or something? You're acting like a child."

"I am a child," he snapped back, and then, as if to stave off the impending fight, he winked and smiled. "I'm seeing my grandpa for the first time. I can't help it."

She resisted the urge to slap him and walked on in silence while he hopped around Aunt Jessie.

"What do you think, Auntie?" JJ asked her.

"About what, JJ?"

"About this whole thing. It's kind of weird, isn't it?" JJ walked sideways and so close to Aunt Jessie he was almost in her face, as if he were attempting to see into her brain and read her thoughts.

Teresa grabbed JJ's arm as hard as she could. "I'm sorry, Aunt Jessie. I don't know what has gotten into him." Teresa turned to JJ. "What's wrong with you?"

The group stood in the hall, unnoticed by passersby, as the busyness of the hospital continued around them. Teresa watched her son's face grow calmer. "I don't know. I guess I'm nervous."

"Well stop it. Stop it right now." Teresa dropped his arm. "Quiet please. I need you to be quiet."

The urge to slap her son subsided as Teresa focused on the visit that was about to take place. She led her aunt and JJ down the hall while she thought of her father.

What had he been up to the last five years? The man was sober, and he'd been living within miles of her and JJ. After her mother's funeral Teresa had stayed in their family home alone, and everyday she dreamt of her father's return. At some point after that, her Aunt Jessie moved her out of the house. She'd told Teresa it was not okay to sit in the dark and cry all day long.

Teresa's BlackBerry brought her back to the current moment as an e-mail vibrated upon its arrival. Kelly had cleaned up the back room and had learned that one of the other part-timers had an emergency and left early on Sunday. Teresa would have to deal with this later. She turned off her phone and approached the nurses' station with her aunt and son at her heels.

"Hello. We're here to see my father, Joseph Torres. Can you tell me if the doctor is available?" she asked.

The nurse looked over the top of her glasses at Teresa and spoke. "Oh, we love Juan. Let me find Willa, his nurse. She's been with him most of the time, and she definitely knows the doctor's schedule."

For a second, Teresa's insides warmed at the thought of so many good folks around her father, and then the feeling died as it collided with her grinding jaw. Her father, the saint, never offended any person, unless of course he was related to them. Teresa took a deep breath and reminded herself this emotional roller coaster would be over soon.

The nurse picked up the phone and spoke softly to someone on the other end of the line. She covered the mouthpiece while she spoke to Teresa. "Willa is in his room right now. It's 424—down the hall to the left ..."

Walking away, Teresa heard the nurse speak again into the phone. "I'm sending them down. I know, I thought he had no family as well."

JJ grabbed Teresa's hand. "Mom, I'm here, and we're family. Don't pay any attention to those do-gooders."

Teresa smiled at how JJ had gotten it wrong and quickly decided not to go there with him. "Thank you, son." Teresa grabbed his chin with her free hand and kissed him on the cheek.

"Yuck." He laughed.

Her Aunt Jessie moved along quickly and now stood directly in front of Teresa and JJ, blocking the entrance to room 424. "Okay, let's talk about this visit."

"I thought we'd just see the nurse and the doctor, if possible, and say our good-byes," Teresa said.

"So that's your plan. I think you need some time alone with your father to talk with him, regardless that he's in a coma." Aunt Jessie had a stubborn look on her face.

"Okay, Auntie. Let's first see what the doctor says. Then we can play it by ear," Teresa answered.

"Do you know when you walk through that door to see the nurse, you'll be with your father?" Her Aunt Jessie crossed her arms and nodded toward the hospital room.

"Yes, and that's why we're here. Are you nervous or something?" Teresa asked.

"I'm concerned for you. But if you've thought this through ..." Her Aunt Jessie hesitated for a moment. "Well, then, let's do it. Let's go see my brother ... your dad."

Saying that, Aunt Jessie moved through the door at once, leaving Teresa in the hospital corridor wondering exactly what had just happened.

"That was weird," JJ said.

"No stranger than you bouncing off the walls a few minutes ago. Come on, let's go." Teresa and JJ stood in the hallway for a few seconds and then entered the hospital room. Her father lay in the second bed, on the far side of the room, tethered to machines emitting a series of steady beeps and wheezes. A nurse stood at the window alongside Jessie.

"Are you sure your brother doesn't have a twin somewhere?" Teresa heard the nurse ask Aunt Jessie.

"Oh, no, Willa. My brother's one of a kind."

"I swear I saw him walking outside with a young girl. It's the strangest thing." The nursed turned and nodded at JJ and Teresa who had entered the room and now stood at the foot of Joe's bed. "Oh, hello. I'm Willa, Juan's nurse."

"I'm Teresa and this is my son JJ. Joe—well, Juan—is my father."

"Well, I'm glad to meet you. Your dad's stable, now," the nurse responded.

"Do you know if the doctor's available? I'd like to speak to him." Teresa licked her lips. Her mouth was dry. She was afraid to look directly at her father, but cast an oblique glance at the figure in the bed—not enough to see his features, but just enough to notice the grey stubble on his face. She supposed they didn't shave him every day.

"Your timing is good because the doctor makes his evening rounds just about now. He'll be here any minute," the nurse answered.

"Is Joe still in a coma?" Aunt Jessie asked.

"Yes. But I've seen his eyes flicker. It's a sign that he might come out of it." The nurse moved to the other side of the room and pulled over a chair. "Sit down, please."

"Willa, you sure are an attentive nurse. Do you have any other patients?" Teresa's voice sounded shrill to her, almost unrecognizable.

"Teresa, that's rude," her Aunt scolded her.

"Oh, no. That's okay, Jessie." The nurse turned to Teresa. "I do have other patients. But I like your dad a lot. He's helped so many folks in this part of town that he's somewhat of a legend. You know, he did the impossible with my brother, sobered him up and got him a job. I've known Juan ... or, Joe, for quite some time."

"I'm sorry. It's not your fault he abandoned his family years ago and drank himself into oblivion." Teresa felt her throat close around the words.

"It's not my fault and it's none of my business. I'll be at the nurses' station if you need anything." Willa left the hospital room.

"Now why'd you do that, Teresa?" her aunt asked her.

"I'm so over hearing about my father the saint. Come on now, you have to be tired of it too."

"Actually, I'm kind of proud of Joe. At least he tried to do something with his life."

"What's that supposed to mean?"

"Mom, Aunt Jessie," JJ interrupted. "Look." He pointed toward the bed.

Joe's eyes blinked. His head moved from left to right as he took in a deep breath of air.

CHAPTER 12

JOE FELT THE HEAVINESS OF HIS body. He'd wished he could've stayed in the dream, or was it reality? It seemed real, it felt real, and most importantly it mirrored everything he'd been going through over the years.

His body was done with this world, and Joe could sense the onset of death in every pore of his being. His eyelids were heavy, and he felt as if a lead anvil had been placed in his stomach. The pain he'd imagined, or experienced, at the beginning of his hospital stay was now completely gone. The doctor must've given him some serious medication.

He sucked in oxygen. Still alive. Joe wished for strength to get through this last phase of his life. On his left side was a continual beep, and on his right a low-level hum from the machines. His right arm lay strapped down, attached through a tube via a needle, to a bag of fluid.

Joe smacked his dry lips and let the realization sink in. All that he was and all that he'd ever be was about to be wrapped up. The final days of his life. He laughed at the sound of it, like a soap opera: "The Final Days of His Life."

Joe moved his left hand. He knew the remote to the bed was somewhere close. He wanted to sit up and couldn't accomplish this on his own. Somehow his head turned right as he fully opened his eyes, and although his vision was rather blurred, his eyes met the eyes of a young man who stood in his room just outside the line of where the curtain would be if it were pulled shut.

"Hello," the young man said.

Joe opened his mouth and a croak came out. He gestured for water with his left hand and somehow poked a finger in his own eye. Joe's hand/eye coordination didn't work well this morning, or afternoon. What time was it?

"Hello, Joe."

Although she was older and seemed much shorter, Joe recognized his sister near the window, off to his left. His brain was intact but his body appeared to have taken on its own agenda.

A whisper came out of Joe's mouth. "Jessie?"

Jessie walked up to the table next to Joe where a water pitcher sat empty. With the pitcher in her hand she bent down to Joe's ear and said in a quiet tone, "I'll get you some water. Your daughter and grandson are here to see you."

"Teresa ... Angela?" He saw two females near the window, up against the wall. The boy stood to the side of them.

"No, Joe. It's just me, Teresa. Angela died years ago." If he could have felt anything, Joe believed he'd have felt an icy chill down his spine as his daughter's voice knifed the air.

Teresa moved closer to his bed, and as she moved, so did the other female, Angela. Joe's chin sat close to his chest as he struggled to hold up his head. Did his eyes deceive him? The girl behind Teresa waved, winked, and smiled. He smiled at Angela as his head landed back on his pillow.

Jessie returned to his side, where she found the remote to the bed. "Here." She put the straw in his mouth, but held onto the cup and he sipped the water as Jessie raised the upper part of the bed.

"The doctor's on his way according to your nurse friend, Willa," Jessie said.

Joe coughed. Water and blood spilled down the front of his hospital gown. His head was clear and he was ready to talk, but his body seemed to have other plans.

"I'm sorry. I'm having a hard time here." His voice was scratchy, but it worked.

"It's okay." Jessie wiped his mouth and then patted his gown with a cloth that had been sitting on the bedside table.

"I don't want to see the doctor. I want to talk to Teresa and meet my grandson." Joe's words slurred together. "No more pain medicine, either."

Jessie turned to Teresa and the boy. "It's okay. Move in closer. He wants to talk to you."

Joe nodded his head as confirmation his body parts still followed his command. A nurse entered the room. "Joe, it's me, Willa."

"Hello, Willa. I'm awake. I'm a little slow, but coming around."

"Joe, you've got a lot of toxins in your body. But we've followed your instructions."

"Remind me ... what the instructions were ..."

"No pain medicine. Tell me now, do you want anything?" Willa asked.

"I want to be left alone for a while, with my family."

"All right, I'll see you later."

"Wait, Willa?" Joe, not able to yell, spoke as loud as he could, and to his amazement his voice felt a little stronger.

"Yes, Joe." Willa stopped at the door.

"How's your brother?"

"Sober and doing great. Thank you." The door swung shut as Willa left the room.

Joe turned backed to his daughter. "Teresa, I'm so proud of you."

"For what?" His daughter had moved to his right with JJ at her side.

"Raising your son, building a business from the ground up to name a few things."

"And how do you know about all that?" Teresa asked.

"I've been sober for a while," Joe answered

"That didn't answer my question."

"Let me meet my grandson."

Teresa sighed, rolled her eyes, and looked from her son to Joe. "JJ, this is my father, Joe."

"You don't look like you were in a coma," JJ said.

Joe gave his grandson a slight smile. "Yeah, well, I'm not sure what I'm supposed to look like. I feel better than I have in years. They keep telling me it's the toxins filling my body and they're coming from my liver which isn't working." Joe smiled a little more broadly. "How old are you, now? What grade are you in?"

"I'm fifteen and a sophomore. How old are you, now?"

Joe laughed, and then stopped to keep himself from coughing. "Sixty-six or so. Today, I feel older, but younger."

JJ snorted. "That doesn't make sense, but okay. If you say so, Gramps."

Teresa frowned and snapped, "Dad, what do you want to say?"

Joe didn't know where to begin, so he froze. The moment he'd thought would never arrive was here, and he couldn't back out now, nor could he move forward.

Jessie cleared her throat and began to talk. "I ought to slap you upside the head, Joe. We looked for you for years. Where the hell have you been? And why did you wait until you were almost dead to contact us?"

Joe had missed his sister's spunk, which always struck him like a breath of fresh air. He took in the moment with a grin. Jessie, his sister, was still a straight shooter, and oh how he regretted the lost years of not being around her.

"Have you gotten shorter?" Joe finally asked.

"No. We're not going to let you change the subject. Come on, Joe, where've you been, and why now?" Jessie tilted her head and leaned in with a "don't try it again" look on her face.

"I'm not sure where to begin. There's so much to tell," Joe answered. His breathing had become a little labored.

"Well you better start somewhere because time is at a premium." Jessie waved her arm at the machines surrounding Joe's bed.

He raised his left hand to his eyebrow and continued. "Yes. Okay, pull up some chairs and sit down. This is going to take a while."

JJ pulled the lime-green chair in from the hall and brought it to Jessie, while Teresa scooted the orangish corner chair up to Joe's bedside. JJ borrowed a third chair from the next room.

Joe, with his family situated around his bed, felt his heart beat a little faster. The moment he'd thought about for years was actually happening, right now. He smiled.

"Joe, what's with the smirk?" Jessie put her hand on Joe's shoulder and pushed gently.

"I'm sorry." Joe snapped out of his silent victory dance. "I'm thinking about how I've longed for this moment for years. And now that it's here, I don't want to blow it."

"Okay, okay. We've got some anger going on over here. So wipe the corny smile off of your face and get busy," Jessie said.

Joe ran his free hand down the front of his gown, avoiding the wet spot. His coordination had improved. Then he somehow managed to put a serious look on his face. They were as furious as he suspected they might be. This wasn't going to be easy and perhaps wouldn't end in the result he wanted to achieve before he died. Joe sighed.

"I'm going to go way back, and start with the car accident. I know this is something you don't like to acknowledge or talk about, Teresa, so it may be painful for you." Joe nodded toward his daughter.

"I'm not sure how you know these things, the things you think you know, Joe." She sounded bitter. "I'm here, I'm listening, and I'm not happy about it. So continue, please."

"When your mother was diagnosed with cancer, I held it together for a time. I thought we could beat it, and well, we all know that didn't happen."

The beeps and whirrs charged on next to him, and Joe's eyes filled with tears. His glance at her met the glare of his daughter, which added a special stab of pain that he believed he fully deserved. Joe turned to Jessie, and she nodded for him to continue.

"I'm sorry. I know that's weak, especially after all these years. But it's true, and I probably would've died without contacting you if I didn't have something more to share."

Joe swallowed and continued, "I lived on the streets, in the storage unit, and in shelters around town, off and on. I'd sober up, get a job here and there and think about finding you, Teresa." He shook his head. "And then lose it again. I'd spend my paycheck on binges and then sober up. Your mother's voice haunted me. Marion, constantly yelling at me about how I ruined our daughters' lives."

Joe stared straight ahead in a daze. "I thought I was dreaming it. So I drank more to shut the voice up." He turned to Teresa. "I loved your mother, and she was my life. But at this point her voice was driving me crazy. And I would do anything to shut it up. Booze, drugs ... anything."

Teresa shook her head. "What's wrong with you, Joe? You're blaming Mom for your drinking problem? Are you insane? Is this what you brought me here for?"

"Teresa, let him finish. He's not ..." Jessie looked from Teresa to Joe as she continued. "You're not blaming Marion for your mess, are you?"

"No, no. I'm not communicating this well ... I didn't know that it was her, at least not for sure. And nobody dropped the alcohol down my throat. I'm fully to blame for this." Joe gestured at his body. "In fact, I didn't truly give up alcohol until I almost died about five years ago. The gallstones led the doctor to look at my liver. I was sick and tired."

Joe took a deep breath and looked over at JJ. "JJ, can you hand me some water? I'm not real mobile. I can't reach it."

JJ filled the plastic cup and held it in front of Joe with the straw.

"Thanks, kid." Joe looked JJ up and down. "Are you in sports? You look athletic."

"Not really." JJ glanced at his mom and mouthed the word, "help," which Joe caught.

Joe drank from the cup that JJ held while his daughter, sister, and grandson watched in silence. He ignored the boy's gesture to his mom and decided to leave behind any more attempts at lightening their mood. "So I found out I was dying back then and healthy'd up as much as I could. I've worked at the church during these last five years, and I spent a lot of time helping folks like myself get sober."

Joe wiped his brow with a heavy limb. "I think you know the obvious stuff. I want to talk to you about something else. And this is the reason I haven't taken any medication. I know what I'm about to share with you is going to sound strange. In fact, you may not even believe me. But I ask that you keep an open mind."

Joe looked from Teresa to Jessie. "I'm not looking for your forgiveness. I don't want anything from any of you for me. I know what a fool I've been and where I stand in your eyes. What I'm trying to say is, this meeting is not about me at all."

Joe shut his eyes and took in another breath, as deep as he could without igniting the pain underneath. "I'll say this, though—it's wonderful to see all of you, and I'm really glad I met my grandson. But if that were all this was about, I wouldn't have asked to see any of you."

As Joe exhaled, Teresa jumped in. "Dad, where are you going with this?"

Joe's body quivered. "It's about Angela." His lower lip shook and tears streamed down his face. He wasn't sure he'd have the strength to wipe them away. "She was so young and ... well, Angela lost her way back then."

"Joe!" Jessie jumped up, grabbed his arm, and shook his shoulder. Joe's eyelids were heavy, so very heavy ...

CHAPTER 13

HER BROTHER, JOE, FELL ASLEEP OR back into a coma as she frantically tried bring him back to consciousness. The bastard. Why did he go away again? "Joe, wake up."

"Aunt Jessie, stop it." Teresa pulled Jessie's arms away from Joe and hugged her. "It's okay. He's not doing so well. I don't know, maybe we were too hard on him."

Jessie squinted her eyes and pulled her cheeks in real tight. "He's rambling, and nothing he says makes sense. What's he trying to tell us here?"

"Who knows." Teresa turned to her son. "JJ, push the button for the nurse, or better yet, go and get her. I think he needs some medical attention."

Teresa led Jessie to the chair by the wall and Jessie allowed her niece to guide her there.

"I don't get this. It's all so odd," Jessie said. And the more she recalled all that had happened, the more surreal the whole day seemed.

"Yes, this whole thing is strange." Teresa looked around the room. "After all these years, and there he is."

Jessie thought about the distress her brother's absence caused her niece, and yet during this visit Jessie was the one who'd been the hardest on Joe. She'd reared up on him and hadn't given him a second to breathe, even though in the past she'd been the one to make excuses for him, over and over again. What had gotten into her?

Seconds later, the doctor and nurse entered the room, and quickly checked Joe's pulse and poked around at him. The diagnosis came that ... Joe was asleep. Evidently being in a coma could be exhausting, so Joe had fallen asleep.

The doctor sent the family out of the room to give Joe some space to recover. At the same time, the nurse requested the family stay close, since Joe was on a day-by-day watch. He wouldn't be sent to an extended care facility because he was expected to die soon. Jessie, Teresa, and JJ stood in the hallway and looked at one another.

"I think I'm going to go home for a few hours and come back later. Are you up for meeting here again in about two hours?" Jessie asked.

"We can decide in a while," said Teresa. Jessie could see her niece was trying to get a grip on herself. "We're going home. I have some work to do and JJ has homework. Call me later and let me know what you're doing."

Jessie hugged Teresa and then headed to her car. She wanted to return home and finish reading the journal Joe had put together. Something he was trying to communicate to them gnawed at her. Jessie believed the writings held a clue or two, and if he woke up, she wanted to have the journal with her, or at least full knowledge of it so she could understand him better.

She realized she needed to relax a little around her brother and maybe even talk to him alone when he woke up—if he woke up again. Such craziness he'd caused, and now for him to be talking in circles ...

At home, ten minutes later, Jessie found the notebook on her kitchen table where she'd left it. Then, with a fresh cup of coffee in hand, she sat down and took up reading from where she left off.

At first, I thought the alcohol was causing me to see and hear things. I was certain these were illusions, or better said, I was delusional. I kept hearing Marion's voice over and over in my head, and at times whispering in my ear. "Save her. Your daughter needs you." I'd drink more to drown her out, but she'd yell louder. "You fool, you've ruined everything! Stop this nonsense now."

It could've been about a year after Marion's death or at some point around this time. I woke up in a dumpster in South Los Angeles with my head pounding, my mouth dry, and my body sore as hell. I think I'd been beaten and dumped in the trash bin, but I couldn't be sure. Up to this point, not knowing what'd happened the night before had been a running theme the entire year. The blackouts occurred so frequently and were so total that I have memory gaps covering weeks at a time. It's either dumb luck that I'm alive, or Marion's angels—or my own angels—because by rights, I should have been dead by now.

So on this day many years ago, I'm lying in a dumpster on a pile of stinky trash feeling like I've been run over by a steamroller or two. Then I heard Marion's voice, plain as day, as if she were standing over me. She said, "Joe, get up and go to the house. Take a shower, clean up, and move as many things as you can into storage."

The woman meant business—I could hear it in the tone of her voice. If that was a hallucination, well, it sure did scare the crap out of me. And I was in bad shape then. But I got up and moved my tired, hungry, hurting body toward the house. And when I made it home, later that day (after a few drinks to stabilize my brain), I saw the notice on the door. Our house had been put into foreclosure. The bank was going to seize the property.

It took me a few minutes to figure out the date the bank was going to take possession. Somehow I understood that I had about a week to either pay up or get out. I think I also realized at this point that I'd been living on the streets for over a year. What a fool I was.

And then, I remember looking for Teresa in the house. As if my teenage daughter would be right there, living and going about her business with her mother, sister, and father all gone. I really wasn't thinking straight, especially when I became disappointed to find the fridge empty.

Teresa's room had been completely cleared out, and Angela's room was how we'd left it. The house smelled stale and stuffy, and it appeared to have been abandoned for quite a while. I opened the windows and went into the bathroom, where I was shocked to learn the water worked. Though there was no hot water and no electricity, I took a cold shower and managed to pull it together for a short while. In fact, I had more time than the notice said. I spent about a week or so at the house and I called in some favors from friends I hadn't seen in quite a while. I somehow got the important pieces out of there.

We managed to put a few boxes and some furniture in a storage unit, though I've not been back to the unit since I sobered up. I want to make sure Teresa has access to these things. She can sell them or keep them, it's up to her. I'll make sure my friend Father Benjamin has the details and the key. Oh, and the unit is paid for five years or something like that. So she can let it sit for a while and get over the ugliness of the situation before she has a look.

I'd like to say I sobered up at this point, but I didn't. Seeing the family home and just simply coping was extremely difficult, and this is not an excuse, but I kept drinking. My demons had taken over and they were winning. After I finished packing up the items I thought would be important to Teresa, like her grandmother's dining room table and some of the kitchen items, well, I left the house and never looked back.

Oddly enough, during that week for those few days, for brief spells here and there I had moments of clarity. I was so clearheaded that I knew exactly what to save and put aside for Teresa. I believe to some extent I was guided or bossed around by Marion. I didn't hear her voice again, for a while, but I believe she was working inside of me. Here I was out of my mind, falling down drunk, and then for a while I pulled it together, getting the house in order simply to lose it.

I wasn't completely finished when they came for the house, but I was definitely intoxicated. As sick as it sounds, I thought I'd hit pay dirt when I found some cash in one of the dresser drawers in the master bedroom. We bought a bunch of whiskey and beer, enough to last throughout the ordeal of sifting through my dead wife's things. Vinnie was with me at the time—he had a beater of a pickup truck. I remember when we made our last pass from the house to the storage unit. We'd loaded up his truck and we were backing out of the driveway when some suits showed up with the sheriff.

Vinnie freaked when he saw the official car, and what he called "the Man." But they weren't there to bug us in the least. I told him they only wanted the house. I kept telling him that, but he refused to stop. We drove off with what became our final load, and I never returned. I did, however, go back to the storage area many times. In fact, I lived in it—off and on for several years.

After Vinnie dropped me off with the load of stuff and what was left of my booze, I put the key to the unit on a chain around my neck. I carried my suspended driver's license and any dollar cash I had in the bottom of my shoes. My change was put in a small bag I tied to my belt loop and kept inside my pants. Oh yeah, I was good at being homeless.

When I first went to stay in our house, I had to throw out the clothes I was wearing at the time. My goodness, I lived with myself for so long I had no idea how smelly I was until I took that cold shower. Because of that experience, afterward, over the years, I made every attempt to keep somewhat clean. You do get used to your own smell and lose track of time going for weeks without a shower, unless you make an effort to think about it. Later on, I often used the water hose on the far end of the storage unit, hidden behind other units and cold as hell ... But, it worked. Some of the homeless shelters had showers, it's true, but too many rules.

After that, my life, my behavior, didn't get any better. I was picked up for loitering, being drunk in public, and a few other things. I went to AA meetings off and on and tried to get sober. I've woken up in so many godforsaken places, yet somehow I'm still here today.

Throughout my ordeal, or more specifically my trip to hell with my demons in tow, one thing remained constant—Marion's voice. My wife was really pissed off at me. Not a little, but a lot. At first I heard words from far away, and it'd be pieces of sentences. She wasn't whispering at all, it sounded like she'd been yelling from a far away place.

One night—I think I was under the bridge warming up by some guy's fire and lit up from some homemade beverage he'd made from potatoes—the voice started in on me, and it sounded like a radio with a broken-down frequency. Marion's voice was coming through to me in my head and I couldn't quite get dialed in properly.

I heard sporadic words, just enough to know what she meant, "... your fault ... daughters ... sober up ... jackass."

I asked my friend if he heard the voice and he just laughed. I remember how pissed I got at the noise in my head or near my ears. It was weird. The sound, her voice, was coming at me from around my head, but sometimes in my head. I grabbed that crappy old moonshine and guzzled it down, anything to shut her up.

My friend laughed more when I told him I thought it was my wife. He said, "Keep drinking, she'll shut up. If that don't work, focus on the fire, and maybe you'll pass out."

That was some bad advice, and it's exactly what I did. Not one of my proudest moments at all. But my gawd, I kept at it, over and over again, and Marion wasn't nothing if she wasn't persistent—she kept at me. Eventually the sound waves must have cleared up or gotten better—who knows, maybe all of her practice at communicating had started to pay off. I could hear her clearer and better over the years.

When I sobered up completely, sometimes for weeks at a time, the voice would go away during the day, but then my wife would haunt me in my dreams.

It started with these beautiful cloud dreams. My daughter Angela would be floating in the clouds, peaceful and serene. Then Marion's voice would come in like a bad voiceover in a B-movie. She'd say something like, "... you see what you've done to our youngest daughter. Put the booze down and fix the mess you created. This is not what we planned ..." She'd go on and on. So I'd wake up and hit the bottle, because I refused to face my life.

At one point I believed I was schizophrenic, but eventually I learned this was not so. I lived through that voice crap. Oh, she'd stop for a while and then as if the mute button would come off, it'd start up again for days at a time. And at one point, about ten years in, I began talking back to the voice. That worked out well for me when it came to street cred. Those badasses all thought I was nuts and not one of them would come near me. "Shut up, woman. Leave me alone!" I'd yell to my right side and then to my left.

One time I helped an older woman on the streets. She was shaking real bad and most folks stayed clear of her. I can't remember her name, or maybe she didn't tell me, but she was in a real bad state. I helped her with her things and actually walked her to a shelter. I shared some cocktails with her, which seemed to help her shake a little less.

When her head cleared up she freaked me out. She said I was haunted and the female who was tied to me would never leave me alone until I set right the error of my ways. Man, that was weird. The old woman told me the dreams would never stop and the voice would keep on talking until I fixed it, though she wouldn't tell me what "it" was. Also, I never told her about the dreams and the voice.

Then the old lady told me to get away from her. She said she didn't like my energy and that I was tied to some "bad shit." She rambled on about how I had a lot to do to make it right with the world. She affected me a little because she knew things that no other living being could've known. I had a chill going up my spine for a while after I met that woman, and I never saw her again.

After that episode I tried to clean up. I went to some meetings and worked hard at staying sober. I was scared. God, I wish I could say at that time I held it together, but I didn't. Like I said, my demons were some bad boys, and they refused to let me go about my business.

What's so odd about this comment now is that as I sit and write about it, I'm not the least bit triggered. Used to be ... speaking about it, or thinking about drinking would set me off. Now, the thought of drinking, or smoking crack, or partaking in any substance abuse makes me sick to my stomach. It's unfortunate that for me to reach this state of being has taken so long. But I am grateful that I have no desire or need to take a sip of alcohol or ingest any other mind-altering substance.

I'm still not sure how I survived that crazy time. And that is all I want to say on the subject. I'm sorry about those I hurt, because the list is long.

So, how did I get from street slug, mood-elevator connoisseur to sober saver of the free world? Ha, ha, ha ... or LOL as the kids would say these days. Over five years ago I had some heartburn that turned into radiating pain. I walked around for a few days with it and when I couldn't stand it any longer I went to the hospital.

The nurses made me wait, and for hours I was doubled up in pain, groaning in the waiting room. I had my own corner because nobody would come anywhere near me. I thought I was going to die—in fact, I wanted to die. I whispered to the voice to take me away, get me the hell out of this world. As you can imagine, the people in the hospital thought I was crazy. I think I heard somebody say that nobody wanted to tend to the crazy homeless guy in the waiting room. But that could've been me being paranoid.

I know I reeked of street gunk and alcohol. I just wanted a shot to put me down like the tired old sick dog I was. Youth in Asia (I don't know how to spell it). Put me out of my misery, please. And although I was talking to the voice, she was gone now, in my darkest hour. And it served me right, because I was gone in her darkest hour. But for some reason, as much as that voice drove me crazy over the years, I was less lonely because of it. Strange as it now sounds, it's true. Probably at some point I drank to hear the voice instead of get rid of it. What a mess I'd become.

Okay, so I'm doubled over, talking to myself, and stinking up the hospital. I'm ready to die and of all the things that could happen at this moment, a frigging priest somehow approached me, or snuck up on me (and it's not easy to approach a homeless guy without him noticing unless he's drunk). I never saw the priest coming at all. I felt a hand on my shoulder and then I see the guy in my face practically. The guy tells me he knows me from some meetings gone by. All I could think was, "frigging priest, get away from me." And I'll be damned (probably for sure) if I didn't say it out loud.

"Joe, it's me. Father Benjamin," he says to me. "You know who I am, from the Washington Street meetings."

I don't remember what happened in that hospital waiting room after that. I woke up about a month of Sundays later and I was cleaned up in a bed with monitors attached everywhere. My gallbladder was gone and I was sober, really sober.

Father Benjamin told me he raised "Cain" to get me some medical attention. He said I was in the hospital for more than a week before I woke up. I went through withdrawal and I was a real handful for that first week, all in my sleep. I guess I was in like an alcohol- or toxin-induced coma. I don't know how it works. But I really got cleaned out and that's when they found the cirrhosis and Hep C. I sure had done a number on this body of mine. And apparently it was touch and go for a while there. They didn't think I was going to make it.

You ever wonder what happens when somebody is in a coma or hanging on for dear life? I had an experience, I truly did. I don't think it was a typical experience, but I had one. It wasn't good, either. No white light, no beautiful music ... But then, I guess at that time I wasn't ready for anything pretty. For several days, I was told, I appeared to be hallucinating and sometimes, in my sleepy state, I would become hysterical. The nurse, Willa, who also became a friend of mine, told me I was covered in perspiration and ranting about things she didn't understand. She said the devil was purged from my system that week, and that's why I never wanted to drink again.

"Joe, it was like an exorcism. One that you had all on your own," Willa said to me a few years later.

At the time, I didn't talk to her or anyone about what had happened. The experience had been too weird to discuss. I'd heard about people dying and coming back to life, but everything I'd ever heard was positive. The words serene, beautiful, peaceful, and such were always used to describe those experiences—but they wouldn't be used to talk about what I went through. My experience was dark, dreadful, ugly, reprehensible, and downright terrifying.

I can't come up with a timeline for what happened to me, but I can give some kind of order for what I underwent. As I sit and think about this now, I believe I created this episode, or my wife did. To be clear, I sometimes waffle on my understanding of the voice and her involvement. This entire process could all be explained away as hallucinations, and occasionally I feel that way, or I want it to be a hallucination. Yet, in all reality, I have to say it's not just something that my brain made up—this was real, and it's a bit scary to look that fact in the eye.

Imagine a dream in which you're falling, and you have no control except for at the very end when you wake up. I began my journey in this falling manner. As I said, the timeline is sketchy, but I know that this happened some point after the waiting room fiasco.

I fall in a fast downward motion where I have no control, and I'm going down, down, down. The falling seems to take forever, but soon I feel as if I'm in a well, or a dark tunnel somewhere. A chill is in the air, not as in cold but as in eerie—in fact, my spine tingles at the thought of this now. I'm still falling downward until the tunnel narrows, and I land hard in some nasty tar-like substance. My senses seem heightened, and this muck smells worse than the gutter, or the street in South Los Angeles.

I stood up and was ankle deep in real crap.

I begin wiping the gunk off of me, a natural reaction, right? A low-level hum filled my ears, and I saw figures rising up through the muck. Arms and bodies, people covered in this putrid mess, reaching up to my legs trying to pull me down to suffer the identical fate. I screamed at them—it was like the Night of the Living Dead, a woman's shape to my left rising up, and arms, a lot of arms pulling and tugging on me.

I knew then if they pulled me in, I'd drown, and not only be dead forevermore, really dead, but I'd be one of the anonymous dead, suffering in Hell for the life I'd lived, suffering in the sludge, unable to breathe, unable to rise, and with no identity except for my suffering. That would be it, for all eternity, and that's exactly the definition that I would give today of Hell.

I didn't know where these people-like things were coming from, as I was on firm ground, ankle deep in the gunk and standing on something. The zombies rose around me as though they were a part of the floor. I thought if I moved I would land in their sinking, stinking world and never return to the "normal" world—that is, the world in which I had my quite abnormal human existence.

Don't get me wrong, I wasn't calm. I was scared to death, petrified, frozen in place, about to throw up with the stomach-wrenching fear, and no longer wiping off the muck. My heart raced, and regardless of the chill in the air, I was dripping with sweat. I think I was literally almost scared to death.

"Get back," I yelled at the freaky things clinging to my legs as I shook them off. "Back away from me or I'll kill you." A funny kind of threat to make in Hell.

The episode was disgustingly real, but yet I still hoped I'd wake up and see that this event was only a nightmare. It felt as if hours were going by as I kicked off the hands and stood in the one spot I knew was on solid ground—but for how long would it remain that way? I thrust the bodies back and tapped my bare toe on the ground in front of me. Ugh,

I finally realized I was standing in that crap with bare feet. Gross, even for someone like me, who'd woken up in some of the vilest circumstances imaginable—in human excrement and garbage of every possible kind.

I continued to kick and tap my way to the wall, where I had to feel my way around the edges of this circular, clammy, cavelike arrangement. When I looked up in the darkness, I observed the rest of this structure, which appeared to have no ceiling to it—but it did have a smell that's best described as the bowels of Hell. Maybe that sounds a bit melodramatic, but those words still don't capture the essence of this odor—and maybe this place really was what the ancients called Hell. Hell, or the pit, was where God threw the rejects, those who refused to turn His way.

I slowly made my way around the outermost perimeter of this place. The wall was smooth and felt like cement, or something equally cold and solid. I leaned my cheek and my body up against it and inched around it by tapping my toe. I wasn't going to fall into the pit, wherever the pit might be, to join the bodies from the underworld. My mind wasn't working very well at that time, but I knew if I fell in with the others, I was lost. I would have no chance at all of redemption, and I was scared. Maybe what my elders had said when I was a child was true—maybe the priests actually had it all right. If I didn't repent, this was where I was bound to wind up.

112

It could've taken only minutes, but hours seemed to pass before my hands finally came upon a hinge to a door. I scooted past the hinge and groped around until I discovered the handle to the exit. I panted hard while sweat dripped off of my brow, and my body shook. The feeling of nausea, too, had never left me.

A low-level hum rang in my ears and the bodies, with extended arms, continued their writhing in the pool of muck. It appeared to be a pool now, with absolutely no floor. Where, then, had I been standing?

The cylinder we were in was dark, but not pitch black, so I could see the zombies freaking as I stood at the door, as if they didn't want me to open it. The entire pool was full of them now and they were coming closer to me. I wanted to pray, but my mind hadn't the habit, and I didn't know how. A man's hand grabbed my ankle and the outline of his head lifted from the pool. He looked like he was trying to speak, but I knew the words would be inhuman ones. So I put my foot on his head and shoved him back.

"Get off," I yelled.

This action created a ruckus in the pool of muck, and within seconds I had slimy hands tugging at my bare feet, reaching up my legs, all trying to get a grip but slipping back down. I grabbed the knob on the door, pulled it open, and jumped. No time to check out the other side since the creatures were gaining ground on me and I had to get away. Sure enough, they slipped off and the humming of their cries turned into murmurs. I thought I heard the words "Wait, don't go ..." and "You'll regret this ..." and "You bastard ..." as the door shut behind me.

I landed in another dark but silent space. The area was dry, giving off only a slight stale odor. I took a moment to catch my breath and slap my face to wake myself up, still hoping this was a bad trip or something explainable. However, deep down I knew what I was going through was real enough, because it felt realer than this moment in which I sit here writing.

For quite some time I stood, unable to move, in the spot where I'd landed. I wiped my feet on the floor, which had the texture of a gravelly type of cement. After my eyes adjusted to the darkness, I could see I stood in an immense vacant area that appeared to have no walls, but only a ceiling, about nine feet above.

"Hello. Is anybody there?" I whispered. Yep, I was scared. On the other side, I'd been in terror of those hellish brutes; on this side, I was nearly out of my skull with fear that no one and nothing existed in this place.

I tapped my toe forward and discovered I was on solid ground. In my mind I had two choices: I could stand here and look at this circular structure and do nothing, or I could move ahead and try to work my way out of this damnation. I advanced with caution; although I wasn't sure what direction might actually be onward. I just wanted to get away from that pit.

"Hello." I spoke a little louder as I moved out of sight of the zombie tank. "Is anyone out there?"

My voice echoed and that was the only noise I heard. Alone, I walked and walked for miles. Miles. I knew they were miles because the soles of my feet, scraping almost noiselessly against the rough floor, became raw. Eventually, I turned around and the circular structure that held the pit was gone. No more pit. I really had to catch my bearings. A guy could get turned around in this vast space without walls and with absolutely nothing to mark the way. I kept going and quit looking every which way for fear of getting mixed up and heading back to the pit.

Alone, alone, I walked on alone. No matter how loud or how long I screamed for attention, no one was in this barren place to hear my pleas. Was this Hell, too? My suffering in my solitary state, with no human connection, was another sort of Hell. I tried to remember my catechism. What, if anything, came next after a descent into Hell?

I must've been at it for many hours, feeling helpless and hopeless, and though I can't remember doing this—I lay down. I must've fallen asleep on that scratchy cement floor because I woke up to a beam of light, but I don't remember lying down and sleeping. Yep, I was on the ground with dried up muck on me and my cheek lay directly on the rough floor, my belly straight down, and my arms splayed over my head. Like I was doing a frog swim! From the distance, this flicker of light had woken me up. It appeared I'd slept through the night and finally daylight had arrived. I stood up and saw the dry muck on my feet and clothes and knew I'd really been through the pit—it wasn't a bad dream after all. Oh and yes, I smelled to high heaven—or heaven had nothing to do with how I smelled. The place I was in was stale and not like the pit, but I smelled like the pit.

My lungs hurt, my legs hurt, my head hurt— this was no peaceful warm feeling of life beyond life. Getting up wasn't easy. I moved slowly, with great caution. My knees clicked and my bones rattled as I stood. Top that off with the quiet and complete aloneness. I hadn't been alone with myself for quite some time, and although I wasn't sure how long I'd been in that current situation, it seemed like forever. The only noise I heard was coming from me. And even those sounds were minimal at best—my bare feet, bleeding and sore from the long journey, made little noise on this floor. As I tried to move forward on them again, I felt a red hot pain shoot up from my toes to my ankle.

Gradually, I moved toward the beam of light and I was happy to see it become brighter and brighter as I approached. The light stretched across the horizon like a line when the television used to mess up before cable—many years ago.

As I got closer, I thought I was in a parking structure headed to the ledge, and then I actually saw a ledge. Hooray! I planted my butt on the end of that floor and dangled my bare feet over the side. I looked out at the sky, or what I thought was the bright-blue sky with a small speck of a cloud in the distance. Fresh air touched my cheeks and ruffled my hair, and boy that felt good. My mood shifted, the fear subsided, as I sat in silence. I had no idea what to do next with my body hurting and my feet all blistered. I took a moment to rest and gather my thoughts.

I stared out as the cloud floated in my direction, as if I were watching a movie in slow motion. I sat in silence and enjoyed the fresh air, not really thinking about anything. I noticed the cloud growing slightly larger as it drew near me. Slow as slow could be, it floated close, and it grew larger and larger. At some point I realized the cloud was moving toward me, and I felt as though I was a target for that cloud.

I had momentarily forgotten the slimy gunk I climbed through in the pit of Hell and the long journey alone through the gray, dank area to arrive at this moment. All of what had gone before had vanished from my mind. My entire being was focused on that cloud growing larger and larger as it approached. I stood up and paced the ledge, watching the cloud in awe of the buoyancy and the softness of its billowy form. I thought it was beautiful, and I felt hopeful that perhaps now I was going to have some peace on this grueling, tortuous journey.

I saw a fleck of something inside of the cloud, or maybe on the cloud. As the puffy substance grew closer I could see movement and I realized something or someone was riding on the pure white pillow in the sky ... A girl and what looked like two little dogs. And the girl was happy. Strange ... Well, the whole circumstance was strange, wasn't it?

That vaporous configuration came right up to the ledge and I saw the girl—or more like a young woman—who looked very familiar. But I had no idea what I was about to discover.

Angela, my daughter, was in that cloud. She was talking to two small puppies. All of them appeared to be comfortably lounging on top of the strange pile of white mist—seemingly with sides for them to cozy up against. What I saw was almost exactly like the dreams I'd had over the years, but now Angela was right there in front of me.

I sat and listened without speaking, but had trouble hearing her conversation. As much as I didn't want her to see me this way, I very badly wanted to talk to my daughter. I wanted to be around my Angela again. Tears flowed down my cheeks as I watched my dead girl right within reach. Until I couldn't stand it anymore.

"Angela. Angela ..." I yelled and yelled and yelled.

My stubbornness didn't help me here. It took me a while to figure out that I was peeking into a world that would not let me in. Angela couldn't hear me, and the dogs didn't flinch at my yelling and ranting. I was able to watch but not interact. So, eventually, I gave up on the yelling and sat in silence. I could hear patches of Angela conversing with the little dogs. Occasionally the breeze would blow a few words my way, which was another odd thing (as if all of it wasn't odd enough—right?). I couldn't hear exactly what she was saying, but I knew she was speaking to the animals.

Torture is how I'd describe these moments on the ledge. For years I'd had these dreams about a girl, my daughter Angela, in the clouds, and this time I was so close to her, and it was so real, but she couldn't hear or see me there. She laughed, frowned, moved around on the edge of the cloud. And those dogs, there was something engaging about those tiny, little creatures.

Oh no, I'm not a dog person, but my wife was before she married me, maybe that was the connection, who knows ... I remember when we were first married I didn't want pets and

Marion went along with it. I seemed to recall Angela loved dogs and vice-versa. Now, these tiny dogs followed her every move in that large cloud. I heard them bark quite a bit and I think Angela understood them because she talked back each and every time.

I was so intent on watching this cloud and my little girl I hadn't noticed I'd sat back down with my hands clenched on the ledge, my shoulders pulled tight, and my jaw in a grinding motion.

If I were only having a dream or hallucinating, I don't believe I would have physically felt all these sensations. I could feel the aches and pains, and I was covered in sweat, which smelled like it activated the pit stench—whew … But, I didn't care. I could sit in my own shit to have this time with my daughter. As one-sided as the event was, I still saw her, and everything about her seemed the same. Well, at least her essence hadn't changed. She was my baby and I was there to witness … something. I have no doubt about this fact. Here we were fifteen years later and she'd remained the same age she was when she'd died—fifteen.

As quickly as I wiped my tears away, the stream was replaced with even more tears (at least gravity worked in this place).

After quite some time, the cloud began to drift back in the other direction in the same manner it had come to me, ever so slowly.

"No, not yet." I stood up and reached out to the cloud and pulled back a handful of ... well, nothing. I paced back and forth.

"Don't go," I yelled as loud as I could.

Eventually the cloud disappeared, and I cried like a baby. Until finally the tears ran dry, and I realized I was alone in the quiet solitude of the ledge.

"What next?" I yelled out to the sky.

When I didn't get an answer, after quite some time I realized I couldn't sit on that ledge forever. I had to move on and figure this all out for myself.

I was exhausted, hungry, and extremely tired. I didn't have any desire to go near that pit again or through the stuffiness of the cavernous space without walls. Walking the perimeter I thought was my best choice, so that's exactly what I did. Slow, but on the alert, I moved to my left and put one foot in front of the other. Despite the numbness in my feet and the pounding in my head, I decided to walk on until I found some way out.

I moved forward over what appeared to be the same stretch of cement I had hiked across before, with the same claustrophobic ceiling and rough ground. I don't know how long I walked because distance and time were elusive in this cavelike place, but soon the sky turned to dusk and the night brought a chill. I sat down to rest, and as if yesterday repeated itself, I found myself in the same frog position the next morning during sunrise.

My mouth was parched again, and my body still felt like crap. When I realized I wasn't in a dream, I sat up and cried like an infant abandoned without a mother's comfort. I was stuck in Hell, wallowing in my own misery. Tears I hadn't cried for years flowed down my face, and then, at some point I was all cried out. So, I stood up and started moving.

I recognized that following the ledge was getting me nowhere, though it certainly was the easiest route. My intuition, or some inner sense of that kind, tugged on me to move away from the fresh air and the blue sky and go toward the inside of the cavelike area. I felt as if I had to go back and deal with something in that direction. I wasn't sure what needed doing, but I knew that something—inside of me or outside—had to be dealt with there. As stale and oppressive as the area was, it had been my way in, so I figured it must be my way out.

I moved away from the sky and the breathable air and walked inward—not toward the pit, but away from ledge. To my surprise, this time around the area didn't smell as musty. A cool breeze moved with me as if it were guiding me on the path I was headed down. My insides kind of lit up, and for some reason the way I was headed felt just right. For once in my life, I believed I was going in the right direction.

So I kept on walking, even though being alone with my thoughts for what seemed like miles and miles—yet again—was excruciatingly painful.

For someone like me, a guy who had ignored his own existence over the last several years and drank to keep the world away, but mostly to keep away from himself, being fully sober and alone in a quiet place showed up as a sort of private hell. I'd been my own judge, jury, and executioner of my death sentence for so long that I really didn't know how to behave on my own in an unaltered state. I was uncomfortable facing my indignities and myself. I tried to ignore my past but I walked for so long my mind started moving there. Where else could my brain go? I thought my future held nothing that wasn't bleak and ugly.

What a stupid fool I'd been for so long. I was 45 or so when I'd begun my downward spiral and 60 at the time I experienced the revelation of the pit. I'd spent about 15 years demolishing my body as if I were on a dedicated mission to do exactly this. I wasn't able to control the cancer that killed my wife, or the car accident that killed my daughter, but I was able to control my alcohol intake and my own personal madness—so that was the path I'd pursued wholeheartedly.

Jessie took a deep breath and placed the notebook upside down on her table. She didn't know what to think. Was the journal fiction? Had her brother imagined the incident? Or was he on a bad trip on alcohol or some weird drug that had induced a bizarre experience?

She flipped through the remainder of the notebook and noticed she didn't have too many pages left. Finishing would probably only take a few minutes, and then she could go back to the hospital.

Coffee cup in hand, Jessie stood up and was surprised by the creaks and clicks of her own body. She entered the kitchen and refilled her cup with lukewarm coffee. She'd been sitting for a long while reading her brother's journal, and she didn't know how to feel about it. Who was she to judge? At least she had some insight now into what he'd gone through, or what he thought he'd undergone.

The phone interrupted Jessie's thoughts. "Auntie, it's me, Teresa."

"Hello, my niece," Jessie answered.

"I've got some work to do. I'm actually headed over to the store. I may not make it back to the hospital tonight. Will you keep me posted?"

"Oh, okay ... Listen, Teresa, I think you should read your father's journal. It's, well ... it's kind of shocking. I'm not sure what to make of it. I also think he recently wrote it as an attempt to explain himself to you. It's not really a journal—it's more like an accounting of events or an event. I'm not through with it yet, but ..."

"I'll think about it, Auntie. I've got to run. Call my cell later?"

Jessie had been surprised when Teresa'd actually gone to the hospital earlier that evening. JJ was a wonderful boy and probably the only person on the face of the earth who could persuade Teresa to do something she didn't want to do.

Picking up the notebook, her purse, and her car keys, Jessie headed out the door. This was as good a time as any to return to her brother's side.

CHAPTER 14

TERESA PUT DOWN THE PHONE AND shivered, a physical reaction to this ugly day. She'd asked Kelly to close the store early because she wanted to go in and clean behind her. Not that Kelly didn't clean well, but no one cleaned like Teresa. She changed into sweats, a T-shirt, and comfy shoes.

"JJ," Teresa yelled from the hallway. "I'll be back later. I'm going to the store for a while."

Teresa waited for a response and heard nothing so she went to JJ's door and knocked. No answer. She opened the door to an empty room, which wasn't like her son. Pulling out her cell phone to dial his number, she saw the text JJ'd sent a while earlier: *Going to Seth's, call you later.*

Blood rushed to her head—the kid didn't ask permission; he just went. Teresa took a deep breath and sent JJ a text, every word typed out: *When did you ask?*

JJ immediately responded with a *Sorry* and a question, *Can I go to Seth's?* She recognized his sarcasm in spelling out the words, or perhaps he was being nice so she wouldn't have to answer with a *What?*

Teresa told JJ to be at home in about two hours if he wanted to go back to the hospital, and they would talk about this issue later. She left the house and headed toward her store. The early-evening Los Angeles rush hour was in full force causing her normal five-minute route to take thirty minutes—so much for an easy-commute day.

Teresa turned into the parking lot where she immediately saw four black and white police cars surrounding the old sedan she'd cursed at this morning for taking her spot. Since this was the only entrance to the parking lot, she drove directly toward the hubbub.

A police officer moved from the open door of the older car toward her vehicle. He waved a white piece of paper indicating for her to stop and then approached her car window with his chest puffed out and his eyes squinting as he attempted to see into her backseat. The officer gestured for Teresa to roll down the window. "Excuse me, ma'am, the mall is about to close, and we have a crime scene here. Where are you headed?"

"Oh my, officer, what happened?" she asked. "I own the Soap Store in the mall. I'm going in to clean up. Is something going on that I need to be aware of?"

The policeman now stood at her window in a relaxed stance with his arms crossed. "We don't believe there's any cause for alarm. Probably some kids joy riding. The car was reported stolen earlier today."

"Well, then I should be okay going into my store, right?" she asked.

As the policeman moved his hand, Teresa's eye was drawn to the print on the paper he held, and she realized the notice had JJ's full name across the top and looked a lot like his learner's permit. Adrenaline shot through her body and sent her senses into a spin. She forced herself to remain calm despite her agitation and immediately decided she had to get to JJ before the police did. She had to find out why they had his driver's permit and what, if anything was his involvement with this stolen car.

Teresa held her breath as the officer spoke. "I think it's okay for you to go into your store. We'll be out here for a while, and there's no need to be alarmed." The officer tapped on her car as he walked away.

With her heart pounding, Teresa parked her car in the first spot she could find and she resisted every urge in her body to run into the store and call JJ. "One foot in front of the other," she said to herself as she waved over at the police officers. "Slow and easy. Smile."

And then ... "What am I doing? We're not fugitives ... JJ's a good boy ... He didn't do anything wrong ..."

And then ... "Stop it."

Teresa stood outside the back door and dug through her bag for the keys. After some time, her hand found the set and she entered the stuffy back room. Here, she felt she was finally able to exhale. She dialed JJ's cell phone and got his voice mail. Teresa then sent JJ a text: *Call me. Now.*

Maybe the officer found JJ's permit in the parking lot and Teresa was just overreacting. No, surely, any trash in the area would warrant further investigation and even somehow be connected to that car. She wouldn't have dropped JJ's learner's permit in the lot, and he hadn't been here with her recently. Perhaps JJ's odd behavior wasn't so odd after all. What if he really was in trouble?

She dialed his number again, and again her call went straight to voice mail. "JJ, it's Mom. Call me at once when you get this message."

Teresa looked around her store and decided to reorganize the front shelf while she waited for JJ to call her back. No need to alert

Heaven or Hell*

Aunt Jessie or anyone else until she spoke to her son. Soon, she moved from the front shelf to the back shelves and then eventually she pulled out the vacuum.

Teresa was ready to throttle JJ. He hadn't called her back, nor had he even acknowledged her text: A full hour had passed.

Finally a text message from JJ: *What's up?*

Teresa dialed his number, and at the click of the phone, before he could even say hello, she pounced on him. "Why haven't you called me back? I've been trying to reach you for over an hour. What's wrong with you?"

"Hello, Mom?" JJ asked.

"Yes, yes, sorry. Listen, JJ, where are you?"

"What do you mean? I'm at Seth's. Why are you acting so crazy?" he questioned her.

"Well, open your wallet and tell me if your learner's permit is there."

"Oh, that. Well, I lost it last weekend. I'll pay the ten dollars to get the new one. Calm down, Mom."

"JJ, don't tell me to calm down. What do you know about this car in my parking lot?"

"Car, what car? You're acting crazy."

Teresa heard it in his voice—she knew her son was lying to her.

"Okay, listen." Teresa spoke in a low whisper, as if the police in the parking lot could hear her on the phone. "The parking lot is full of police. A stolen car is in the lot and it was searched, and it looks like your learner's permit was inside the car."

"What car, Mom?"

"Don't even try it. I can hear it in your voice. I'm locking up right now, and I'll come and get you. Stay put."

Teresa set her alarm and locked the back door. A tow truck had just arrived and a crime scene van was leaving the lot. The dark powder on the outside of the car led Teresa to believe they'd fingerprinted the stolen vehicle. She also noticed only one police car remained. The officer nodded at her as she walked by.

Teresa made her way to Seth's house and found JJ sitting on the front porch with his backpack at his side. She thought about Greg, her ex-husband, and wondered if she should've pushed him into being more involved with JJ. For so long she'd been a one-woman show, financially and emotionally, for her son. Maybe he needed a male influence in his life.

JJ slouched in what appeared to be a defeated walk as he moved toward the car. "Hi," he said as he plopped into the passenger seat.

"Hi? That's it?" Teresa responded. "I think you have some explaining to do."

"I thought I told you I was going to Seth's house. You just didn't hear me."

"No, you didn't. Why would you send me a text when we were both in the same house? What is going on with you, son?"

"I'm sorry, Mom. I really thought I asked."

"I'm not talking about Seth. I'm now talking about grand theft auto." Teresa's mouth tightened and her face filled with heat as she drove the car through the neighborhood.

"What? Nobody stole a car," JJ said.

"Well, then why was it reported stolen?" Her voice rose as she spoke. And for some reason she put her palm up to quiet JJ's response and decided to access their home messages remotely— something that she rarely did. With one hand on the steering wheel, her earpiece in her ear, she managed to dial the access code and listen while driving. Sure enough, the police department had left a message for the parent of Joseph John Reynolds and asked for a return call immediately. Because the voice on the machine made it seem as if JJ had been in a fatal accident, if the boy hadn't been sitting right next to her, she'd have called back that instant.

Teresa hung up her cell phone and turned toward JJ, who was busy texting on his phone with a smile. Something about his nonchalant attitude disturbed her and before she realized it anger filled the space between her ears until she saw red. Teresa slammed her foot down on the brake pedal, hard. The car jolted to a stop. JJ's phone flew from his hands and landed between the dashboard and the window.

"Geez, Mom. What the ..."

Teresa grabbed the cell phone and quickly moved the car out of the road. Her heart dropped as she deciphered JJ's text messages. She learned that he'd been in that parking lot with his friends on Saturday, and some of them had been drinking alcohol. A fight broke out, and the kids had left their bottles and trash behind.

"JJ, what's this?" Teresa held up the phone.

"I'm sorry, Mom. It's not a big deal."

"It definitely is a big deal. Yes, it is, JJ. You didn't have permission to go hang out in a parking lot. Especially my parking lot. What were you thinking? And the police are investigating a stolen car. They're not concerned about the trash you and your friends left behind."

"I was just being a teenager, not a criminal. The guys talked me into going on Saturday night. I got tired of them teasing me, so I went along," he whined.

"Why didn't you tell me?"

"It wasn't anything. A stupid night that I wish would've never happened. There's nothing to tell." JJ put his face in his hands. "This is stupid."

"How many kids were there?" Teresa asked.

"There were tons of people there."

"How'd you get there?"

"A friend of Seth's drove us."

"Did you know this guy?"

"No, five of us were packed into the car."

"Was it his car?"

"It's the one he drives to school every day, so yeah, I think so. God, Mom, what's with the interrogation?"

"You might be in a load of trouble, son. This is no joke."

"But I didn't do anything."

"Why the parking lot by my office? What were you thinking?"

"None of this was my idea. I was dragged into it."

Teresa put the car back into drive and decided to go to the hospital and find Aunt Jessie. She dropped JJ's phone into her purse, then turned her own phone off. The police would have to wait.

Something about JJ's story didn't ring true. He wasn't sharing everything. The boy wasn't a criminal, but a little voice inside told her to proceed with caution. What did her dad's Uncle Joe used to say? "Anytime you're on the wrong side of the law, be careful ... They can spin it how they want to ..."

Within minutes they arrived at the hospital, which seemed so much busier this evening than earlier that day. As Teresa and JJ walked through the waiting room she was so focused on finding Aunt Jessie that she didn't notice the heavyset woman moving quickly toward them. At first she was a flash in the corner of Teresa's eye, but that quickly turned into an almost full-on collision—by this time it was too late to avoid contact.

"Teresa, Teresa! It's me, Anna."

"Oh, yes. How are you?" Teresa cursed herself for not sneaking in.

"I'm fine, thank you. How's your dad?" Anna put her hair behind her ears. On the woman's shoulder she carried a huge bag and in her other hand knitting needles and the makings of a blanket. Anna must've been sitting in wait, ready to jump on her prey as they entered the door.

"He woke up from the coma earlier today, and he's sleeping now. That's all I know." Teresa watched Anna turn her face toward JJ. "Oh, this is my son, JJ."

"I'm Anna. Pleased to meet you." Anna shook JJ's hand.

"Pleased to meet you," JJ responded.

"Have you seen Joe yet at all?" Teresa asked.

"I got here about fifteen minutes ago. I didn't want to interrupt Jessie—she's in his room. I really want to give you and the whole family time with him. I'm just here out of support. We finished serving dinner at the kitchen so I thought I'd stop by. I'd like to give you my cell number. Will you call me if anything changes?"

Oh good, Teresa thought, Aunt Jessie was here. "Sure." Teresa absentmindedly took the piece of paper Anna handed her.

"Okay, well, I'm going home. Please, no matter how late, call me." Anna grabbed Teresa and pulled her into a smothering bear hug. "I'm so sorry about your dad."

The air was literally squeezed out of Teresa's body in the grip of this woman, and for a moment she almost forgot the task at hand. "Okay. It's okay," Teresa said as she eventually pried herself away from Anna and did her best to scoot the woman toward the door.

"All right, thank you." Anna wiped the tears from her cheek and waved to Teresa and JJ as she exited the hospital.

"Gosh," JJ said with a chuckle. "I thought I was going to have to jump in and save you, Mom."

"Yeah, well, no doubt about it, people love my dad," Teresa said. "JJ ..." She stopped talking when she felt her voice ripple.

What a messy day Monday had become, and oh how she wanted Sunday night back, when everything was normal. "I'm not certain what the police believe you did or what really happened, but I think we need a lawyer."

"Mom, why don't you just call the police and ask them? I didn't do anything."

CHAPTER 15

ANGEL SAT IN THE CLOUD WITH Kail on her lap and Belle at her side and thoroughly explained to them her connection to Teresa and the visit from her dad.

"We saw him," Belle said. "He was in the cloud with you. By the time we got here, though, you were both gone."

Kail sat quietly in Angel's lap wagging her tail. "Why do you think *we're* here?" the pup asked.

"The man, my dad, said that my mom use to have dogs. He also said that Angela was real good with dogs. I'm sure we're connected somehow ..."

Angel looked out at the clear sky, checking the weather. The cloud would be fine through the night, no rain or wind. She thought about going back to the hospital.

"You should go," Belle said.

Angel smiled. "How do you always know what I'm thinking?"

"I heard you. You spoke."

"Oh, no. Not this time." Angel laughed. "Why don't we all go to the hospital?"

But the cloud seemed so cozy to Angel, with just the three of them relaxing and floating in the night air—in complete silence. Soon, Angel fell asleep snuggled up with her girls under the lip of the cloud. She'd been in a deep slumber for a while when she felt a tap on her shoulder.

"Wake up," he whispered.

Angel rolled over and wrapped her arm around Kail.

"Angel, it's me, Dad. Wake up."

Angel stretched her body and sat up. Her heart jumped when she saw the man who seemed to be her dad petting her pup Belle.

"So, you can understand them?" he asked Angel.

"Well, yes. Can't you?"

"No. But I've seen you talk to them, and I've heard them bark back."

Angel shook her head in wonder. "Well, they do bark sometimes. But usually they speak to me."

The thought never occurred to Angel that she was the only one to hear the pups speak. For so long they'd been together in the clouds, she just assumed they could speak to anyone else in this state, and not that she was the only one who could understand them.

"They're beautiful. You all look so good together," her dad said.

He sat on the edge of the cloud with Belle in his lap gently swinging his leg. He held his head up to the sky and closed his eyes.

"Your leg is moving us." Angel pointed at the cloud. "Like an oar in a boat—we're slowly moving in a circle now. And with each kick we lose a bit of our cloud. Can you sit still for a while?"

"Oh, yeah. I'm sorry. I can't move much down there, and it feels so good up here." Her dad turned his body inward and sat on the inside of the cloud with his back perched up against the edge.

"So, how'd you end up here this time?" she asked.

"I'm not sure. My eyelids got really heavy when your Aunt Jessie, Teresa, and JJ were visiting me. The visit was a step in the right direction, but I couldn't stay awake. Down there ... well, my whole body feels weighty—and while I'm in it, I'm weak, tired."

"Oh." Angel frowned.

"I'm not leaving you here. Don't worry about that." He reached across the cloud and attempted to touch her on the chin.

"Dad, I can't feel anything here. But the gesture is nice." Angel nodded.

"I feel so good up here. I don't want to go back to that beat-up old body."

"And I'd give anything to be in one. I'd like to feel the sun on my face and eat a cinnamon roll again. I miss being heard." Angel picked up Kail and placed the pup in her lap.

"What about us?" Kail whispered.

"What's she saying?" Joe asked.

"She wants to know what's going to happen to them."

"Tell her they'll be taken care of, and thank her from the bottom of my heart for watching over my daughter."

Angel looked at the pups and then back to her dad. "Dad, she can hear you and understand you. I don't have to translate. Did you want me to bark at them?"

"No, no. I'm thinking it's another language," her dad said with a chuckle.

Angel smiled. This man, her father, felt so familiar to her, and right now their sitting in the cloud together seemed like the most natural thing in the world. Her dad's body was lean in this form, not the puffy yellowish shape he had in the hospital bed.

They sat together for quite some time in a comfortable silence.

"I feel like I'm in a quiet hot air balloon floating over the world," her dad said. "My body hasn't felt this good in years." He rotated his shoulders and moved his arms, causing the cloud to tip in his direction.

"Careful, Dad. I keep telling you movement isn't good for the cloud." Angel ran her hands over the edge of the soft formation. "See, you can shape it, but eventually it evaporates."

She scooped a piece of the cloud into her hand, held it directly out toward her dad, and then inhaled and blew. Pieces of the cloud gently floated down around them and melted back into the soft pillowy substance. Angel felt her cheek muscles pull tight across her face and realized she was smiling one of the biggest smiles she'd ever felt.

"Happy?" her dad asked.

"It's great being here with you. Can you stay a while?" Angel asked.

Her dad nodded, and they floated in silence enjoying the fresh air.

After a while, he spoke. "I can't hide out here forever. In fact, it'd be nice to hide from all the stuff that's happening down there. But I've got this feeling I'm needed back in my body so I can die. Sounds funny, doesn't it?"

"Yes, it does." Angel laughed, though within moments the seriousness of the matter occurred to her. "Are we real? Is this really happening? Are you going to die and leave me in this cloud?"

Then she panicked. "I don't want to stay up here and forget who I am ... Okay, forget who you say I am since I can't really remember who I am ... I don't want another decade to go by while I'm stuck here doing nothing ... Well, I'm actually not doing nothing, but it's close."

The man who was her dad sat still in the cloud. "Relax. Everything is going to turn out how it's supposed to turn out." He slowly moved to a standing position with Belle in his arms.

"Careful ..." said Angel.

"I have this. Everyone relax." Her dad held Belle's small body in his left hand. He put his right hand on the pup's head and spoke directly to Belle. "I'll take care of you, no matter what happens. I promise."

Angel was shocked to see Belle relax at his touch. "What can you tell me that I can remember about my life in the flesh?"

"In the flesh? Is that what it's called?" he asked.

"Well, I don't know. I suppose I could call it being human, but I still feel human. Do you know what I mean?"

"Yes, I do. I still feel human."

"Because you are, right?" Angel asked.

"Yes, but technically I'm not in the flesh right now. So, I think that saying works."

"What about my life?"

"Okay, okay. Where did we leave off?" he asked.

"I asked you where you've been all these years and you changed the subject."

"Ah ha. And you wanted some sort of confirmation, too." He touched his chin and remained standing. "I need to tell you, I was messed up for all those years. I had no way to communicate with you. I didn't know for sure you were up here until I actually came here. And I still don't know how I happen to be here."

Angel nodded.

"I think it has to do with the coma and the sickness." He paused and placed Belle gently on the cloud. "When I first got sick I had a dark experience that really terrified me. Something

I can't talk about, but it pretty much scared me straight. I haven't been tempted to drink since I had that ... vision.

"After that, I really got into helping the hardcore cases like I was. It's how I ended up out at Skid Row—often helping the guys that society considers 'throwaways.' The police, fire department, social services, and any other government employee want nothing to do with such pitiful people." He shook his head and continued, "I threw myself into my work. Dedicated every waking moment of my life to fixing these folks who seemed beyond repair. In retrospect, I think I was trying to fix myself because I didn't want to leave anyone behind. And when some of the guys would mess up, I never gave up on them. I was a diehard."

Her dad took a deep breath and cautiously sat down in the middle of the cloud, crossing his legs. "I'm trying to tell you, when I sobered up it was so easy to get real busy with my new addiction of helping people. I'm sorry it's taken me so long to get here and be with you. I'm sorry." He put his head in his hands.

Angel sat with Kail in her lap and listened, which she was used to doing. She rarely had opportunity to interact with people, so out of habit, she sat and quietly listened.

"I started helping people and I couldn't stop. My personal penance became my saving grace, and maybe it worked—because I've lived longer than I was supposed to. Now, I'm ready to say good-bye to that tired old body and take my daughter home to her mother."

"How do I know for sure I'm Angela? Why can't I remember?" Angel asked.

"My Angel, relax, it will come. My best guess would be to follow your gut. Does it feel right?"

"Yes, at this moment it does."

"You know my mother, your grandmother, gave all of her kids names that start with the letter 'J.' It seemed to be a family tradition. I was named after my Uncle Joe, and I think JJ was named after him too. Marion didn't want to follow that naming convention. She was a strong woman, your mother. She said she knew the names of her daughters before both of you were born." Her dad looked out at some distant place.

"Why the name Juan? And why use it now?"

"It's my name. It was Uncle Joe's name too. Juan Joseph Torres. I go by both Joe and Juan."

"When did I become Angel?"

"I always called you Angel. Your mom wanted you to go by your name. She'd get so mad at me when I called you Angel." He raised his voice to a shrill tone, "Her name is Angela."

Angel felt a tiny tickle inside her belly, like butterfly wings beginning to wreak havoc on her insides.

"Angela, you'd be in your thirties right now if you were in the flesh, and I'm a granddad. It's amazing—where did the time in between go?"

The question bothered her though she couldn't say where in her being she felt thrown off balance. "Instead of being thirty, I've been trapped for all these years. Don't get me wrong, I love the girls and being with them, but for a long, long time, I've known that I've missed out by not moving forward. Maybe wherever my mom is there's another life for me." Her body deflated a little.

"When you were ten you were teased by the kids at school because you insisted Santa Claus was real. Remember how I created a boot print going up the chimney, and you set out milk and cookies? Every year I ate the cookies and kept the mystery alive. Oh gosh, that part was fun."

Angel shook her head to signal no.

"When you were twelve, you graduated from elementary school. The whole family showed up, including Uncle Joe. You graduated with straight As, and we celebrated with a huge barbecue at home. Teresa and your mother put a big banner up on the garage. In fact, years later, I think the idea for the bumper sticker came from that banner. Remember, the sign said: 'Our Angela is an honor student!' The whole thing was a huge surprise to you, and, Angel, you were so shocked and happy that day."

"No. I don't remember," Angel said. She felt strange—both herself and not herself.

"Okay, the day of the accident. You were upset. Some girls were messing with you at school. Your mother was sick and you were trying to get by without asking for help. Your sister was busy getting ready to graduate from high school. Your clothes were wrinkled and not looking so good. It was Teresa's idea ..."

"Okay, okay. Those mean girls, Sara and Nancy, made fun of my hair and my clothes. Oh no, Dad, they were awful." Angel put her hand to her mouth and frowned. "It started as whispers and eventually it seemed like the whole school was in on it."

Angel felt a familiar pain in the pit of her stomach. She sensed this emotion was something she'd avoided for at least decades. Her head felt foggy, as if a dark cloud were putting pressure around her ears and on top of her skull. Oh gosh, it was so familiar, and now it was making her feel sick, but she hadn't felt this way in years. The darkness was about those cruel, cruel girls and that time in her life as Angela.

She'd overslept that day and had forgotten she didn't have any clean clothes. In a hurry to get to school, Angela pulled some wrinkled clothes out of the hamper and ran a cold iron over them. To make matters worse her hair was in tangles and needed to be cut and styled. She was a mess, and she hadn't been shopping for new clothes since the previous school year.

Her mother's illness had changed things around the house, and her father hadn't spent much time with them. Angela had come home crying—as much as she tried to hold it back, she couldn't.

Her dad nodded and for several minutes they sat and stared at each other. "And now, my daughter, we're going to get all of you out of here."

CHAPTER 16

JESSIE HAD SAT QUIETLY AT HER brother's bedside for quite some time before she decided to pull out his journal and finish reading his crazy story. It seemed as if all of his life the man tried to be normal, but everything he touched was extraordinary—for better or for worse. Joe had a zest for life, but the pendulum rested on the far side of good or the far side of bad, with little balance in between. The man knew nothing about moderation.

She flipped through the book to find her place and continued reading.

Something or someone was making me face my demons. And yet I felt some pleasure from moving in silence and being with myself, facing my inner desperation. Later, I slept again and when I awoke I thought I was in the light. It was light, all right, the light in the hospital. And I was in a world of hurt—but I was grateful to be back, no longer in that other horrific and disorienting realm.

I made a lot of deals on my walk through Hell—all the things I'd do if I got out. The deal I felt the most committed to was helping the helpless, the folks who were as bad off as me—with no hope and no one at all to reach out to them. For years I had been completely and totally hopeless in that way, adrift.

I'm no saint, that's for sure, and my intentions weren't and aren't altruistic. I made a deal, with my higher power I guess, and a deal is a deal. I got out alive, so I've helped as many people as I could.

When I was fully awake in that hospital bed, I was surprised to see Father Benjamin at my side. I shared with him parts of my experience in my own private hell, and he told me he'd been watching me on my journey. I was out for a few days after the surgery, where they'd removed my gallbladder and left me knocked out. The doctor put me in some type of induced coma to get me through the DTs as easy as possible. The priest said it was the worst he'd ever seen. Hell, I don't know how, but soon Father Benjamin became my friend. Who would've thought I'd be chummy with a priest?

I didn't share my whole life with the father, either. In my shame, I left out the family part. He didn't know that my dead wife, Marion, was yelling in my ear, and that I had visions of my dead daughter, Angela, stuck in the clouds, haunting me. I conveniently left out the fact that I'd abandoned my only

living child, Teresa, in the cold to fend
for herself. He had no inkling that I had
remaining family. Living the lie was easy,
too. I was still out of it when he asked me,
and I never confessed when I was able to. It
never came up again and I wasn't about to
volunteer the information.

The father helped me through the program,
and he got me a place to live. I was diligent
at staying sober and fixing the world—in fact,
manic is a better word. Father Benjamin worked
hard at keeping up with me. I put in a lot of
time repairing things around the church so
he made me the handyman. It's odd I was sober
and didn't experience a single trigger from
anything around me. The pit in Hell surely
woke me up. I really went to work at making
amends by helping these guys out on Skid Row,
and ignoring the rest of my life.

I learned quickly to go alone to the Row
and find some helpless guys and bring them
back to the church. If I brought one of my
newfound friends home, well, sometimes it'd
take an hour or a day, but they'd go back out.
The drink, the streets were a pull to these
folks who had known nothing else for so many
years. And for the life of me, I can't figure
out why, because it stunk—really, really bad—
with the odors of puke, alcohol, urine, and
terrible hygiene. Who am I to judge, though?
I lived in it for so long, too. Disgusting
what we do to ourselves because of this evil
disease.

So I pulled a few guys out, and the next day they'd go back to their haunts. I'd return to bring them in, and do this over and over again. Then one day, a guy stayed on. At last, the feel of success, so I kept at it, going through the same routine repeatedly until another one stayed off of the Row. For every ten I lost, I'd keep one. Juan Torres, the saint, they'd say. I'd just smile and tell myself, "A deal is a deal."

The ultimate test came the day the old guy we called the General sobered up. He started talking smack about a hit and run he'd been involved in years ago. Well, it might not have been smack, but it pissed me off because in my mind it was Teresa and Angela's accident. He went on and on about it during my meetings when I first became a counselor.

The General said he woke up after a night of drinking and his car was wrecked, but he couldn't remember what had happened. Memories of an accident came to him over several weeks in small fragments. He didn't know where it had happened or what other car was involved, but he knew he'd gotten in an accident and somehow he'd made it home—a place he couldn't remember now.

I've always thought it strange that the General claimed to not know his own name but he could remember this accident. He insisted it was because this event drove him over the top, and the more time that went by, the greater the torment—though he continued to be too scared and too drunk to do anything about it. He drank to forget the accident, and instead he forgot everything else, including his name.

Of course, I obsessed over this guy, the General. I thought of the irony of him showing up at my program, and he'd be the one who killed Angela. I got everyone on the staff to try to find the General's identity under the guise that this old guy's family should take care of him. We all did a ton of research. My team is good at finding families and identifying people, but we found nothing on the General. As weeks turned into months, the old guy and I sort of became friends. I could relate to his experience, more than I wanted to.

To this day, we don't know who the General really is and if he actually was involved in a hit and run. Eventually, I did confront him, and as a result he's one of few people who has some knowledge of my past. When I heard about his accident and couldn't find out a single thing, it was just too much for me to handle. So he and I had an ugly confrontation, which we eventually worked through.

As bizarre as it sounds, the General soon became a link to my family. First I wanted to kill him, and then I wanted to make him my family.

Here's the other thing I find fascinating about this situation: Most of these guys can't keep their tongues still about things they've heard—and well, the old guy kept his mouth shut about my girls' accident (which was really all I told him about, not about Teresa or Marion).

The General would come and go, and sometimes he'd come back sober and physically clean. But for the most part, the General was a mystery. He'd dry up—this wasn't an easy task—and then a few months later he'd be back at the bottle again. Over this last year, his health kept getting worse. When he'd go missing, we'd head out to the streets and bring him home.

Thoughts of the General weigh heavily on my mind, and as I sit quietly and think about it, the old guy might have Alzheimer's disease or some form of dementia. I think he'd sober up and forget he sobered up, and then he'd start drinking again. I also believe this plays a part in his having no memory of who he is.

Now we've been trying to find the General for the last few days. I've got a dreadful feeling about him going missing this time. I believe I'll never again see the old guy alive.

Jessie closed the book. She stood up and stretched as she approached her brother's bed, where he lay asleep with tubes still attached to various parts of his body.

"Joe, you sap. How could you not call or see your daughter before this?" Jessie spoke in a tone just above a whisper.

Her brother had always attracted messes into his life, but his wife Marion was different. She was the best thing that ever happened to him, and for several years they'd lived with their girls like the perfect family. Could it be that Marion was strong enough to reach across the grave and get to Joe? Well, if anyone could do it, it would be Marion. What about Angela? She'd had such a hard time at school and dealing with the other kids. That little girl was smart, for sure; her sad life and her death were a genuine tragedy.

Joe coughed, and his eyelids flickered.

"Are you waking up?" Jessie asked.

He turned his head toward her and opened his eyes with a squint. "It's bright in here," Joe whispered and coughed.

Jessie moved to the doorway and dimmed the switch. "It doesn't seem that bright to me, Joe. I think your body's sensitive."

"Ya think?" Joe said.

"Okay, smarty pants. You want some water?"

"Please." Joe's face shined over with a mist of perspiration on it and his breathing appeared shallow and too fast.

Jessie found the fresh water pitcher, cup, and straw that Willa had placed on the ledge by the window. She poured a cup for Joe and held the straw to his lips so he could drink. Joe placed his free hand over Jessie's hand holding the straw.

"We need to talk," Joe said with a stronger voice now, a few steps louder than a whisper.

Jessie nodded. "Yes, we do."

He sipped the water and moved his nose toward the table. Jessie got the hint and placed the cup down but continued to stand next to her brother in silence. He blinked his eyes and appeared to be trying to move his body. Jessie frowned at her brother's self-inflicted condition. If only his life hadn't gotten so out of control. She pulled the remote up from the side of the bed and placed it on Joe's chest.

"You've got quite the imagination, Joe," Jessie said as she waved the notebook in front of him.

Joe held the bed remote in front of his eyes to examine the settings but turned to look at the notebook and nodded toward Jessie. He then squinted again at the remote and pushed a button. His feet moved up. "Oops," he muttered and continued to push buttons until he'd positioned himself as upright as possible.

"I don't have much time." Joe's voice was almost inaudible. Jessie nodded.

Joe continued, "I'm not good at talking about any of this. I didn't have enough time to finish that notebook."

"It looks like an unusual attempt to give your daughter an excuse for your actions. What really happened, Joe?" Jessie asked.

"I've seen and talked to Angela, too. Since I've been in this coma, I mean. My daughters are stuck. Both of them, and it's my fault." Joe closed his eyes.

"Wake up and talk to me." Jessie didn't recognize her own strained voice.

His eyes opened. "I'm awake. I've just seen better days."

"I bet," Jessie said.

Joe smacked his lips. "I've been hearing things for years, and when I meditate quietly I can speak to Marion."

"Are you crazy? That's what you're going to tell Teresa?" Jessie felt a splash of heat on her cheeks.

"It's the truth."

"The truth? Joe, I think you don't know the truth." She frowned.

"Let me explain. I know you're angry, and you've every right to be ..."

Jessie interrupted. "You're a son of a bitch. After all this time, you offer a tall tale. Did it ever occur to you that you were hallucinating?"

"I've had hallucinations, and that's not what this is." Joe swallowed. "If you'll listen to me—this is real. More real than the moment we're sharing now. My little girl watched you and Teresa visit the church. Angela saw the picture of her and Teresa—you know the one with the boots. The photo in my office, you saw it too. She watches Teresa get ready every morning, and she's been at Teresa's side for years. Angela knows JJ. I didn't make this stuff up. I wasn't there. She told me herself."

"Well, the priest was there, and he certainly could have described our visit to you. So your knowing what happened doesn't tell me much." Jessie pursed her lips together.

"Father Benjamin will tell you—he hasn't said a word to me about this."

"Come on now, Joe. I find this hard to believe." Jessie shook her head.

"I know." Joe sighed.

Jessie pulled the chair closer to her brother's bedside and sat down. "What do you want?" she asked.

"I'll be gone soon, and I'm going to take Angela home to be with her mother. For some reason I find it necessary to communicate this to Teresa. Marion is insistent that Teresa has missed out on a lot during her life. She says both of our daughters are stuck, just in different ways."

In reality, though Jessie had challenged Joe quite harshly, to some extent she wished she could accept his version of events. She wanted to forgive her brother for the heartache he'd given them. But his so-called "experience" wasn't very believable, and right now all she could hope for was to prevent him from doing any more harm.

"Teresa has a successful business and raised her son—on her own. She's not on the streets, no drugs, no real suffering other than the pain you inflicted, and the damage you're about to create after all these years. Why now, Joe? We spent years trying to find you. You broke that little girl's heart. I can't believe any of this is about her. It's about you, isn't it?" She needed to show him how selfish he was being in trying to convince them of this crazy story.

"Jessie, my daughter is unhappy and lonely. Do you know what she does most of the time? She cleans." Joe stopped, took a deep breath, and continued, slower now. "Sure, Teresa's made some good decisions in her life, but she's also made some bad decisions and you know this in your heart. My daughter is miserable. This isn't the life she was supposed to lead."

Jessie knew Joe was right, but she didn't want him to see her niece in that way only, and she didn't want him messing with Teresa's head. "So what do you think you can do about it now? Teresa, in spite of your failed support, has turned into a wonderful human being. Your daughter doesn't need you." She conveyed not only Teresa's hurt, but also her own on Teresa's behalf.

"Jessie, I want to try to help my daughter. I'm not sure what I can do about it. I know I played a big part in messing up her life, so I need to try to help her to fix it. And for her sake, sometimes just knowing things can help."

"Knowing what? This ludicrous story you've concocted?"

"It's the truth, as I see it." He might've been weak but the look he gave her was filled with conviction.

"The truth isn't always the best solution, Joe. But my goodness, if your truth is contained in this book, it sounds like fiction." Jessie waved the notebook above her head. "You know, Teresa lived her own version of the truth, a very solid, real one. Say your good-byes now and leave the girl alone. No more melodrama, please." He said he wanted to help his daughter, but from Jessie's viewpoint, the best way he could do that was not throw her into further turmoil.

Joe coughed and she could hear the phlegm build-up in his chest. He wiped a hand across his mouth. "I know you did a lot for her, Jessie. Thank you for stepping in and taking care of Teresa. I made a promise to Marion, and if I live long enough I'll keep that promise."

"Does Father Benjamin know about all this?" Jessie asked.

"No. This is a family affair," Joe mumbled.

"He wouldn't believe you either, would he?" Jessie leaned in closer to Joe.

"Jessie, very few people, if any, would believe me." Joe shut his eyes.

"We finally agree on something." Jessie laughed.

"I'm sorry, Jessie. If I could do it all over differently this time, I would." Joe opened his eyes part of the way; peeled dry skin was stuck to his lips. He spoke slightly above a whisper and wheezed a little. "Have you heard about the General? Did he ever show up?"

Jessie felt the muscles in her shoulders loosen as she relaxed a bit. "I don't think so, Joe. I'm sorry about that."

"Well, let me know if you happen to hear something about him." Joe closed his eyes.

"You guys ever try to find out who he is by fingerprints?"

"Oh yeah," Joe said opening his eyes. "We tried missing persons, the media, fingerprints. Nothing came up."

"What about hypnosis?" Jessie asked.

"That's a good idea. I never thought of that." Joe nodded. "Jessie, what've you been up to all these years? Is Uncle Joe around?"

"Does Marion see him?" Jessie raised a brow and let out a touch of a chuckle.

"Not that I know of." Joe winked.

"That's because he's alive. Uncle Joe's had some hip issues and health problems. He's in an old folks' home."

"I missed a lot." Joe looked away from Jessie at the moment she thought she saw his eyes fill with tears.

"That you did. Was it worth it?"

"Nope. Not a bit."

Jessie sat at her brother's bedside and looked at the mess he'd made of his body. Skinny limbs, a bloated belly, the man appeared to have no muscle in his entire body, and he looked older than Uncle Joe, though the gray was merely speckled across his full head of hair.

"What's your plan with Teresa?" Jessie asked.

"I'm not sure. I was hoping she'd read the book."

"I'm not certain that's a good idea. Teresa wanted no part of this, you know. She sent it home with me."

"I know."

"Did your priest friend read this?" Jessie waved the notebook in front of Joe's face.

"I don't think so. As I said, I wasn't finished. My big plan was to let her read it and then she'd understand."

"Understand what, that her father's a lunatic?"

Jessie watched Joe take as deep a breath as he could, and then her brother made eye contact with her and spoke. "It is what it is. You either believe me or you don't. So stop it, please."

"I'm sorry, Joe. I just think it's insane. I'll quit bringing it up."

"Good, because I'm exhausted, and I've only dealt with you. I'm not sure I can handle Teresa, too."

"Your daughter is a normal woman. Stop and look. It's not like she's on the edge of losing it all."

"Marion says she's miserable, lonely, and unable to connect with other people. She said that Teresa's living in her own personal hell, one that I helped create. Is any of this true?"

Jessie thought about her niece for a moment. Teresa didn't have close friends or a man in her life. The girl spent time at work, doting over JJ, and cleaning her shop and her house. She wasn't involved with anything or anyone. And come to think of it, she really hadn't been working that many hours lately. What did Teresa do with herself these days? She was a bit of a loner.

"Well, it might be somewhat true." Jessie didn't want to admit defeat.

"What does 'somewhat' mean?"

"Joe, she's not miserable. At least not that I'm aware of ... And I think I'd know. I've been around Teresa most of her life."

"She's been miserable most of her life, her adult life that is. Jessie, you're too close to it to see it."

"What is this RED ALERT on Teresa? You can't just waltz back into her life and make an impact!" Jessie wasn't exactly sure why she felt so angry on this topic, but she certainly was.

"Why not? I did it when I went out of her life, didn't I?"

Jessie tried to choke back some of her response, but the effort failed. "Here we go again—you're back and leaving. I'm going to be picking up the pieces with Teresa once more. I recommend you state your apologies, say your good-byes, and leave it at that. Can you do that, Joe? Can you do that for me?"

"No. She needs to know everything."

Jessie had chewed on the inside of her mouth until she felt the taste of blood. Joe was going to stir it up again. After years of relative peace for the women, his train wreck was headed right at Teresa.

Jessie stood with the notebook in her hand and lifted her purse over her shoulder. She then heard words spill out of her mouth in an unrecognizable voice, one that she had no control over. "I'm going to the ladies' room. I'll be back."

"I know what you're thinking, but Jessie, sometimes calm isn't good. I promise it'll all work out," Joe responded.

"I said I'd be back." Jessie's voice was louder than she intended as she exited the room without a glance in Joe's direction.

The nerve of that man. It simply wasn't okay for him to show up, and like a tornado turn their world on end, and then leave again. Jessie had to sort through her own thoughts on the topic of her brother. She wanted to make sure this wasn't about her, and that she was simply trying to protect her niece.

CHAPTER 17

TERESA'S AUNT BURST FROM HER DAD'S hospital room and took off in the opposite direction from JJ and Teresa. "Aunt Jessie?" As she sped up in an attempt to catch her aunt, Teresa half-turned to her son. "Wait here. I want to find out what's going on."

Wow, the tiny woman moved fast—her power walks were paying off. "Aunt Jessie? Wait up." Teresa reached her aunt at the end of the hall.

"Oh, Teresa, I'm sorry. I didn't see you." Aunt Jessie turned toward Teresa, who was shocked to see her aunt with a pale face and droopy eyes.

"What's going on? Did he die?" Teresa's heart skipped a beat. She didn't know if this was at the thought of being an orphan or if she truly felt something toward her father. Damn this situation.

"Not yet. But the man's in rare form," Jessie snapped.

"What did he do to you?"

"He can't do anything—it's what he's saying. I wish I hadn't encouraged you to see him. The fool has concocted a pack of lies to ... Well, you're probably going to need to talk to him and decide." For the first time in Teresa's life, her aunt seemed old. The woman's knuckles whitened as she gripped her purse tighter.

"What? We know this about him. But he didn't lie when he was sober. Maybe it's the pain medication?" Teresa suggested.

"No, my dear. He's refused all pain medicine. The man's quite sober." Jessie crossed her arms in front of her chest.

"Well, maybe he's delusional. We just need to take it all with a grain of salt." Teresa tried to digest what her aunt had said.

"That, my dear, is an excellent idea, and I'm hoping these old wounds stay healed."

"Or buried—whatever the case may be," Teresa said. Her stomach clenched at the thought of those buried old wounds.

"Yeah, I'm sure you'll get an earful on that one," Jessie murmured.

"What?" Teresa asked.

"Never mind. I'm just an old woman babbling. I'm going to the restroom. I'll be back in a few minutes. Teresa, you and JJ should go talk to your father and let him get it over with. Better yet, maybe I'll go and get some coffee, too, and let you all have some time together."

"Whatever you want." Teresa hugged her aunt and decided this wasn't the time to bring up JJ's current legal issues. She'd wait until later when Aunt Jessie had calmed down. "We'll just say our good-byes to Joe and leave it at that," Teresa said.

"Okay, good luck with that, my dear." Aunt Jessie's shoulders hunched over as she slowly walked away from her niece.

Strange behavior, indeed. The old melodrama that seemed to follow Joe everywhere had seeped back in by way of her aunt. Teresa was determined to cut the visit short tonight once they said their final good-byes. After years of peace, reviving the disturbances of the past wasn't worth the upset. God only knew why her dad had waited so long to contact her, and at this point why he'd bothered at all.

Teresa recalled her father drinking, but never being drunk. Most of this madness took place after her mother became ill—although her dad had gotten much worse after Angela had died. Teresa's mother had tried to get Joe to quit drinking during that period, but to no avail—though maybe her failure as well as his inability to quit were both because her mom had been extremely ill. In fact, the doctor said her mother's reaction to chemo was unusually severe—something the doctors couldn't have foreseen.

Teresa's memories of this period were blurred on purpose, and now as she focused on the forgotten time, feelings of indignation toward her father filled her entire body. It had to be his binge drinking and disregard for everyone that had hastened her mother's death.

Fortunately, Teresa's aunt had been the only relative to come across her father when he was knee deep in the bottle. Her aunt had tried more than once to bring her dad home from the bars, and each attempt appeared to elicit a worse reaction than the previous one. However, Aunt Jessie always refused to discuss what'd happened and how her dad's behavior changed when he drank. Teresa could see her dad's drunken ugliness on her aunt's face—and on Aunt Jessie's body sometimes, too. The woman usually returned with a new bruise and tears in her eyes.

Wound up and in a less forgiving frame of mind than a minute before, Teresa entered her dad's hospital room to find JJ at Joe's side—laughing.

Her son stood on the opposite side of the bed facing Teresa as she approached. "I thought I told you to wait outside," Teresa snapped at JJ.

The boy's smile left his face. "Not exactly, Mom. You told me to wait. So, I waited in here."

Teresa's jaw tightened, and she turned her attention to her father. "Joe, we came to say our good-byes and we'll be leaving soon. I'm not sure this was a good idea. I don't want you getting so comfortable with my son, either."

"I'm leaving soon, too," her dad whispered.

"They're releasing you?" JJ asked with a sparkle in his eye.

"Not exactly that," Joe answered.

Teresa frowned at her father's interaction with her son and the obvious awe in JJ's eyes. "Okay, we get that you're dying, Dad. You've got Aunt Jessie upset, and you're stirring things up with me. I'm not sure any of us are ready for this or that we need this."

"Well, I like that you called me Dad. It's been a long time." Joe spoke slowly, between shallow breaths. "I've really screwed up, and it's way too late to do much about it. I'm sorry."

"Why'd you wait so long? Why now, when there's no time left?" Teresa asked. She felt her eyes sting from salty tears forming.

"I was scared before, but I'm dying now, so it's different—I don't have anything more to lose." Joe's face turned red.

"Once again, you're only thinking about yourself. What about us? We looked for you, for years," Teresa said. She'd waited a long time to deliver these charges against her dad, and despite her vow to not get into it, couldn't resist saying those words.

He looked sad and ill, but Teresa wondered if he had any genuine remorse.

"I know, I know. I was sick. Alcoholism is a disease, and I was in no position to be anything to anyone."

"I don't get it. You sobered up and still stayed away ..." Teresa shook her head.

"I got real busy thinking I was doing the right thing saving souls, not realizing the most important souls are right here in this room with me tonight. I'm sorry," Joe mumbled.

"Joe, it just sounds so weak," Teresa said. Fine words, but too little, too late, she decided.

"Well, it's what I've got at this point. I've got no excuse." Joe's voice sounded hoarse.

"Aunt Jessie says you've made up some reasons ..."

"Oh, no. She's talking about the notebook ... It's not an excuse. I'm responsible for all of this. My actions, my responsibility," Joe said.

"You know, it's really hard to be here," Teresa told him. "I didn't want to do this at all, and now it's really hard not to be mad and walk out of here for good." She made no attempt to hold back the anger in her voice.

JJ's eye's widened and his face went a lighter shade of pale. He nodded at Teresa in what appeared to be a form of encouragement, and for one brief moment she understood how lucky she was that he'd turned out to be such a good person.

In a calmer voice, Teresa continued, "You've got a grandson you could've met years ago. Your sister, your uncle, your cousins, everyone in your family worried about you for years. Everyone thought you were dead. About ten years ago, I would've welcomed this moment. I would've opened my arms, and taken you into my home. But now, I'm not up to this drama."

"You seem to be doing pretty darn good to me." Joe nodded a little, as much as he seemed able to move his head.

"It's just too much, Joe. I don't want my son sucked in ... I don't want my aunt sucked in ... and I don't want to be sucked in ... into your death. Why couldn't you just die quietly?" Teresa felt the vein on her forehead pulsate and a splash of heat rise up through her cheeks.

"I would've, but this is special circumstances." Joe spoke slowly.

"Everything with you is special circumstances, Joe." Teresa heard a high-pitched stranger's voice leave her mouth. For a moment she froze, closed her eyes, took another deep breath, and sat in silence. In her head she began to repeatedly tell herself, "Do not let this man get to you. He'll be gone soon."

Joe interrupted her internal chant as he plowed onward in conversation. "I've got some things to share with you, Teresa. I wrote it out in that notebook your Aunt Jessie has. It's not every detail, but most of it's there." Joe spoke in a surprisingly calm manner. "I'm really curious, although this may sound strange, I want to know if you've ever felt like something or someone is watching you. Have you ever heard strange noises in your house? Or have you seen anything ... unusual?"

"What are you asking me, Dad?" Teresa snapped. She couldn't follow his line of conversation.

"I'm talking about Angela."

"Are you losing it? She died over twenty years ago." Teresa's control was about to crack—as if she had any restraint remaining.

"I know. I was there, remember?" her father asked.

"Yes, but it's not the most positive memory. Do you remember that?" Teresa responded with her personal mantra still ringing in her ears: "He will not get to me."

"Okay, I deserve it all, but this isn't about me. I want to talk to you about your mother and your sister."

"Are you still in denial, Dad?"

"Teresa, it's all going to sound ... well, a bit outlandish."

JJ leaned in and loudly whispered, "Are you about to tell a ghost story because I swear I sense something in our house at times."

"What are you talking about, JJ? Are you nuts, too?" Teresa resisted the urge to slap her son.

"No, Mom. I've felt the hair on my arms go up at times. I can't put my finger on it, but something's there." JJ's cheek muscles flexed when he spoke.

"See, Joe, you're bordering on psychotic, and you've already infected my son."

"Just listen for a moment." Joe raised his voice as he continued, now speaking well above a whisper, and with what seemed to be a renewed energy. "For several years, your sister Angela has been following you, Teresa. She forgot who she was, but she's been connected to you since her death."

"You're a deeply disturbed man. This type of thing happens in movies, not in real life." Teresa folded her arms across her chest.

"I'm going to share some information with you now. I ask that you keep an open mind and try to remember this conversation for later on. It won't matter right now because you're not going to believe me. But later, when I'm gone, it'll all make sense." He turned to JJ, "Can you help with this?"

JJ nodded.

Teresa's head pounded and a flaming red heat spread across the skin on her face. She spoke slowly, enunciating each syllable. "Why? Why can't you just leave quietly? Why now, Joe?"

Hot tears fell down Teresa's cheeks as she struggled to maintain an expressionless stare. JJ moved from the other side of the bed to Teresa's side. He put his arm around his mother, obviously mistaking her angry tears for sadness. "We can leave now if you want, Mom."

"No, JJ. Let's hear what Joe has to say." Teresa glared at her father.

Joe turned his head away. Teresa suspected he had tears of his own.

"I'm sorry, Joe. Did you say something?" she pushed.

"What? No, I ..." Joe wiped his face with the back of his hand and cleared his throat. "It's probably Angela. She's here."

"Oh, now you've completely lost your mind," Teresa said.

"No. I can feel it. I think if you calmed down you could feel it too," he whispered.

"What is this, Joe?" Teresa asked.

"Your sister was supposed to go to wherever we go when we die." Joe raised his voice.

"Heaven?" Teresa interrupted.

"Okay, heaven," Joe agreed. "Listen, Angela didn't want to leave you to deal with your mother's death alone. Because I disappeared, she stayed on, and after a while she forgot who she was. Angela hung around for years, not knowing why she was drawn to you."

Joe reached for his water. His left hand shook causing the straw to fall to the ground. Water splashed down his face the moment he attempted to drink directly from the cup. Teresa watched in silence and remained in place staring at her father. With his hand still shaking, Joe reached for a tissue. The box fell on the floor. Joe rolled his eyes, coughed, and used his hand to wipe the water off of his face. JJ came over to pick up the box and took out a tissue—then mopped Joe's sagging cheeks.

"When your mother died, she tried to take Angela with her. Angela refused to leave." Joe's voice weakened as he spoke.

Teresa took a deep breath. She'd heard enough. "I think we've talked plenty for tonight. We're leaving."

"Wait, wait, wait." Her father raised his free hand and his yellow-tinted eyes begged her to stay.

"Joe, really. We've heard enough," Teresa said as a calm wave flowed through her body.

"All I ask is that you hear me out. You don't need to come back tomorrow, or any other day—unless you want to, of course.

But right now, I'd like to finish." His arm dropped back onto the bed.

"It's okay, Mom. We can go if you want." JJ put his hand on her elbow.

"What else, Joe?" she asked.

"Well, I was hoping to have a few minutes so I wouldn't have to rush."

"Mom?" JJ said. "We can go."

Teresa, standing next to JJ, whispered directly in his ear. "No, JJ, let's get this over with. He's going to hang on until I listen."

"I might be dying, but my hearing works. I can hear you ... Please, just sit down. You'll need this information for later on."

Teresa turned to her son and nodded as she took a seat. "Let's let him finish, JJ." JJ pulled over another chair.

"Thank you." Joe exhaled. "I thought this would happen differently." He stopped, rested, than began to speak again. "I've got to start with your mother, Teresa."

She nodded, all the while silently singing the words, "He can't touch me."

"JJ, your grandmother was a very strong woman. Well, she *is* a strong woman. In fact, it's because of her that I knew you'd resist me. Well, not me, but what I'm about to tell you."

"Joe, it's what any reasonable person would do. Mom has nothing to do with this," Teresa said.

"Okay, well I know at your mother's funeral—the one I didn't go to—you had to be physically taken away from the viewing, Teresa. I know that those stupid twins, the cousins three times removed from your mother's side of the family, put something in the restroom toilet at the gathering after the funeral. Remember, the toilets backed up? And I know that at your college graduation, your future husband brought you a bouquet of peach-colored roses." Joe reached for the cup again while Teresa stopped JJ from getting up to help. Joe made contact with his lips and managed to drink the remaining water without spillage.

JJ had sunk back down into the chair next to her. "Mom, is it true?" JJ asked.

"Yes, well, I didn't know that's why the toilets backed up at the funeral home," she said.

"Marion gave me this information as a form of proof. She told me to give you time so it could sink in and make sense, after all." Joe licked his chapped lips and mumbled, "I think she didn't know I wouldn't have much time."

"My crying and hanging on to my mother's dead body, well that's not a very obscure fact." Teresa had forgotten how difficult her mother's funeral was, another unpleasant part of her history she'd worked hard to erase. Just a teenager, lost without her mom, she'd learned to be an adult on her own, because certainly her dad was nowhere to be found.

"Marion was upset with me, and she still is." Her dad shook his head. "Your mother was the love of my life. She was my backbone, and at the time, I thought she was all of my strength. I couldn't cope with either of the deaths. I had some type of breakdown, I believe. It wasn't long after your mother died that I started hearing her." He stared intently at Teresa before opening his mouth again.

"At first I didn't know what all the noise was. Later, she told me that when she started speaking to me, she didn't really know what she was doing. Learning how to communicate into this world took her quite some time. Apparently it helps if the person you're trying to communicate with is open-minded. I guess being in an altered state helps, too. You've got to understand that I was inebriated when I first heard her, and I thought I was just hearing voices, so I drank more. I wanted the screeching, nonsensical sounds to go away."

Joe smacked his tongue on the roof of his mouth. "JJ, can you fill this cup again, please?"

JJ stood up, scooped the pitcher in his left hand, and poured the water in one swift move.

"Oh, a lefty, that's different to the Torres family," Joe said.

"JJ's last name is Reynolds," Teresa countered, wanting to put him in his place.

"Yes, but he still has Torres blood in his veins."

Teresa waved her hand and frowned. "Okay, okay. Let's continue from the voice."

JJ found a few straws behind the pitcher. He handed one to Joe. "Here you go, Gramps."

"Thank you, son," Joe said.

Teresa's stomach tightened listening to her son's expression of affection toward her dad. She rolled her hands as a signal to her father to speed up.

"Oh, right, the voice." He took a sip through the straw and managed a half smile. "So, the voice kept telling me how I ruined her baby's life. After a lot more drinking to shut up the voice, and a few further crazy incidents that we don't have time to discuss, I learned the voice was your mother. Over time I found out she was angry with me because of the position I left you in, and then, eventually, I figured out your mom was talking about both you and your sister. Your mother's been adamant that I fix the things I broke." Joe wiped his forehead with the back of his hand.

"This is more difficult than I thought." Joe swallowed and continued in a tone just above a whisper that Teresa had to lean in now to hear. "I wrote this out in a book for you. I really thought you'd refuse to see me."

Teresa opened her mouth to speak, but her dad put his hand up to stop her. "No, please, let me continue. You know if anyone could somehow communicate anger from a different world it would be your mother. As strange as this sounds, it's about to get stranger ..."

Joe put his hand on his cheek and went on, "Your sister has been with you through your divorce, and she's watched JJ grow up. When she's not around your family, she floats in the clouds. Weird, isn't it? Remember when Angela use to lie in the grass and look up at the clouds?"

"It's weird," agreed Teresa with a smirk. She thought her father was strange, probably crazy, and yet she resisted the impulse to run. As bizarre as the whole story sounded, in some freaky way she enjoyed hearing about Angela and her mother. It'd been years since she'd thought about her family in the intimate manner her dad took on in referring to them.

"Angela loved dogs. Remember? For years she begged for a puppy. Did you know your mother wanted one too? Marion had dogs when she was growing up." Her father managed to take a deep breath. "I never allowed it, though, because I didn't want the house to smell like a dog. One of my many regrets ... Anyhow, when Angela couldn't find her way to ... heaven, I guess—she forgot who she was. Angela wouldn't go near people, of any kind. So your mother sent her prized dogs to watch over Angela, and it seemed to have worked."

The more he said, the more made up his story sounded. Teresa shook her head, but decided to appease her dying father. "Assuming this is not a complete hallucination, why didn't Mom just go and get her?"

"It's not that easy." Joe raised his left brow. "Angela's stubbornly tied to this world. She thought her name was Angel, and at one point she thought she was going to be your child. Angela avoids anything and everything that comes near her, except those two little dogs. That's the reason your mother sent them." Joe paused as if to gather his strength, and then spoke again. "Oh and this is only the abridged version of a much larger story. I know, I know, it all sounds crazy."

A psychotic break brought on by a flood of toxins from the liver was the only explanation Teresa could think of. "Go on." Teresa nodded, as if trying to encourage him.

"I realize you're not believing a word of this. It's the reason I want you to remember it for later. Okay?"

"Yes," JJ answered.

Joe winked at JJ and continued, "Here's the plan. When I die in the next few days, I'm taking Angela with me. We're going home."

"Okay, and why did you feel the need to share this with us?" Teresa was surprised at how nonchalant her own voice sounded.

"I can't just make this right with one daughter when I go. I've got to try to make it right with you as well. It might not be today, but a few years from now you'll understand." Joe closed his eyes for a second and then opened them again to speak. "I sleep and have these dreams. I meditate and can communicate back and forth with your mother. It's not the same as you and I talking right now. It's more like symbols or visions that I sometimes don't get or I get the message wrong. It's like looking at those 3D optical illusions. I almost have to cross my eyes and let my mind go somewhere else to translate the message. It's not easy." He sighed deeply, as though just thinking about the difficult process required a great effort on his part.

"One time your mother was trying to tell me about a recipe. The spice cake she made from scratch. I thought she was telling me the food was poisoned."

In spite of the craziness, Teresa smiled. The spice cake recipe was something both she and Aunt Jessie had tried to replicate for years.

"Did you happen to remember the recipe?" Teresa forced herself to stop smiling for fear of her dad taking it as some type of approval.

"Oh, I had no choice once I figured out what she was telling me. She said I would have an opportunity to give it to you and Jessie. Marion went on and on about how important the recipe would be."

"JJ, go and get a pen and paper." Teresa, excited now, gestured JJ toward the door. "Ask the nurse, go on."

"You know, I argued with your mother on this topic. I really didn't want to spend my time memorizing the recipe. Marion let me write it down, but she insisted I memorize it. She said our meeting wouldn't be under ideal circumstances."

Within seconds, JJ had returned with a pad of paper and a pen and sat down ready to take dictation.

"Okay, Joe. Let's hear it," Teresa said.

Joe closed his eyes and relayed the recipe in detail. When he'd completed the task, he opened his eyes. "Will you share that with Jessie so I can forget it? I've been working on that for the last few years. I could go a lifetime without having to repeat that recipe again."

"I'll make sure Aunt Jessie gets a copy," JJ said.

"I've got more details and stories, but, Teresa, I've told you the most important pieces. Your sister got lost and I'm going to save her ..." Joe paused for a moment as if he were considering the next move in a chess game.

Teresa, distracted by the recipe that she now held in her hand, only partly listened to her father.

"The other thing your mother believes is that I ruined your life, Teresa. What happened to you, because of me, made it real difficult for you to have a family and lead the life you were supposed to live."

"I'm sorry, Joe, what'd you just say?" Teresa asked. She folded the recipe and put it in her purse.

"I said, I ruined your life too. You know I did," Joe responded.

"No. Stop that." Oh how this man seemed to wear her out.

"I understand what I just said was quick and to the point, but you've been about to leave since you walked through the door," her dad told her.

"And let's say my life is your responsibility. What could you possibly do about it now? Aren't you a little too late?" Teresa stood up.

"Well, yes, for me, but you've got a lot of time left. Gosh, I don't know what to do about it now. I was hoping for a brilliant answer to come to me." He crinkled his face as if he was in pain. He probably was—the expression wasn't in upset over her, she decided.

"You're kidding, right? That's all you've got," JJ said.

"No, son, I'm not kidding. I can tell my story, and I can apologize—and I do mean it. But beyond this, I think it's up to your mom to figure things out, because as hard as I try, I can't go back in time and change my actions. Believe me, if I could I would. I'd rather have been the one in that car or with the cancer. Both Marion and Angela wanted to live and couldn't go on, and what a waste my life has been." Joe looked at Teresa as tears rolled down his cheeks.

Teresa, numb from the day, stood and pulled JJ out of his chair. She put her arm through her son's. "I think we're going to leave now, Joe. You could use the rest, and I'm not buying your little scheme, whatever it is. So for now, we have to say good-bye." A stranger's flat monotone voice had filled the air, and then she realized it was her own.

Teresa tugged on JJ's arm as she headed toward the door.

"At least try the recipe—you'll see. And, JJ, don't forget that attorney's name I gave you. If we don't meet again, I'm proud of you, my grandson. I'm proud of both of you ..."

Teresa and JJ moved down the hall toward the lobby, and for a few steps further she heard her father's voice. She ignored him and squeezed her son's arm tightly. Together, they continued in silence to the automatic doors. Once they'd exited the hospital, Teresa was relieved to feel the night air splash against her face.

She took a deep breath and then spoke. "What's this about an attorney?"

"I told him about my driver's permit and the car. You know, when we were waiting for you. He said to call his friend, Steve Haut. Your dad said he's the best." JJ stood at the passenger side of the car speaking to his mother over the roof. "But, Mom, you've got to admit, there's been some weird noises in the house over the years."

"JJ, we live on a fault line in the middle of earthquake territory. He's crazy, and the toxins in his body are making it worse ..." Teresa's voice trailed off into a whisper.

"Well, I'm sorry then. It was my idea to see him," JJ said.

"No, no. You're not to blame. What did you tell him about needing an attorney?" Teresa asked.

"Just what happened, nothing more." When the lock clicked open, JJ got in the car. "I think I would've liked your dad," he said while he put on his seatbelt.

"Oh, that's the problem. He's so likable," Teresa answered.

"Well, he said the guy has connections at the police station."

"Okay," Teresa answered, distracted by the conversation with her dad. "We might do that." She bit her lip and thought for a moment about her life. So what if she was absent a husband and liked to clean a little? At least she was content. What had her father tried to say to her? First he said he was proud, then he said she hadn't led the life she was supposed to. The man was delusional.

CHAPTER 18

ALONE IN HIS HOSPITAL ROOM, JOE gulped in air as quickly as he could and exhaled in the way the respiratory therapist had showed him to. Father Benjamin had somehow managed to get his daughter to visit, and Joe had blown it. She'd rushed him and pushed every button possible. Teresa was very much like her mother; he realized he couldn't demand she listen or believe him, but Joe was disappointed at how he felt forced to minimize his own experience. Then he'd hurriedly blurted out to Teresa that her life basically sucked.

Maybe Jessie was right. Perhaps Teresa was okay, and she didn't need him around stirring up this old crap. Marion might have this one wrong, although he couldn't remember a time when she *was* wrong, especially from the grave. She seemed to know everything.

Joe was so uncomfortable; he wanted to jump out of his own skin. His attempts at adjusting his body didn't help and moving the bed up, then down, didn't work, either. He silently prayed for his soul to hang on for at least one more day.

"One day at a time," Joe whispered as he pushed the nurse's button.

Either he'd fallen asleep or Willa had been standing right outside his door. "Did you ring?" she asked with a smile.

"I think it's time for some pain medicine," he said.

"You've been crazy to wait. This is supposed to be one of the most painful ..." Willa stood with her hand on her hip and a frown on her face.

"It's kind of uncomfortable, but not real painful yet," Joe said.

"Well, then you got some kind of angel on your side, Joe," Willa responded.

"More than I can share." Joe laughed and then coughed and coughed.

"Easy now." Willa pulled Joe forward and slapped his back a few times. "I'll be right back with some medicine."

He must've fallen asleep this time. It seemed as if she'd just said she'd be right back when he heard Willa speak again.

"Sorry that took so long," Willa apologized.

Joe popped his eyes open. "How long you been gone?" he asked.

"Almost an hour. I'm sorry."

"Wow, I didn't notice. I think I fell asleep or something ..."

Willa put the morphine directly into his IV. "There, this will help you get some rest. Dying can be exhausting." She smiled wryly.

"That's kind of silly, isn't it?" Joe responded. Everything in his whole life had been hard. So why couldn't leaving the world at least be the easy part?

"Maybe some good sleep will help you get through tomorrow. One day at a time, baby," Willa said as she moved the bed to a flat position and turned out the lights.

Joe was snoring before the room went dark.

"Wake up." Joe heard a female voice and felt a gentle push on his shoulder. "You're in my cloud. Now wake up."

"Okay, okay," he said, opening his left eye. "What?"

"You were lying here when I got back. Wake up."

Joe opened both eyes and saw his youngest daughter, Angela, standing over him with her arms crossed. "How'd I get here? Am I dead?" Joe asked.

"That's a good question," Angel said in all seriousness.

"Have you forgotten who I am?" Joe asked.

"No, I'm just skeptical," the girl responded.

"Oh, big word." Joe sat up and scratched his head. "I know that Willa gave me some medicine and now I'm here."

"I was there. I saw it all," Angel said. She plopped down carefully onto the cloud. "I've been thinking." One of the dogs ran over to her and she picked up the puppy and set it on her lap. The other dog followed, fluffy tail wagging. "I'll go with Mom. Can you get her to come and find me now? Instead of you having to sacrifice yourself. I think Teresa and JJ need you here."

Her mouth was set with determination and Joe smiled, remembering her babyhood. "My body is quitting now," he answered. "A day or a few days at the most and I'm done. I can't even keep my eyes open down there, and I'm not so sure that your mom can just swing back by."

Angel sat on the edge of the cloud staring out at the stars. Joe stood up directly behind her. If he could feel right now, which he really couldn't, he believed he'd sense a chill in the air this evening, and the thought of this sent a tremor through his body.

"Can we move the cloud? Can you take me somewhere?" Joe asked. An idea had lit up some sense of hope in him.

"Yes, why?" she answered.

"Can you see things and know things that people in the flesh can't?"

"What are you getting at, Dad?" Ah, she'd called him "Dad."

"I'd like to see if we can find the General out at Skid Row," he said.

"Oh, I'm not psychic if that's what you're asking."

"Well, let's see if we can head north and check out the area. Don't you hover?"

She turned and looked at him, her eyes big. "How do you know about that?" she asked.

"I know some things," he said.

Joe blinked, held his arms straight out, and smiled. His body worked really well up here in the clouds, and so did his mind. In fact, his mind was wide open; he was grabbing ideas from out of nowhere. Hovering, what the heck was that?

Angel's face was pulled tight with an effort of concentration as she leaned to the left and then to the right, guiding the cloud as if it were a sled. This felt familiar to Joe and yet odd at the same time. Although for years he knew something was going on, he hadn't really completely believed it until he saw it with his own eyes—for the first time after he'd escaped the pit. Truly this moment lifted any doubt left. Something about being in the flesh clouded people's perceptions. "We still need to see it to believe it, and that includes me," he whispered to himself.

Last week, none of this had been in his plans. Now, he had one daughter in a physical state furious at him, while the other daughter, in a spiritual state, relishing any second she had with him, remained in a sort of limbo. And his wife waited out there, somewhere, a few inches closer to peace. He was at a loss as to what to do for Teresa and his sister, Jessie. If only he could show them where he was now, that would seal the deal.

"Angel, do you know how to get into people's dreams?" Joe asked.

"I'm not sure," Angel responded. The question seemed to confuse her a little.

"I'm thinking if you could somehow show your sister or your aunt something in a dream that might help." He stared at her intently.

"Like what?" Angel asked.

"I don't know. Something I haven't told them because they would probably dismiss the dream as their own and not from you if it didn't show them something different," he said.

"I tried for years to talk to Teresa. Only recently has she heard a few words. I'm not sure how I'd go about getting into her dreams." Angel frowned and the cloud stopped moving.

"Maybe it's different now that you know she's your sister," he suggested.

"I wish we had a handbook or something." She smiled and the cloud moved on. "Oh yeah, but you never read the directions, do you, Dad?" She chuckled.

"Yep, I just figure it out." Joe sat down and leaned back on the ledge of the cloud with a smile on his face and his arms crossed over his chest. At the moment, this seemed to be the most normal thing in the world, and he wanted to be present through every second of it.

"Usually, I think about a place and I'm there. It's that simple." Angel reached down and caressed Belle's head while Kail took up residence against Joe's leg. He peered over the side of the cloud and within seconds recognized his old stomping grounds. Somehow Angel had maneuvered the cloud into a low hover about ten feet above the ground in the middle of Skid Row—no stinky smells, but the streets were the same. Folks were lined up against the buildings with makeshift tents, homemade beds—whatever they could find to sleep in and cover up with. Some were passed out, though others sat up, somewhat alert. Sleeping on the streets wasn't easy or safe. Most of these people managed to keep one eye open at all times.

"Let's go down to the corner and turn right," Joe whispered.

"It's okay, they can't hear you," Angel said.

"Oh, yeah," he chuckled to himself. "Can you sense things? Is it possible that you could tune into the General?"

"I don't think so." Angel shook her head. "I stay away from almost everyone."

"I'd think you'd have some type of special powers in this form."

"I'd think you'd have some, too," she snapped.

He laughed. "Okay, okay. I get it." She hadn't changed much over the years, and how he'd missed his smart little girl.

"Take a peek at these people and see if you recognize him."

Joe made an effort. "It's hard without waking them up to see who they are. Can we go lower?" Joe asked.

"We can, but somebody is going to see us if we do. Any one of them could have the talent. We're already too low for me. I'm not so sure I want to risk it."

"Aw, come on Angela. What could possibly happen?" he asked.

"We could lose our cloud and get separated. I don't want to risk that with the girls." Angel's lower lip slipped out.

"You're pouting," he said. Even seeing that old pout was precious to him.

"No, I'm not," Angel answered too quickly. "Why not relax from here and see what you can?"

"Can we walk on the ground?" he asked.

"I can. But I'm not sure what you are, so I don't know if you can," she responded.

"How do you get down there?"

"I think about the ground under my feet and I'm there. Close your eyes and think about the street below."

Joe opened his eyes and both he and Angela were standing on the street just below the cloud. "Not quite the father/daughter outing I'd planned," he said.

"Well, at least if they see us they won't think we're floating. Look up." Angela pointed.

"Wow, that's cool." To Joe the cloud seemed to be a natural part of the sky.

"Okay, what does he look like?" Angel asked.

"He's an old guy with stripes on the shoulder of his jacket. If he's out here it'll be in this area." Joe gestured toward the end of the block with his hand. "Let's stay together and walk up and down this block, and if he's not here, we'll go back."

"What if he's here?" Angel asked.

"I don't know yet. Let's take a look first." Joe moved to the first tent to his left and tried to pull back the tarp. Whoa—how weird. His hand went through the material at a slightly slower rate than going through the air and left a slight buzzing feeling in his fingers. He stood there, somewhat stunned.

"You can't move anything like that. You need to really concentrate and use your brain along with the motion of your hand." Angel's eyes widened as she stared down the next tarp and moved her hand through it. The fabric lifted as if the wind had swept over and hit this single tent in the middle of the street.

The body beneath the tent stirred a bit but remained limp under the tarp.

Joe focused hard on the fabric in front of him and moved his hand through the fabric again. An ever-so-slight movement of the sides of the tent caused the habitant to yell obscenities. "Get the hell away from me," the man shouted, following that up with a few other choice words.

"That's not him, he doesn't curse." Joe laughed and continued down the street. "This isn't easy, is it?"

"No. Imagine living this way for twenty years," she said.

"Well, we all choose our own hells. My world wasn't much better, either." Joe attempted to put his arm around Angel, but he stopped midway when he realized it wasn't going to happen. "I know. I know. I keep forgetting."

"Well, sometimes I do feel things. I can't explain it, but it happens. It might be coming from my emotions," she said.

"Oh yeah. Then I'll keep trying." Joe pointed toward the corner. "This area in here is really a lot of folks passed out or trying to keep warm. It's a rough crowd down here. The General usually hits the bottle and then finds a spot on this side of the street. I really don't think he's here right now." He tried to follow the General in his mind. "I wonder where he went."

"He's not here," Angel said as if she hadn't a shred of doubt.

"How do you know that?" Joe asked.

"I don't know. I just think he's indoors—like a bin or something."

"How do you know that?" Joe pressed.

Angel wrinkled her nose. "It's what I feel," she said.

"It does feel like he's not here, doesn't it?" Joe nodded. "Let's go, I don't like having you down here, even if they can't see you."

Joe reached for Angel's hand, and she smiled and put her hand near his. It looked as if they were holding hands, but the moment he moved in the opposite direction the optical illusion disappeared.

"Keep trying, Dad. One day it might work," Angel said. Then she added, "I wonder how come we can hold the pups."

"Maybe it's because I'm not dead yet. Maybe that's why I can't touch you." Joe shook his head.

"Death isn't as final as most people think, is it?" she asked.

"I guess not," he answered. "How do we get out of here?"

"Same way we got here, focus on the cloud."

Joe felt a steamroller of emotions overcome him as he floated up onto the cloud with his dead daughter while his body remained in a hospital bed thousands of feet below and probably miles away. Unbelievable—and stranger yet, that he'd just walked down Skid Row with this same daughter looking for the General. Maybe Teresa was right—maybe he was in the middle of a mental breakdown.

CHAPTER 19

ALTHOUGH ANGEL'S PAST HAD ONLY COME to her in bits and pieces, she believed she'd changed quite a bit since she'd been in the flesh as Angela. But she still didn't understand why she remained in this limbo state.

For so many years she'd tried to figure out her purpose and why the isolation; now, these most recent revelations had astonished her. She hadn't ever imagined her pups being a part of this plan or Teresa as her sister. As tired of her current existence as she might be, Angel believed who she was and where she came from amounted to much more than her simply being Angela.

Turbulence filled every inch of what remained as her being because the thought of moving on at this moment—which had been her main desire for years—also frightened her. Leaving the pups would be difficult, but more difficult still was facing the unknown. She wondered what really did happen when most people died. Well, Angel could certainly answer what happened when they got stuck.

The unscheduled visits from her father and the interruptions of her daily routines troubled her. Initially, the diversions weren't at all welcome. Now, she expected the visits and feared her disappointment if they stopped.

Thinking of her sister, Angel could only imagine what Teresa was going through internally—most likely a complete dismissal of the whole crazy story.

"How much time do you have here?" Angel asked her dad.

While the cloud floated thousands of feet above the streets of Los Angeles, Angel lay with her head resting on the edge of the pillowy substance and her legs stretched out across the middle. The pups sat to the right of Angel, and Joe stood at the prow of the cloud with his back to his daughter, looking down.

"I'm not feeling it either way, but all signs point to soon." Her father turned toward her then sat. "I don't know what happens next."

"Teresa's not going to believe any of this," Angel said.

"I know. It's more about prepping her for the future, in hope that one day some of it will make sense to her and help her deal with her past," her dad responded.

"It doesn't make sense now, does it?" Angel asked.

"Some of it doesn't make sense at all. Like how are we sitting in a cloud?" Joe laughed.

"Well that part makes the most sense to me." Angel blinked. "I've been here for a long, long time."

"Oh, sorry."

"No, it's not about being sorry. Because I don't get at all how you're here, too. How'd that happen? And it sounds like bullcocky, your saying you talk to Mom. If it's so, then why can't I?" She sat up so she could face her dad directly.

"I know, we've got a lot of unanswered questions. It does sound like ... what'd you call it?" Joe snickered. "Bull ... what?"

"Bullcocky." Angel giggled.

"It does sound like bullcocky, doesn't it?" Joe burst out laughing.

"How come I can't talk to Mom?" Angel's smile left her face, and she placed her hands over her stomach as if it ached—but it didn't. "I'm serious. I'm not in the flesh. It would make more sense that she could communicate through me."

Joe gently moved closer to Angela and spoke softly, "Well, I think your mom has always tried to speak to you. But you're blocked."

"I'm blocked?" That surprised her, but maybe it shouldn't. Stuck and blocked might be the same thing.

"Yes, you're blocked. Think about how much you keep to yourself and push everyone away. She sent the girls to you for that reason."

Angel, who had been shocked by this claim of his, turned to Belle and Kail and asked, "Does this sound right to either of you? Did my mom send you to me?"

"It could be. But I don't remember," Belle answered.

"What'd she say?" Joe asked.

"They don't remember." Angel laid her head back on the edge of the cloud and closed her eyes. She was exhausted and confused and wanted some peace and quiet. Her regimens had been interrupted, and the emotions tied to this drama were affecting her. Perhaps her dad was right, maybe she was blocked. She'd chosen the clouds as a safe haven, years ago, away from everyone else. The isolation was her idea, due to her own fears.

Angel recalled seeing a few lost souls in a similar situation to hers when she'd first arrived in this state, whatever it was. Those rootless ones tended to band together, and sometimes made trouble for the living. At the time, she believed remaining alone and learning to get by on her own would be safer until she could figure out the "who, where, when, and why" of her own situation.

To Angel, getting involved with complete strangers didn't feel right. Yes, she was a little blocked from years of dodging contact with others.

"I've got a feeling things are going to be changing real soon," her dad whispered.

"Can you hear what I'm thinking, too?"

"Too?" her dad asked.

"The girls can hear me when I think."

"I can't hear what you're thinking. I'm watching your face and your brow is furrowed together in an intense stress pattern. I understand that you'd like to get on with your life."

"Well, now that's interesting." Angel opened her eyes and lifted her head as she spoke, "Since I've been dead for twenty years or so."

"Angel, as you of all people should know, death is not the end."

"Well it certainly isn't life as we know it." She giggled nervously.

"That's a fact, isn't it?" Her dad winked.

"Where's Mom? Where is it that people go when they die?" Angel asked.

"As I said, your mom calls it `home,' and that's about all she'll share with me, other than ... `You'll see for yourself, Joe .... you'll see for yourself.'" He mimicked her mom's voice.

"Why is it such a secret?" Angel asked.

"I think it's indescribable and that's why it seems like a secret she won't tell. No word can capture the feeling and the look of the other side—or as your mother calls it, `home.' My personal belief is that the years spent in the flesh, on earth, is like a speck of time on the other side. Or better said, time doesn't exist over there—no deadlines or schedules." Angel could see in his eyes some of the fear she herself had—and some of the eagerness she used to feel as well.

"Your mother is waiting for her family, and somehow she's found the ability to watch out for each of us, and this is a rare feat, I imagine. When we do arrive, I think that to her it'll be like it happened right after she got there, too, and not twenty, thirty, or forty years later. I'm in my sixties, and looking back now, my life went by like that." Joe snapped his fingers.

"'I wonder about it all, you know ... Why even be born into the flesh?" Angel asked him.

"It's the circle of life. Learning and loving. I've been told being human is the most difficult job in the universe," Joe answered.

"I know, so why bother?" Angel's lip started to form itself into her little girl pout.

"It's also supposed to be the most rewarding job in the universe," her dad answered.

Angel put her head back down and closed her eyes. A moment later, she felt the lift of the cloud when her father left. She didn't bother to open her eyes and say good-bye at that point because she knew the cloud would be empty. With her chin tucked into her neck, Angel curled up in a ball and fell asleep. After what seemed like hours, and because she was a creature of habit, Angel woke up, and within seconds found herself in Teresa's home.

A predawn light leaked through the shades of the living room. Angel knew the house wasn't haunted by anyone except her, and as she became more aware of herself, she also became more aware of the environment around her. Although she couldn't see everything in the house right this second with her own eyes, she could feel the truth of what was here—down to the very core of her being. Without looking in their bedrooms, she knew that both JJ and Teresa were asleep.

What if she could enter Teresa's dream, or JJ's, as her father had asked?

In less than a split second, Angel drifted over Teresa, who slumbered quietly in her bed. Angel hadn't a clue how to make a go of this, but she felt the urge to try. She floated directly above Teresa and slowly guided her body down, lower and lower, all the while focusing on entering the living body that lay peacefully below her. It wasn't a task Angel had attempted often, or even ever before, her soul merging with another breathing human being. But once again, she somehow knew it could be done.

Within moments Angel felt cramped in a tight spot that had poor visibility. Suddenly, she sensed another presence push up against her in an attempt to shove her out.

Hey, I just got here. I'm not leaving yet, Angel thought as she struggled to stay inside of the narrow space. She believed Teresa's soul, perhaps unconsciously, was trying to protect her territory. In wrestling to remain in place, Angel stretched her left arm straight up as a sort of anchor onto the spot she'd settled in. Amazingly, this caused Teresa's arm to dart up, too. A shocked Teresa opened her eyes, and it was at this point that Angel's vision became much clearer, though not as omni-directional as it was outside of the human body. She realized she was seeing the world through her sister's eyes, and that she controlled the arm. Angel put Teresa's hand in front of Teresa's face and wiggled the fingers. Yes, she definitely controlled the arm.

For the first time in years, Angel felt what it was like to be in the flesh again—if only for a fleeting moment. Teresa closed her eyes, breathed in deeply through her nostrils, and Angel smelled the cleanness of the house. Teresa stretched her legs, yawned, and rolled over to her side. Angel felt every heavy movement the body made.

"Go and see Dad," Angel whispered.

In her sleep, Teresa completed a turn that felt like a flip, shifting her body to the other side. Angel felt the sensation of the pillow on her check and the blanket landing back down on Teresa's body. With all the energy Angel could muster, she focused on her dad and his recent visit with her. Angel repeated to Teresa the conversation she'd had with her father in the cloud earlier that evening. She hoped by doing this the images and words would be able to enter Teresa's dreams.

"Tell him to describe his visit to the cloud, and he'll dictate exactly what I shared with you. He'll confirm this craziness is true," Angel said.

Exhausted once again, but happy to have experienced some of the human senses Angel had taken for granted when she was in the flesh, she exited Teresa's body by imagining herself in her usual state. At the moment she escaped the confinement, a loud pop left an unpleasant ringing noise in her ears—a sound, Angel hoped, that only she could hear.

How wonderful being light again felt. Though she'd only spent a few minutes in Teresa's body, the constraint of that tight place had been horrible. The heaviness of the body, too, was almost as disturbing as the confinement—but smelling the scents of the house had been pleasurable.

Angel went to JJ's room; she wanted to give him a sign as well, but hesitated. She had no desire to squeeze into the enclosed space of a human body anytime soon. Angel stood next to JJ and put her face up to his eyes, which appeared to be in full REM mode.

"Wake up so I can tell you about your gramps!" Angel yelled.

Angel jumped back as JJ's eyes opened. "Shoot," she said. "You scared me."

JJ closed his eyes and rolled to his side. "Oh, he didn't hear me," Angel whispered. "Well I'll sit next to your ear, JJ, and talk to you about your family. I guess you can think of me as your Aunt Angela. Please call me Angel ..." For the next hour, Angel told JJ about the cloud, her pups, her dad, and some piecemeal memories of her mom and Teresa.

She had no idea if he'd remember a single bit of what she shared, though telling him all this seemed like a good idea, and the words flowed from her mouth as easily as water from the kitchen faucet. Her mind raced while her mouth hurried to keep up. Finally talking, when mostly she just listened and watched, felt good. So Angel spoke to him until the alarm clock went off, and then she waited to see the effect of her efforts.

As JJ and Teresa got ready for the day, Angel hung back to allow them their privacy. She floated around the door and watched both mother and son eventually exit the house.

CHAPTER 20

THE PRIEST ENTERED THE HOSPITAL EARLY, before sunrise. Although Father Benjamin had said his last good-bye to Juan already, he'd felt a tug, as his mother would've called it, to drop everything and go at once to the hospital. He couldn't validate whether this was a pull of curiosity, because he did want to know what happened with Juan's family, or if the tugging was a simple need to see his friend again.

A weight lifted from Father Benjamin's shoulders as soon as he entered the room and realized Juan was still alive and at this early hour, awake.

"Well, how are you my friend?" Father Benjamin asked with a smile on his face as he approached Juan's bed.

"I've seen better days." Juan squinted. "It's bright in here."

The priest turned off the lights. "You must be sensitive to light."

"Thank you. For the prayer."

Father Benjamin's cheeks burned with heat, his voice filled with excitement. "You heard me?"

"Sort of," Juan said. "I can't explain it, but I was pulled back. I know how you feel, and I appreciate it."

"Did you go back to the pit from Hell?" the priest asked.

"No. It was Angela this time," Juan said.

"I'm sure that's an interesting story. What about Jessie and Teresa? How'd it go?"

Juan smiled, filling in his sunken cheeks. "Funny you should ask that question. I managed to anger both Jessie and Teresa yesterday. Both were here on separate visits and both left in a hurry after I'd annoyed them. I've got a way with words, Father."

Father Benjamin sat in the chair next to Juan's bed knowing he was spending time with a man who had few precious hours left on this earth. Yet Juan seemed to have energy and awareness in his corner this morning—kind of like a second wind. "Is there anything I can do for you?"

"You did great, Marcus—better than I could've expected. I want you to know, you're like a brother to me, and you were right. I should've handled this a long time ago."

He reached out toward the priest, who immediately grabbed the offered hand.

"I'm ashamed of my behavior toward you. It's not in my nature to be so judgmental. I'm sorry. I'm glad I got the chance to say this to you while you're ..." he hesitated. "... awake."

Juan smiled and retracted his hand. "Father, I'd like to continue planning for when I'm gone. Cremate my body and hang on to my ashes until the day Teresa will want them. I think it might be a while, but I know you'll have no issue placing me in a vase up on a shelf." Juan's breaths appeared short but he somehow managed to chuckle.

"Yes, I'll take care of it. I'm sure Father Kramer will have an issue with the cremation, but I'll handle it." Father Benjamin thought about his peers for a moment but decided to save Juan from putting any energy into this issue.

"Oh, yeah, the Catholic Church and all. I should've thought about that. Well, if ten years go by and she doesn't claim me than you should dump me in the ocean." Juan laughed again. "It sounds kind of funny."

"Brave is a better word." The priest was overwhelmed with sadness. He swallowed in an effort to hold back his tears, and it seemed to work.

"Oh, Father Marcus Benjamin, there's nothing brave about me. You're turning into a softy. It wasn't but a few days ago you were ready to tan my hide."

Juan turned his head toward the window, then pushed the buttons on the remote. After his body was propped up, he moved a hand to his brow and wiped his forehead. "I've kept some unusual events from you, Father. Things that have happened to me over the years."

"The voices, the nightmares. I'm sure there was more to it than just that," the priest said to encourage his friend to speak. This wasn't confession, but he wanted Juan to relieve his mind.

"Well, yeah. I guess I did share some of it with you," Juan whispered.

"Have you had any pain medicine?" Father Benjamin asked.

"Willa gave me something last night and they're going to put me on the morphine pump today. I wanted a clear head to talk to Teresa and Jessie, and to meet JJ, though I don't think it helped. I doubt they'll be back. But I've made my own peace. I'm ready to go."

Father Benjamin remembered the waiting room fiasco about five years before, when Juan was left to drown in his own bile. At the time he would never have thought they'd work side by side and become such good friends.

"Do you want your last rites?" the priest asked. He had come ready for just that.

"No, no. I'm thinking I've got a little life left in me and I don't want you to jinx it." Juan winked. "Don't you find it strange—I'm talking one second, and the next second I could be dead."

"Yes, death is difficult to deal with. I'm glad you've had some type of a warning." Father Benjamin looked down at the floor. He'd attended dying parishioners before, but this was harder. This touched him personally.

"I appreciate you seeing me as a friend and not a priest."

Father Benjamin smiled. Although Juan never admitted it, the priest knew that he prayed and believed in God. Juan worshipped in his own way, and that was okay with the priest. It had created some controversy with the elder clergymen, but they had gotten over it. A big part of their distaste dissipated when they learned Juan was working out on Skid Row, a job many of the folks at the church shied away from. It was okay for them to turn their backs on what they deemed Juan's "lack of faith" as long as he was doing their dirty work.

At least that was Father Benjamin's view of their hypocrisy. The priest silently reprimanded himself for being judgmental again.

"Any news on the General?" Juan asked.

"No. I keep thinking he'll show up for dinner, but nothing," the priest responded bringing his mind back to those poor souls he felt responsible for.

"Did we ever check the shelters across town, out of his area?" Juan put the back of his hand on his forehead. His breathing was labored.

"A couple of the gals made some calls. Why are you asking? You should be more focused on yourself, now."

"That's funny, Father." Juan chuckled and then coughed. "Most of my life was all about me, which is why I'm in this situation."

The priest spoke in a hushed tone. "Not really, Juan. You give yourself no credit for the last five years." And surely God forgave Juan for all his decades of alcoholism when he wasn't able to help even himself.

Juan ignored the priest's prodding. "Well, I think the General is inside. Some kind of confined space."

"What makes you think this? Did you have a vision?" Father Benjamin resisted the urge to laugh.

"Now you're making fun of me like no priest ever should." Juan somehow managed to wave a finger at the priest and then wink. "Angela did. She had the vision."

The priest laughed and Juan joined him as well as he was able. "I'm sorry, it's not funny," said the father. "I'm trying to deal with my best friend's death."

"It's okay. I can take it. I'm a big boy." Juan's tone sounded condescending to Father Benjamin.

The priest laughed harder, and Juan appeared to be attempting to join him in his laughter, but he paused and coughed a while. "Hey, Father, I think you're taking twenty minutes off of my life making me laugh." Juan snickered and then cringed slightly as if from pain.

"Well, at least you go down with a smile on your face." Father Benjamin couldn't believe he'd said something so insensitive.

"You got that right!" Juan winced as his voice rose up.

"After all, laughter is the best medicine." The priest chuckled, hoping that was true and that he hadn't added to Juan's discomfort.

"I do feel a lot better," Juan said, and then with a sober look on his face he continued. "No, really, I do."

Father Benjamin sat up straighter in his chair and tried to focus on the more serious matter of Juan's death. "Laughing is also a defense mechanism, isn't it?" he observed.

"Well, yes. But it was more fun not thinking about that part of it. You know? It's hard to believe my life's almost over," Juan murmured. His legs moved restlessly under the covers.

"Well, if you go soon, maybe you can find out where the General is and somehow tell me." The priest wanted to take his words back as soon as they left his mouth. "I'm sorry, that was a really bad joke."

"I'll tell you what, Father, I don't know whether to laugh or cry."

The words removed the smile from Father Benjamin's face. "Yep," he responded.

"Well, it's all I've been dealing with for the last week. A part of me wants my simple life back." He offered a weak smile.

Father Benjamin sat quietly and listened.

"I know it's pathetic, but I had my routines. I felt safe. Now, I'm scared," Juan said.

"For this God is our God for ever and ever; he will be our guide even to the end," Father Benjamin whispered. He knew this was true, but he imagined he, too, would be frightened when leaving this familiar world for the next.

"No, no, don't start, please," Juan requested. He seemed to lie more heavily against his pillows, and he closed his eyes.

Father Benjamin sighed, sat in silence with his friend, and prayed for him.

CHAPTER 21

JESSIE OPENED HER LEFT EYE AND saw the tattered black and white essay book sitting on her nightstand. Darn, she'd hoped all of it had been her imagination at work, but she couldn't be that lucky. Joe was back and definitely leaving chaos in his wake.

She sat up in bed and reached for her clock since a small bowl she'd used for popcorn last night along with the paper wrappers from her Big Hunk candy blocked her view. Joe had really rocked her world. She hadn't eaten that late in years, and such junk to top it off.

The clock displayed 5:00 a.m. Why was she up so early? Usually she slept in later and stayed up late. As she began to age, she'd noticed she needed fewer hours of sleep at night, but yet her energy levels seemed to be diminishing. So difficult getting old—something that her brother, Joe, wouldn't have to worry about.

Jessie decided to get up, make some coffee, and then head over to the hospital. She felt it in her bones—he was going to be gone real soon. Even though he'd handed them such a cockamamie story, she wanted to be around her brother for a while and help him through this last phase of his life. Her brother was a real deliverer of tales, and this was the most difficult part for her to comprehend. Why couldn't he just stand up and be accountable for his actions? Crazy, crazy man.

Jessie hurried through her morning routine. She'd arrive before visiting hours, but she trusted that the hospital staff would let her in. Something about Joe's rapport with these people during his dying days made her believe this would be okay. If the hospital in general were strict, Willa would look the other way—assuming she was there this morning. In the few moments Jessie had spent with Willa, they'd become fast friends.

A heartbreaker was what this would all come down to. Joe, or Juan—whatever the hell his name was—would stay alive long enough to make his family care again, and then he'd die. Leaving his daughter, grandson, and everyone else scratching their heads and wondering what had just occurred. Not much Jessie could do about it now, except for trying to talk Joe out of sharing his craziness with Teresa. Or if he'd shared it already, maybe she could get him to help convince Teresa he was mentally disturbed. Then he could, kind of like ... take it back.

Jessie was glad she'd get to see Joe again, because the more she thought about it, the more she liked the idea of having closure. Finally just about ready to start out, Jessie allowed herself to leave a few dishes in the sink in order to exit quickly for the hospital. Opening the front door, she shuddered as the chilly early morning air slammed against her face. She laughed at her reaction, and told herself, "The people in Bismarck would think you're crazy for being cold right now. Or crazy for talking to yourself. Ha!"

Jessie trotted to her car and immediately turned the heater on. "Sissy." She aimed her insult at the air vent. "Crazy," she then said to her reflection in the mirror and followed it with, "Torres family curse."

As she backed out of the driveway, Jessie realized she'd neglected her weeding, and her yard was starting to look a bit frayed around the edges. She made a mental note to return to her yard work that afternoon. A little a day kept the messiness away. But at least the seediness wasn't easy to recognize in the dark morning hours. God help her when she saw the yard in the light of day.

Jessie clutched the steering wheel and zipped through the neighborhood. Speeding over the morning roads made her feel a whole lot better. Control was what she'd lacked during the last twenty-four hours, and at the steering wheel she felt in control again. Yesterday had simply been no picnic whatsoever. Joe had sucked the life out of all of them in one fell swoop. Grief, sadness, regret, anger, hate, and love—just a few of the turns on the roller-coaster ride he'd been offering. Now, how much time did she have to convince him to leave it alone and simply say good-bye?

Jessie pulled into the hospital parking lot ten minutes after she'd left her house. With her head tucked down, she hurried through the front of the hospital and through the halls trying to show confidence, as if she were a hospital worker. She laughed to herself when she realized she didn't need to feel she was going to be arrested. The halls were almost empty this morning, and the silence was soothing.

Jessie stopped short when she entered her brother's room and saw Father Benjamin seated next to Joe. Both men were silent.

"I'm sorry, Father. Am I disturbing something?" she asked. These priests—who knew what nonsense they might hand out to a man at the threshold of death.

"Hello, Jessie." Father Benjamin stood up and gestured toward the other chair. "Have a seat. I'm glad you're here."

"What's happening? I woke up and thought I needed to be here," Jessie told them both. "Joe, what does the doctor say?"

Joe appeared to be awake and more alive this morning.

"I'm still here. They don't know for sure, but soon is what I'm hearing, and sometimes feeling," Joe answered. "Earlier, we were talking about what to do with my remains."

"Oh," Jessie said, and she sat down.

"Your brother asked me to hold his ashes until Teresa's ready to take them," the priest explained.

"I thought you wanted them scattered in the ocean or something like that," Jessie said.

"Why?" Joe asked.

"I don't know," Jessie said with a nervous chuckle. "Just something I thought you mentioned long ago."

"I was probably drunk. I'm not much for water," Joe answered without much emphasis.

"I know," Jessie replied. "I always thought it was a strange request from you. So we could put your ashes near Marion's grave. That'd take the decision away from Teresa, and she could visit once she ... you know, once she gets past this ..."

Joe's eyes moved from Jessie to the priest. "What do you think, Father? It's not a bad idea."

"It works for me. I'll research it and see what we need to do to get it done," the father answered.

"What about the Church, Father? You're okay with cremation?" Jessie asked. "And will Marion mind, Joe, that you'll be next to her?" What, really, was she asking? Not if Marion, now, would mind—since his wife was long dead. Jessie meant, of course, did he think it would be respectful to her memory. But Marion wouldn't have minded, would she have—what was she thinking?

"Marion always said the body is a shell, and she'd left hers years ago. So no, she won't mind," Joe answered Jessie.

"I'm okay with cremation. The Church, in general, has a different opinion," the priest added in.

"How'd it go with Teresa and JJ last night? I haven't talked to her yet." Jessie was, frankly, curious.

"Not so good. She didn't want to hear any of it. She pushed me to deliver and it all came out wrong." Joe closed his eyes and mumbled. "Teresa's really mad at me now. Worse than before we talked."

"I'm not going to say it, but I'm thinking it," Jessie said. She'd told him so.

"I had to try," Joe answered her.

"Why?" Jessie shook her head.

"Come on now, let's not start," Joe whispered.

"Well." Father Benjamin stood up. "I think I'll head out and leave you two alone."

The priest reached out for Joe's hand and held it for a moment. Jessie watched Father Benjamin's eyes meet her brother's. The priest then nodded, turned, and slowly left the room.

"He's not happy about you dying," Jessie said. "That priest is going to miss you, Joe. How the hell did that happen?"

Joe laughed and suddenly cringed as if with pain. "I know," he whispered. "It makes no sense at all. I've got a priest for a friend. Fancy that."

"And no laughing, you." Jessie pointed her finger at her brother. "Enough of this craziness—it's time for you to relax."

"I think I'll able to relax a lot here in a few," Joe said.

"How do you know that? You don't know anything for sure, do you, Joe? So listen up, it's time to let go, get pain medicine, and say good-bye. Enough already!" Jessie's voice echoed against the clean, white walls. "Sorry, that was too loud," she then whispered.

"Oh God, I missed you. I did." Joe managed a slight smile.

"Well, what's done is done." Jessie slapped her hands together. "I'd like to take you to breakfast, but I see you're all tied up."

"Very funny."

"But seriously, do you want me to find Willa and get you some pain medicine? This is crazy—you're turning gray," Jessie said.

"What? Where did my yellow tint go?" Joe asked.

"Don't be so silly—it's there. Underneath the gray," Jessie answered.

"You're serious, aren't you?" Joe asked.

"Yes."

"Do you think Teresa and JJ will come by again?" Joe questioned her then.

"I don't know. I haven't talked to her since before she saw you yesterday. I think this is real tough on her. So, it's hard to say." Jessie sighed. She didn't know what would be best for Teresa—seeing him again, or just avoiding further contact.

"How've you been? What've you been up to all these years?" Joe turned his head toward Jessie and maintained eye contact.

"It's been a long time, hasn't it? I wouldn't know where to begin. Teresa lived with me for a while and we got her through college. I retired from the school a few years ago, but I keep busy."

"Jessie, you've never liked talking about yourself. You haven't changed a bit, in that respect."

"Hmm, thank you … I guess," Jessie said.

"What happened to Robert? Did you marry him?" Joe asked.

"Robert Nunez? We were never going to marry. He went to jail." Jessie wrinkled her forehead and squinted her eyes. She hadn't heard the Nunez name in years, and hearing it now was a shock to her system. Robert!

"What? No way. That guy was as straight as an arrow," Joe rasped.

"He got into drugs or something, but that was long after he and I broke up. Robert just wasn't meant for me." Jessie couldn't tell if her brother was truly interested, or if he was merely pushing the focus off himself. At this point what did it matter though? She'd play along.

"So, who was?" he asked.

"Well, evidently no one, Joe. I never married," Jessie snapped.

"I thought you had somebody in your life ..." Joe's eyebrows lifted.

Jessie smiled and put as much lightness in her voice as she could, almost as if she were talking to a child. "No, I don't have time for that. I'm a busy lady. I can't say I've saved the streets of Los Angeles, like my brother has, but nothing romantic to speak of, either."

"What happened with Teresa and Greg?" Joe asked.

For a moment Jessie thought of the arguments between the two, and Teresa's obsession over getting pregnant. The strain was simply too much for their relationship. "I'm not completely sure," she answered. "But he's been remarried for quite some time, and he has a beautiful family, which I'm sure secretly bothers Teresa."

"That's too bad," Joe said as he closed his eyes.

Within seconds, the machines began making noises—a different rhythm than previously. Several medical technicians, nurses, and doctors ran into the room and shooed Jessie away from Joe's bedside.

"He's got nine lives, you know." The priest entered the room and the two of them stood by the empty bed near the door.

With her face pulled tight and her jaw clenched, Jessie leaned against the wall farthest from Joe's bed. Her stomach began to turn. As quickly as he'd reentered their lives, it was over. Her brother was about to die. A tear fell down Jessie's check. Speaking now would only cause her to cry hysterically. Oh, that stupid priest. Why didn't he go away and leave her alone?

"Jessie," Father Benjamin said. "He might pull through."

Jessie nodded and made a weak attempt at a smile while she watched the hospital staff come and go on high alert. To Jessie the moment seemed surreal; her head spun, and she fidgeted on her feet, murmuring, "This isn't happening right now. Not yet."

Many sets of scrubs stomped in and out of Joe's room for what seemed like hours; then all at once the flurry of activity came to an end. Jessie's purse fell to the ground as she moved quickly around the empty bed and trotted to her brother's side.

"What happened? Joe?" She pushed her way through the sea of green that were surrounding his body.

A woman who she thought was a nurse spoke directly in her ear. "Juan was very specific about *not* attempting resuscitation. We can't do anything else. I'm so sorry."

Joe's eyes were closed, and the machine's rhythm seemed familiar, but Joe was barely breathing. His pale skin seemed almost transparent.

"Joe, it's okay to go," Jessie whispered.

She touched her brother's cheek and he opened his eyes but stared right past her. His eyes shut again, and he gasped for breath. The breath soon exited him, and she waited for him to take another gulp of air, which never came.

Tears welled up in her eyes and slowly spilled over. If the room was still filled with hospital workers she wasn't aware of it. It seemed as if she and her brother were all alone, yet connected again at the moment of his death.

Jessie stood at Joe's bedside and held his lifeless hand until the warmth left his body.

CHAPTER 22

TERESA DROVE HER CAR THROUGH TRAFFIC as if she were on autopilot. She'd managed to get an earlier start than the previous day, but her head was foggy, and she felt like she could easily go back to bed and sleep the day away. She hardly noticed that JJ was unusually quiet as well. She sipped her coffee and shivered while she drove with one hand.

"I had some weird dreams last night," JJ said.

"Oh yeah, about what?" Teresa asked.

"Aunt Angela talked to me, practically all night long. She told me things like what your Dad was telling us yesterday. Well, she said she was my aunt."

"Hmm ... I think I slept pretty deep, because I don't remember anything." Teresa sipped her coffee as a memory of her fingers flashed into her head. "Except for my fingers."

"What?" JJ asked.

"Yes, I woke up and my fingers were moving in front of my face. Sounds crazy, but I had no control of my arm ..." Teresa gripped the steering wheel harder. "I think we both experienced a Joe Torres tall tale night."

"My dream was strange. I've never experienced anything quite like that. Aunt Angela went into detail about those little dogs, your dad, and that cloud," JJ said with a yawn.

"Aunt Angela? Where'd you get that from?"

"In my dream. I told you," he responded.

Teresa shook her head and cleared her throat. "This is nuts," she whispered.

"I know," JJ said. "But just in case, this morning I wrote down what I could remember."

Teresa raised her eyebrow and glanced over at her son.

"I know that look, Mom," JJ said. "But, I want to track my dreams. What if I have more? And what if they tell me something we need to know, even if it is my overactive imagination. I think you should write down your dream, too."

"Mine wasn't a dream. I woke up and my hand was over my face, and my fingers were moving in front of my eyes. I went back to sleep," she said.

"Okay, then, I'll write that down." JJ pulled a notepad out of his backpack and began to write.

"Oh, stop this. Don't be so silly. It's all coming from Joe." Teresa put her hand on JJ's pen.

"Mom, steering wheel, please!" JJ pulled away his pen and pointed toward the road.

"Oops." Teresa grabbed the wheel and for a split second thought she saw the gold interior of the old family wagon she and Angela were driving in the day of the accident. JJ's voice brought her back to the moment.

"I want to keep track of all of this weird stuff." JJ wrote while he spoke. "I'm also documenting your hostility."

Teresa chuckled and let down her guard a bit. "Okay, okay. I guess it's good exercise for your brain."

She thought about last night and how she'd tossed and turned after the incident of her fingers in her face. A restless night would be an understatement. It was as if she'd fought with herself all night long. She yawned and was back in automatic pilot mode when her cell phone rang.

"Hello," she answered.

"Teresa, this is Father Benjamin. I'm afraid I have bad news."

"Is he gone?" she asked.

"He's gone," the priest responded.

"Okay, we'll be right over." Teresa moved the car through traffic as she dialed JJ's school to say he'd be out for the day. Heaviness weighed in her heart, a sadness she thought she'd never feel toward her father again. Her throat tightened, and she used every bit of her energy to focus on something else—anything else to help her resist the urge to sob. She told herself she wasn't going to cry. Damn that man. He was only gone as he had been last week and the week before. It was that simple. No more pain.

"I'm sorry, Mom," JJ said.

Teresa dared not open her mouth for fear of losing control, so she nodded toward JJ and drove in silence. Her Aunt Jessie would need to know, and somebody would have to call Uncle Joe at the home. She absentmindedly reached in her jacket pocket looking for that woman Anna's telephone number. How silly of her—the priest would surely tell the folks from the center.

What about Greg? Well, he didn't need to know. She hadn't been married to him for many years now. And he'd never met her father, had he? The people she'd be spending time with today were folks in her father's life. Strangers whom she didn't know.

"Are you okay?" JJ asked.

Teresa nodded. She'd have to make arrangements at the funeral home. Should she call Aunt Jessie now? No, that could wait until she got to the hospital and saw for certain that her father was gone.

"It's going to be okay," a woman said in a hushed tone.

Wait a minute, that voice wasn't JJ's. "I'm sorry, did you just say something?" she asked.

"Like an hour ago. What's up, Mom? I said, 'Are you okay,' and you nodded." JJ leaned into her, touching her shoulder with his head.

"Oh, I thought you said ... it's okay ..." Teresa supposed the voice had been her imagination.

"I guess you're hearing things, or your dad's here." JJ laughed.

"Stop that nonsense," Teresa snapped.

"Okay, okay," JJ responded.

Dazed by the news of her father's death, and a little confused, Teresa drove like an automaton to the hospital. Which seemed a lifetime away. The unpleasantness of the situation seeped into her bones as she maneuvered the car through the hospital lot, and out of habit looked for a safe place to park.

How could Joe have done this to her again? The man seemed to be continually abandoning her—Joe's perpetual motion.

JJ and Teresa entered the hospital and went directly to Joe's room, where Aunt Jessie stood outside the door. The priest must've called both of them. Well, of course he did; he must have their numbers on speed dial—judging by the urgency with which he'd tried to get them to visit her dad, and that was only yesterday. Had it been just about twenty-four hours since she'd learned of her father's illness, and now he was gone?

"Aunt Jessie, you're here early." Teresa hugged her aunt.

"I woke up, got dressed, and came right over. I felt like I had to. I didn't know he was going to die while we were talking." Aunt Jessie dabbed at her bloodshot eyes and frowned. "I know it was inevitable. I suppose it's inevitable for us all. But I wasn't ready for him to go just yet."

"I know," Teresa said.

"Aunt Jessie, I'm sorry." JJ hugged her.

"He's still in there, if you both want to say your very final good-byes," Aunt Jessie told them.

CHAPTER 23

JOE OPENED HIS EYES AND STRETCHED his arms without any restrictions imposed by the hospital equipment. Then he sat up on his own. The hospital room, his noisy home for the previous week, was unusually quiet. The lights were dim, as if some type of power failure had occurred in the hospital and the back-up generators had kicked in.

The unbelievable heaviness of his body seemed to have disappeared and was replaced by a freer, airier feel. Joe stood next to his bed and wondered why he wasn't hooked to the machines anymore. Had he gotten better?

With one foot in front of the other, he walked from his bed to the other side of the room and smiled. It seemed like years since he'd been able to walk so upright and strong. Grinning from ear to ear, he danced a few steps to the door.

"Wow," he whispered, and then put his head through the door. "Hello. Where is everyone?"

The hall was empty, and the hospital appeared to have been abandoned. Joe trembled and tried to shake off the foreboding feeling that had snuck up on him. He looked at his arms, no needles or marks from the IV bag. In fact, his skin was a smooth tan color, glowing, and no longer yellow. The burning in his throat and stomach was completely gone along with the pain that had pervaded his entire body. He hadn't realized how bad the pain had been until he felt its absence.

"Angela, Angel, are you here?" Joe walked the hallways of the vacant hospital, unsure of his new reality, but more than happy to be out of that tired, sick body.

"I must be dead, or someone's playing a cruel trick on me, because ... I feel good, like I knew that I would ... now ... and ... I feel nice, like sugar and spice. So good." Joe laughed at his James Brown impression as he continued to dance his way down the hall.

Joe picked up the phone at the nurses' station—no dial tone. He moved to the light switch—no control of the lights. What kind of heaven was this, anyway? Out of the corner of his eye, Joe saw movement—sort of like a ripple over reality—as when a pebble breaks the surface of clear water. Yes, the world rippled a little.

His head turned quickly to the right when he witnessed another ripple, but he only caught the tail end of the movement. And it seemed as if this entire setting was fake, that the world he now inhabited was like a window blind or some type of veil. Then the hospital rippled, and the world appeared to be something completely and totally counterfeit at that moment—like a liquid movie set, one that Joe was somehow walking and living in.

The front doors to the hospital reflected beams of sunshine that seeped into the empty lobby. Joe stood in front of the exit. He felt no fear; his life had brought him to this point and he was ready to continue with the plan his dead wife had assigned him to. He'd tried to make it right with his daughters before he'd died, and hopefully his next steps would complete the attempt. He really wasn't bothered that he was encircled now only by silence and stillness. In fact, his solitary state was kind of relaxing. Perhaps the benefit of his journey through the pit was that the experience somehow enabled him to live in this moment.

Suddenly, the interior of his body lit up, and he wanted to laugh because he felt as if he were being tickled. The light inside his being gave him a sense of invincibility, and the strength of his body felt good—like an old memory from many years ago.

At the same time, the airiness of his being and the absence of constraints caused by the heavy human frame were marvelous to experience. He enjoyed a sense of freedom he'd never known during his life as Juan Joseph Torres. Oh yes, by now he fully understood that he'd really died, and it suited him just fine.

The world rippled in the corner of his eyes, again not letting him see this special effect directly. He sensed this strange veil had to do with the place his wife called home, which was much closer than most living people were ever aware of.

Heaven was not a million miles up. Oh no, it was about three feet—or maybe three inches—from the physical dimension. Not directly up but sort of diagonally set—or simply moving at a different speed. And so, Joe's vacation, or his education, was about to end and he was finally going home. Some vacation, he thought, and then he changed his mind and told himself it wasn't a vacation after all; it was simply time he'd spent in the flesh, having a range of experiences.

Joe sat on the couch in the lobby contemplating his next move. He didn't want to leave his mission with Teresa so unfinished. If he'd only had a few more days, he might have gotten through to her. As stubborn as she was, he felt as if she would eventually have come around.

His concern was exactly what Jessie had suggested: Joe had come back into Teresa's life, only to leave again and without making an impact. He wasn't ready to go through those doors, not yet.

He closed his eyes and thought of the cloud and his daughter, Angela. When he opened his eyes, he was still in the lobby. A ripple, he thought, to his left—and then again to his right.

"Umm." Joe felt a tremor in the depth of his being. Something didn't seem right. This wasn't exactly part of the plan, although the plan hadn't really been laid out in detail.

Joe stood up and headed back to his room. In his peripheral vision he saw ripples trail behind his movement. The ripples seemed to follow him down the hall and become more frequent, yet the vision was still too elusive to catch full on. With each turn to confirm what he thought he saw out of the corner of his eye, the world flattened again as if the ripples were a part of a sort of daydream.

As he approached his room, he noticed the door was closed, yet he didn't remember shutting it. Odd that he could touch the door and feel it. Based on his time with Angel, Joe thought he wouldn't be able to feel anything solid. He moved through the door—but then to his amazement he entered a room that wasn't part of the hospital.

He recognized the old couch and the special bed to the left in the living room of his family's home. Joe was standing in his wife's hospice room, the room he'd set up over twenty years ago. Beep, whirr, fizz went the familiar sound of the machines that appeared to be attached to his wife's body in the bed. Joe closed his eyes for a moment—he thought for sure this was a hallucination. He opened his eyes and understood immediately that this wasn't an illusion, after all. He was there.

Joe watched the young woman, well, the girl, administer a wet cloth to his wife's forehead. He heard Marion whisper to her daughter, their daughter—and he suddenly recognized the girl was Teresa at nineteen.

"Hello," Joe said standing next to the bed, hoping they'd be able to hear him speak.

Teresa bit her lower lip, turned, and wiped her eyes with the back of her sleeve. "Dad will be home soon, Mom," she said with a forced smile.

Joe's heart dropped, and he was overcome with sadness. Tears spilled over the rim of his eyes. The contents of his stomach churned as he burped up the flavor of ... tacos? He knew he hadn't eaten a taco before he'd died; in fact, he couldn't remember the last time he'd had a taco. Then, when he saw the Taco Bell wrapper on the dinner table, he realized this experience wasn't about him. A deep sorrow seeped into his gut.

Teresa touched her stomach, bent over, and threw up in the wastebasket below the bed, out of sight from her mother. At the same moment, acid reflux or some type of stench erupted from Joe's stomach, and a sickening, regurgitated flavor filled his mouth. Joe coughed, and spittle flew down his chin. He wiped his mouth with his shirt. Sweat covered his forehead as his body reverberated with an aching, deep pain, unlike anything he'd ever experienced in life. Marion moaned loudly while the pain spread through Joe's body.

"Okay, Marion, I'm on to you now. We can do this together," Joe whispered. Unable to bear the pain standing, he bent down on one knee and doubled over, gripping his stomach. He remained close to the bed, but below eye level, so that he couldn't see Teresa or his wife. "Oh crap," Joe whispered as his body spasmed involuntarily. The pain was worse than what he'd been through during his own dying process. He lay in a ball on the side of Marion's bed.

"We don't have any more pain medicine." Teresa's voice trembled as she spoke. "I'll call the hospice nurse and the doctor. They didn't leave any more morphine, Mom."

"Okay," Joe answered from the floor at the same time his wife, Marion, whispered a response.

"It's okay," Marion said in a low, almost inaudible voice.

Teresa held a washcloth to her mother's forehead. "I'll be right back, Mama." She left the living room, grabbed the phone with the long cord, and walked down the hall to the bathroom. She shut the door behind her, the phone cord fitting neatly under the door.

Somehow, Joe continued to feel the pain with Marion in the living room, and at the same time he was in the bathroom with Teresa. He knew he wasn't at eye level or within viewing distance of either one, but he could see both of them. A feeling of loss and despair mixed with complete confusion rumbled through his body. He was literally in two places at the same time.

"Aunt Jessie?" Teresa cried as she spoke into the phone. "Dad is nowhere to be found. He didn't go to work and I can't locate him."

Teresa sat down on the toilet seat, pulled some toilet paper off the roll, and blew her nose. "Mom's hurting and I can't get in touch with anyone. The doctor or the nurse."

Teresa wiped her eyes and blew her nose again. "Okay, okay, I will. Hurry, please." Teresa put the phone back in its cradle, wiped her nose again, and moved quickly through the house toward her mother's bed, placing the phone back on the counter. Joe stared for a moment at the phone. Something seemed out of place. "Oh yeah," he whispered. "No cordless phones back then."

Marion lay still in the bed. Her body must have shrunk with the illness, so much so that the bed almost looked empty. Her pale, gray face blended in with the color of the blankets, while

215

the red-flowered scarf on her head was the most visible item on the bed. At first it looked as though a stuffed animal was lying there.

Joe still wasn't sure how he was seeing all of this, as his body remained at the side of the bed, his breathing labored and his insides feeling that they'd been turned facing out.

He wasn't sure how much time had passed; it was as if he'd fallen asleep on the floor under the bed. Eventually, Jessie's voice woke him up. She hadn't been there earlier, hmm? Teresa was asleep in the chair next to the bed, so Jessie was essentially alone with Marion. Joe seemed to hear her voice in his ear.

"This will help you." Jessie leaned over Marion with a cup, then put a straw in Marion's mouth and said, "Drink."

A bitter flavor filled Joe's mouth. It took several minutes, but eventually the pain faded, never quite leaving his body but becoming more tolerable. After more time passed, Joe was able to stand. It was at this point that he saw both Teresa and Jessie sleeping in chairs next to Marion's bed. Jessie's shirt was ripped and she had a few bruises on her arm and face.

He went to his wife's bedside and held her hand in his.

"I'm sorry, Marion. I didn't handle this well at all," Joe said.

He touched her cheek and was about to speak again when Marion's eyes opened. Joe stiffened from the shock—it'd been twenty years since he'd seen his wife's beautiful brown eyes.

"Joe," she whispered.

"I'm here, I'm here," he responded with a sniffle.

"Thank you. I feel better now. The pain ..." Marion said.

"I know. I felt it too," answered Joe. "God, I've missed you."

"Don't be so silly, Joe. I'm not dead, yet." Marion sighed.

"I'm such a fool," he whispered.

"Yes, you are. Teresa needs you. You need to put the bottle down, now. Enough." Marion seemed to have lost her breath, and she closed her eyes.

"I have. I promise you I have," Joe said squeezing her hand a little.

Suddenly Marion's eyes opened with complete clarity. "You bastard." She sat up, pulled the needle from her arm, and detached the heart monitor. "I can't believe you'd let me think this actually happened. You didn't stop drinking."

Marion stood up with confidence. The scarf was gone and her hair was in place as she tapped her finger on Joe's chest. "You listen to me, Juan Joseph Torres, both of your daughters need you now. You cannot leave this undone again."

Joe backed up with each tap on his chest, his eyes wide open and all of his senses on alert. "I did stop drinking. I know it took me a long time. God, I'm trying to make this right." He stammered and backed up all the way to the far wall in the living room. Fear filled his veins.

"What now, Joe? You died too soon." Marion sat down on the couch in the living room. Her lips puckered, a look Joe recognized as anger. "Did you know your sister, Jessie, paid a huge price when she got those drugs for me? And she didn't tell a single person about what happened." Marion's tone lightened a little. "I think she gave me heroin. It worked though, didn't it?"

Joe took a deep breath and stepped away from the wall.

"I'm confused," he whispered.

Marion turned to Joe and looked back at her body in the bed, and then she turned toward Jessie and Teresa sleeping in the chairs. "I think you know what this is. What's so confusing about it?"

"You're not real." He stumbled over his words.

"Oh, I can assure you that I am. I'm more real than they are in that state." Marion pointed at the women.

"What is this?" Joe moved toward the couch, but as he bent to sit down, he landed hard on the ground in his empty hospital room. His tongue bled from the pinch between his teeth when he hit the tile floor. "Damn."

He stood up and walked out the hospital room door. And to his surprise, he entered the same living room again—only this time it appeared to be the next day. Teresa and Jessie stood at Marion's side, and he overheard their conversation. "No, he wasn't here, Mom," Teresa said.

"He was here. He said he stopped drinking," Marion whispered, and then in a stronger tone, she continued. "It's going to be okay."

"Oh, Marion," Jessie said. "I'm sure he'll be back sometime today. But I've got to go to work right now."

Teresa followed Jessie to the front door and spoke directly in her ear. "She's seeing things again. Yesterday, it was Angela in a cloud."

"We need to get some morphine from the nurse," Jessie said. "She's not doing good, Teresa. You need to be prepared for the worst, and we can't let them leave her without medicine, ever again."

"I know. I'm trying to keep it together for her. Where is he? Where's my dad?" Teresa whined.

"I think she needs to return to the hospital," Jessie said. "I'll be back later today. Let's get the doctor over here, too. The hospice nurse will be here soon, right?"

"Yes. But can't we get my dad back here?" Tears flowed from Teresa's eyes.

"I think you should stay out of school today. I'll try and find him, again." Jessie exhaled.

Joe closed his eyes. Oh God, he knew what came next. He remembered this one. Passed out on his own front lawn in a pile of puke—he'd walked home after a night of bingeing.

Joe opened his eyes to find himself back in the hospital lobby. What was going on here?

If he remembered correctly, it wasn't long after this incident that his wife passed away, or maybe his memory was playing tricks on him. Marion may have really seen him during her illness, because time wasn't linear on the other side. Of course, he suspected he was on the other side himself, yet he was beginning to feel a bit like Angela, stuck in between.

He should've held it together and been there for his wife all of those years ago.

The front door to the hospital rippled and this time Joe witnessed the effect. Outside, a normal day moved along. Cars drove by, people walked. It was as if the world was right in front of him, a stone's throw away. Joe hesitated at the door, because he wasn't sure if this led away from the world as he knew it or back into the world.

He sensed a finality in going through that door.

Behind him, a vacant hospital; in front of him a thriving world: The choice was obvious. Joe pushed through the door and stepped onto the sun-drenched sidewalk. His smile widened at the noise and activity outside the door, a day like any other day.

He walked to the corner and approached a man waiting at the stop sign.

"Excuse me, sir. Have you got the time?" Joe asked.

The man looked at his watch, then glanced across the street toward the top floor of the office building on the opposite corner. His lips didn't move, but Joe heard him say, *I'm going to be a few minutes early—good. I've got this job. I just need to get through the interview.*

"What?" Joe asked.

Joe looked at a woman walking by on the pavement and heard her whisper, though again her lips didn't move. *I can do this. I know I can. It'll be over in a few minutes.*

Thoughts—he was hearing people's thoughts. He knew this when he caught a glimpse of the man the woman was thinking about. Gross.

"Hello." Joe moved quickly along the sidewalk and waved his hands in front of anyone he could find. Sooner or later somebody would be able to see him. He was sure of it. He decided to make a commotion until he found that one person who would notice him.

He continued at it for quite some time, so that when the moment finally arrived, he almost missed it.

"I've been waiting for you." After a second or two, Joe realized he'd heard a voice directed his way. He saw a man with a ragged coat and worn-out shoes leaning against a brick building where he thought the voice had come from. "What's taking you so long?"

Yep, it was that man. Joe looked behind him to see who the guy was talking to.

"No, you. I'm talking to you. Joe, Juan, or whatever the hell your name is." The man stepped forward. His fingertips protruded from the frayed sweater gloves, and he held a smoking pipe in one hand and a lighter and a baggy full of tobacco in the other.

"You can see me?" Joe asked, somewhat surprised.

"Not only can I see you, I know you. Don't you recognize me?" He pointed to the stripes on his jacket.

"General? You look so different. Where've you been?" Joe asked. He was startled but pleased, but then wondered if his reaction was appropriate. Did this mean the man was no longer alive?

"I've been waiting for you, son." The General lit his pipe.

"What? You don't smoke a pipe. You look so ... young," Joe said.

"My name's Nathaniel Becket. I am young—at least I am, now." He laughed. "You can call me Nate, or General. Whichever you prefer. What the hell do I call you? Joe or Juan?"

"Call me Joe—it seems right." A grin filled Joe's face; he thought he'd never see the General again. And then his smile faded as the seriousness of his own situation brought him back to his new reality. "General, where are we? I have no idea what's going on here."

"Let's walk this way, and I'll tell you all about it." The General directed Joe forward on the sidewalk. "I'm treating you to a cup of coffee. It's my turn to treat."

A few moments later, the General emptied his pipe at the double door to a small establishment that seemed to have appeared out of nowhere. "The Cafe" blinked on a neon sign in the window of the small brick store that the General signaled Joe to enter. He then pointed toward a table and followed behind Joe, stopping at the counter to pour two coffees into paper cups along the way.

"Black, how you like it." The General winked as he pulled up a chair across from Joe.

The cafe seemed a lot like a school cafeteria, with that pale, cheap linoleum flooring. As familiar as it felt, it was a place Joe had never been to, or had seen in his life, although it reminded him of his first AA meeting: folding chairs and tables, stark walls, and free coffee. The place was mostly empty except for a few folks scattered in the seating area.

"You like the setting? I thought it was appropriate," the General commented.

Joe looked at Nathaniel Becket and slowly began to recognize the General in the man in front of him. Nate was a much younger, cleaner version of the old guy who Joe'd become so close to over the last few years.

"This looks a lot like my first AA meeting room, but I'm sure I've never been to The Cafe," Joe said.

The General saluted and winked. "It's all about comfort, my friend."

"What ... Where do we start? I'd like to know who Nate Becket is first," Joe said, sipping his coffee and leaning back in the plastic folding chair. He was amazingly at ease in this strange place.

"I thought you'd want to know my story once and for all." Nate stood up and turned completely around, and when he faced Joe head-on again, Joe saw the General as he'd last seen the man. Gray hair, familiar wrinkles around the eyes, but much more clarity within the eyes. "This might be easier for you if you can see me how I was when you knew me."

Joe smiled. What a pleasant surprise, seeing the General.

"Well, I think my heart gave out or something. I'm sure my body is still rotting at the trash dump. Drunk as a skunk, I crawled into a trash bin about a week ago. I never made it through my first night outside. I sat inside that trash bin, dead as a doornail. I felt bad that you guys were out looking for me for so long when I was dead and in the next world already."

"So what happened when you died?" Joe asked. He wanted to learn from the other man's experience.

"Oh no, we're not going there just yet. Let me go back a ways first." The General took a sip of his coffee. "I got a brother in Cincinnati, and that's about it for living relatives. I was a mechanical engineer with a seemingly bright future. I moved to Los Angeles, had a nice job with Pasco Industries and a beautiful girlfriend. Until my brain thing happened. Yep, I had brain damage." He smiled sadly.

"Brain damage?" That would explain quite a bit, Joe realized.

"Yes, so bad I lost everything. I hurt my head in a fight at the bar when I was just a kid, barely in my thirties." The General let out a nervous laugh. "The only car accident I ever had was with a tree, and really I think that was my memory of an accident."

"Interesting." Joe looked into his coffee cup while he spoke. "Okay, so what's with the pipe?"

"It's something I enjoyed a long time ago. I forgot how much I liked a pipe, until I died ..." The General examined the pipe and then set it back down. "Though it's really not the same here as it was back in the flesh."

"Aha, is that a common term to use? You know, the `in the flesh' saying," Joe asked.

"I learned it from Angel." The General tipped his head and held his cup up as if to cheer the girl.

"You've talked to Angel?" Joe asked, dumbfounded. He couldn't have been more shocked if the General had turned into a ... giraffe.

"No. I learned it from you. You learned it from Angel." The General winked.

"Oh, you've been around me, then," Joe commented. He tried to think if he'd use that expression at the church.

"Yes, I have. But, I don't know too much about what I'm doing here, either. If that's any reassurance to you ..." The General's voice trailed off.

"No, it's not," Joe said. "I'd like to know what to do next."

"You seem to be doing all right so far," the old guy responded.

Joe wasn't exactly sure how long `so far' had been—an hour? A week? He felt very muddled about time right now. "So, what happened to you when you died?" Joe asked.

"I noticed a clarity in my mind that I hadn't had in years. It was as if the limitations of my body were completely gone. I felt unencumbered, free. Did you notice that?"

"Yes, that's what I noticed first," Joe agreed. "It's like the body was holding all of this energy in check, and my soul, or the essence of who I am, popped out of that tight confinement all of a sudden. I felt liberated, but that word doesn't quite capture the moment." Joe's mind went back to his feeling at the second when he'd died.

"I understand what you mean. I felt as if I'd had on a scuba suit that was too tight. And then somebody came along and undid the zipper." The General chuckled.

"Yep, that's a good way to describe it." Joe laughed along with his friend.

"When I clobbered my head, it was on a table in the bar on my way down to the floor. Some guy decked me. I was so drunk I couldn't stand the force of the punch. It was an accident. That poor sap spent some time behind bars over the fight. He didn't mean to damage my brain. But I was never the same after that injury." The General sighed.

"And they didn't help you or keep you in a facility?" Joe asked.

"They tried, for years. Before my parents died, they kept tabs on me as best they could. I was placed in a facility that let me come and go—it was sort of like a rehab house. Once my folks died, my brother lost track of me. Then again, I was an alcoholic even before the accident. Drinking was my favorite pastime." The General took a sip of his coffee and paused as if looking right into that time so many years before. "The moment I died I knew what had been wrong with me, and who I was—and that I wasn't the person who'd hurt your daughters."

"That had a big impact on you, didn't it? My girls' accident," Joe said. He felt regretful at having passed on the pain to the General, who was innocent after all.

"More than I thought, but you know now—don't you?" the General responded.

"Know?"

"Well, yeah, you know what happened?"

"I'm not having the same experience you are. I don't know what happened ... Do you?" The sensation of blood rose up through Joe's body to his brain—an extremely physical feeling. The incident that so thoroughly affected the latter part of his life, and had set the stage for all of his mistakes, was about to be made completely clear.

"Oh gosh, I assumed everyone went through the same thing. You just got here, didn't you? Have you had any revelations?" the General asked. He stared at Joe intently.

"What do you mean? Like who killed Marilyn Monroe?" Joe asked.

"Well, yes, but that was an accidental overdose, and Robert Kennedy's people came and took her diary. Did you see the JFK thing?" the General asked.

"I guess you must've been a history buff, and it sounds like you still are." Joe laughed. "Hey, my body feels good—really good."

"I know. I feel the same way. I was thirty years old when you first walked up a few minutes ago. It seems to be a good age around here."

"What happens now?" Joe asked, becoming somewhat more serious.

"It sounds as if you still have everything in front of you, Joe." The General took a puff of his unlit pipe, looked at it, then set it down with a frown. "Sometimes the past leaks in, and my mind doesn't work too well, though I'm healing more and more the longer I'm in this place ... Well, anyway, I'm here to introduce you to Flavio."

"Flavio? Who's Flavio?" Joe asked.

"He lived in the Los Angeles area about twenty years ago. He was an illegal immigrant who was driving the vehicle that got into the accident with your daughters' car. Joe, Flavio wasn't drinking that night. He was rushing to the hospital to be with his wife, who had just lost their baby. It was an accident, nothing more."

The General fidgeted with his pipe and stirred his coffee before he continued. "Flavio left the scene when he heard the sirens because of his immigration status. He knew there was nothing he could do about the wreck—or the condition of your daughters—and help was on the way. Ironically, both he and his wife were deported that week anyhow. The whole accident wasn't what everyone thought."

Joe felt a pain in his left leg where he'd seen Teresa's injury from the accident still caused her discomfort. His insides swirled. He really didn't know how to behave; everything his life had been about for the last twenty years instantly felt wrong.

"I didn't know about this," Joe said slowly.

"I understand. It was the beginning of the end of your family." The General bent his face down to look into Joe's eyes, and then he continued as if he were giving a lecture. "Flavio wants to meet you now. He's not to blame for this event. It was an accident, something that couldn't be controlled, or avoided."

"Why does he want to meet me then?" Joe asked. He felt hesitant—scared, maybe.

"You've carried a huge emotion surrounding this event for many, many years. A lot of energy was put into that grudge, your anger over what happened to your daughters. Whether you know it or not, this thing has affected everyone around you. Including those who weren't ever around you but were actively involved in the incident."

"You call this an `event,' an `incident,' and an `accident.' The car wreck killed my youngest daughter." Joe felt a tear run down his cheek. "And yes, it was the beginning of the end of my life as I knew it."

"You know how people say there are three versions of what really happened? Yours, mine, and the real version." The General waited for Joe to nod. "Well, there's one version here, on this side, and it's what really happened. I want you to understand, the accident wasn't Flavio's fault."

"What are you saying, Nate?" Even as the name left Joe's mouth, he didn't like the sound of it.

"Oh, I think I like it better when you call me General." The General puckered his face.

"Okay, General, what are you getting at?" Joe asked.

"All these years, everyone blamed some drunken driver. Well, that drunk driver didn't exist. The car crash was an accident." The General maintained eye contact with Joe.

"This was Teresa's fault?" Joe asked. "Teresa did this."

"Not really … It was an accident," the General answered.

"What?"

"It's hard to let go, isn't it? Especially after all these years, all this anger toward the driver who killed your daughter. Joe, sometimes accidents happen. It's that simple."

Joe thought about all the hours he'd spent seething over the killer of his daughter. The man whom he thought had refused to stand up and be accountable for his actions. But somebody was at fault, certainly … Somebody had to be blamed. Joe balled his hands into fists and set them down on the table.

"Let it go. It didn't happen the way you thought it did," A thirty-year-old Nate Becket said in a soothing voice.

A flash of how the car looked at the tow yard entered Joe's mind. The cut-away, torn, and twisted metal roof sat on top of the mangled vehicle. Later, several days later, Joe had gone to the accident site. He recalled seeing a few sets of skid marks and some debris on the road.

The police were dumbfounded as to how the driver of the other car was capable of leaving an accident that had injured two young girls. Every single person involved in the investigation, or who had any knowledge of the accident, concluded the fault had to lie with some drunk driver. Not a single one of them thought of any other reason why someone would leave a fatal accident where a child had died. The idea that the driver was an illegal immigrant hadn't ever even entered Joe's mind, though it made sense now.

"Where is he?" Joe asked. This was one of the hardest truths he had ever faced. The truth was supposed to be redemptive, so why didn't he feel a sense of relief now? Because ... because if he let go of that long-held anger, well, what might he feel?

Joe began to feel the terrible grief of Angela's death.

"He's on his way," the General answered.

He was coming over from the land of the living? "You mean, literally ..."

"Oh no, he's been gone for quite a while. He's coming from another place," the General said.

"Another place?" Joe asked.

"Yeah, another place," the General repeated.

The front door to The Cafe opened, and a short Hispanic man entered. He pulled a black beanie off his head and scanned the room. The man smiled when he recognized the General, and then he moved quickly to their table.

"General Nate, how are you?" Flavio spoke with a slight accent.

General Nate, I kind of like that, Joe said quietly to himself.

"And you must be Joe." The man reached his hand out.

Joe stood up and shook Flavio's hand and nodded somberly. His whole world was turning completely around. But of course it was. He had died and had to accept a whole other state of mind, another set of realities, or truths.

"Please sit down, Flavio." The General gestured toward the empty chair.

Flavio kept his eyes on Joe as he slowly sat in the chair across from the recently deceased. "I've felt much pain deep inside over what happened to your daughters. It's a feeling that comes from all who were involved or touched: your daughters, you, your wife, and your sister. Everyone has been affected."

Flavio, a frown on his face, folded his hat in his hands.

"Say, Flavio, do you want some coffee?" the General asked.

"Yes, I would like that. Thank you very much." Flavio looked toward the General and then back at Joe. "The General has helped me a lot, recently."

"So, Flavio, I just learned you were involved in the accident that changed many lives several years ago," Joe commented with as much indifference as he could manage. Oh God, this was hard. He resisted the urge to jump across the table and strangle this man. And then, somehow, he did feel some peace surrounding the accident. How could he blame this man who sat in front of him, wide open and hurting, even as Joe himself was? But Joe still felt that he had to blame somebody.

"More lives than you know, Joe," Flavio said.

"What happened that night?" Joe's insides churned.

"I didn't really know for sure until the day I died. Which, in a timeframe that makes sense to you, was about five or six years ago," Flavio answered as the General returned with his coffee and sat down next to him.

"Here you go, black as you like it." The General looked at Joe, "We've had quite a few discussions here over the last few days, Flavio and I. Ain't nothing like a good cup a Joe for conversation. Right, Joe?"

"Yep. Many discussions went on and decisions were made during our old coffee sessions in the kitchen." Joe smiled. He was relieved to have felt his jaw start to relax and his wall of defense begin to release in the presence of these men. Especially in the presence of the man whom the General claimed was completely innocent regarding his participation in the accident that'd killed Angela.

"I was working at my second job, cleaning toilets and dirty dishes at that twenty-four-hour diner on Third Street, when my wife called me and told me she thought she was going to lose the baby. She was six months along. She said her sister was going to drive her to the hospital and would I meet her there? Of course I would. I'd driven our car to work, if you could call it that. It was a car registered to one of my cousins. The tags were expired and the car operated when it wanted to. An old Buick Regal, a car that was made out of real heavy metal and was sometimes difficult to control." Flavio paused and took a napkin off the table to mop his brow, though Joe noticed that the man wasn't actually sweating the slightest. He must just have the emotional feeling associated with sweating …

"I was in a hurry and headed in the opposite direction than your daughters. Being in a hurry didn't help in this car, it shook when it went over forty miles an hour, and I know one thing for sure—it wasn't shaking. I had it going at a steady thirty-nine miles an hour while I leaned forward, trying to make it go a little bit faster. I was in a hurry to get to my wife."

Flavio paused, took a sip of his coffee, licked his lips, and wiped his hands on his legs. Joe could sense he was nervous.

"I'm sorry. It all happened so fast. I don't know if she took her eye off the road, or if she leaned in, but your daughter's car crossed over the line. I honked, but it happened just like that." Flavio snapped his fingers. "The front of my car hit the side of your daughter's car, causing it to flip. The Regal spun slightly out of control and had some damage to the front end, but nothing else. The metal on that car was really strong. I stopped and got out, but as other cars were pulling up, and as I heard the sirens, I got back in my car and slowly drove to the hospital. I knew that help was there with your daughters."

Flavio took a deep breath and looked at Joe. "For years my heart has been heavy with this. I was sent back to Mexico where my wife and I tried to have another child. It didn't work out. I began to drink too much, and eventually she left me."

The General spoke. "Tell him what you were doing in Mexico when you died."

"I sobered up and started a crusade to help those like me— alcoholics. I didn't know what else to do. It kept me sober. I remarried, though we never had kids." Flavio sighed. "I stayed in Mexico. I couldn't return to your country after what had happened."

A tear fell down Joe's face. He felt himself somehow to be a reflection of this man. Or perhaps Flavio was a reflection of him. "How'd you get deported?"

"At the hospital that night with my wife, I think the insurance folks called INS. Within twenty-four hours of that accident I was back in Mexico, even though immigration wasn't as hot a topic at the time as it is today with Homeland Security and all. We still got deported. I'd parked the car on a side street near the hospital, and I never saw it again." Flavio, who seemed to be holding his breath, exhaled and sipped his coffee.

Joe looked at the General and back at Flavio, "All these years, I didn't know. I don't know what to say to you today."

"Please, accept my apology," Flavio said. He appeared more than sincere. "I'd like to see you let this go and move on with what you need to do next."

"It's a little late for that, isn't it? I should've handled this whole thing differently." Joe bent his head down and began to cry.

The two men sat patiently at the table without saying a word to Joe while he sobbed on for what seemed like eons. Eventually, his need to cry faded, and he began to feel restored. He wasn't sure how much time had passed but he was aware some type of healing had taken place within him.

"I'm flabbergasted." Joe shook his head. "I don't know what else to say."

"Well, you've got a long way to go, my friend," the General answered. "And we're only working on your major issues right now. You have minor life-altering influences to deal with as well."

Flavio cleared his throat and said, "It caused me great pain, personally, to know that you blamed me all these years. I would take every moment of that accident back if I could. In fact, it would've been easier if I'd have died and your daughter lived." Flavio's eyes filled with pain.

"Oh, you don't know how many times I've asked for that, too." Shame flooded through Joe's insides.

"Yes, I do. And that might be why it would've been easier to have died myself." Flavio spoke in perfect English now—his accent completely gone. "You've no idea how much those intense thoughts affect people, on both sides of the spectrum—or better said, in both worlds. Look, this wasn't your fault, nor was it my fault. I don't think it was Teresa's fault, either. Accidents happen. I'm asking that you find a way to let go of the emotions surrounding that accident."

"Yes, I get this now. I'm sorry," Joe mumbled.

"Listen, General Nate spent a lot of time convincing me to speak with you and clear the air. Coming to this place was difficult." Flavio paused for a second. "It wasn't easy making my way back this far. He had to convince me, and I'm glad he did. You'll understand, eventually. But for now, I'm hoping you can let this go."

"Wait a minute. You're here to save me? And at the General's request? You're not here to save yourself?" Shocked, Joe released the last bit of tension from his body as this surprise swept through his being.

"That's correct." Flavio nodded.

"I thought you said I was holding you to this thing with my emotions," Joe stammered.

Flavio smiled. As he spoke, his accent returned, "Okay, let me explain this in the simplest terms. Once a person figures out what's holding him back, that's all that's needed. I didn't need your permission to release your emotions that were affecting me. I just needed to figure out what it was and then *I released it*."

The man picked up his beanie and bent his head down to catch Joe's eye. "Hey, Joe, that's all you need to do here. It's okay that it was an accident. It's time to let it all go. All of it."

Joe looked into his coffee cup and mumbled, "I know, but look at the chain of events that my reaction caused."

The General cleared his throat. "Think of the good that came out of it, too. Both of you have saved quite a few folks from the wretchedness of the bottle. And don't you think there's some irony to the fact that you both spent the last years of your lives saving people?"

"Now you're going to tell me that everything happens for a reason, aren't you?" Joe asked.

"I don't know that one," the General said. "But I think it smells of truth."

"I heard that quite a bit in Mexico," Flavio put in, "and then later on the other side of the spectrum. I think if you look hard enough at something, you can always find a reason. But I don't necessarily see some big plan for all of us. We have too much free will for it to be so calculated." Flavio set his beanie on his head and swallowed his last sip of coffee.

"Interesting," whispered Joe. "But what is this thing you keep calling 'the spectrum'?"

"We're in it, my friend." Flavio stood up, shook Joe's hand, and leaned over to hug the General. "I've got to get back. Good luck, Joe."

"Wait, wait, wait." Joe rose from his chair. "What do you mean we're in the spectrum?"

Flavio stopped on his way toward the exit and spoke over his shoulder. "It's the place in between." Only seconds later he was out the door.

For a while after that, Joe sat with his head in his hands looking down at his coffee. All this time he'd been wrong. They'd all been wrong about the accident. And to think, the General had asked Flavio to speak to Joe so that *he* could help Joe.

"What now, General?" Joe looked up, but the General was gone. Joe was sitting alone in The Cafe.

CHAPTER 24

ANGEL WAS IN THE BACK SEAT of Teresa's car when Teresa got the call from the priest. Their father had passed away early that morning while Angel had been messing around with Teresa's and JJ's dreams. Panic overcame her. Where was he?

Her head spun as she focused on the cloud. Maybe he was with her girls waiting for Angel to come home. Within seconds she landed in the empty cloud. She noticed it was time to find a new resting place—this cloud was becoming sadly wispy—and she feared her father wouldn't be able to find her if they switched clouds.

The cloud could possibly make it through one more night, but either way they'd have to move because the scent of rain was in the air.

The hospital was the next most likely location to find her father. Angel closed her eyes and thought about her father's hospital room. Immediately, she found herself sitting in the chair across from his bed where his body still lay. Father Benjamin and Aunt Jessie were there, but Angel knew Joe wasn't in the hospital—from the moment she entered the room she could sense he was gone.

"What now?" she whispered.

Aunt Jessie held a tissue to her eyes while she held Joe's lifeless hand.

"I'm so sorry, Joe," Jessie said. "I didn't do enough years ago when you went over the deep end. I'm sorry. And I was hard on you today ... Or, I mean yesterday. I just want Teresa to be okay."

Jessie dabbed her nose with the tissue. "I can't believe this happened so quick."

Where else could her father be? Angel closed her eyes and thought about her father. A sadness filled her head, but at the same time tiny lights tickled her insides like butterfly wings. Angel believed she was picking up on some of her aunt's emotions, yet feeling something else simultaneously.

As she thought about her father, suddenly she was sitting at a table with candles in front of her. Yes, this was her fifth birthday party. The house was filled with relatives, and Angela had on a dress. A dress! Angela hated dresses—she remembered. The little girl wanted to wear that corduroy pantsuit, but her mother had won the battle that day. Angela had pouted a little, but deep down she was happy, anyway. The five-year-old blew out the candles while her second cousins danced around the table. Her father picked her up, hugged and kissed her, and set her back down alongside all the other children at her party.

Angel blinked, and she found herself sitting in a classroom. Mrs. Kennedy's class—this was the second grade. Beyond a doubt, Angel confirmed she was Angela as memories began to flow. The classroom was hot that day; it must've been the first part of the school year, a September heat wave.

Angela's head lay on her desk; she was tired after running from a group of boys. The same group of boys that had caught her and held her down while one of them messed with her puffy shirtsleeve during recess. Then they laughed and told her they'd put a bee inside her sleeve. Which she thought was a lie, until she heard a slight buzzing noise coming from the left side of her blouse.

The shirt was homemade from a flowery fabric with elastic on both sides of the sleeve. Her mother had spent hours making the shirt. Angela didn't like the flower print on the blouse, but didn't want to hurt her mother's feelings—so she wore the shirt to school.

The little girl's heart raced when she realized a live bee was trapped inside her shirt. She was too shy to scream out, and so very quietly Angela pulled at the elastic in the sleeve until it snapped. Angela knew her mom would be upset over the ripped seam, but she'd panicked over the bee. As quickly as she ripped the material, the bee was gone—it flew to the window. Within seconds, Julia Tinsdale yelled, "A bee, a bee!"

The children in the classroom jumped up and ran to the far wall, screaming and shouting. Mrs. Kennedy yelled above the screams. "All right, all right! It's just a little bee." The teacher spoke as she moved toward the window.

Angel was overcome with fillings of guilt. She knew that little girl, Angela, blamed herself for letting the bee go free in the classroom.

"Where did it come from?" David laughed and looked at the other boys.

Angel felt heat in her face, and her head pounded. The second grader was consumed with self-blame over the drama in the classroom, and in that moment Angel experienced exactly what Angela, her younger self, had gone through.

In the classroom, Angela cowered in the farthest corner from the windows, behind the rest of the kids. She dared not tell the teacher or anyone else how that bee had gotten in the room, for fear that she would be punished. It disturbed Angel now to know the boys had gotten away with such meanness, and how distraught it had made the young Angela. She wished the girl could have handled it differently.

Mrs. Kennedy pushed open the window and shooed the bee outside. "Okay, it's gone. Everyone, back to your seats ..."

When the kids moved slowly to their seats, Angela was the last child to be seated. As Angel witnessed this incident, she was overcome by the loneliness Angela felt. She remembered Angela choosing to be isolated from the rest, even though some of the kids tried to be friends with her. She was so insecure and shy that she preferred to remain alone. At home and with her sister, Angela was happy; at school with the other kids her age, she was a mess.

When she turned around, Angel realized she was back in the hospital. Strange, since she wasn't thinking about the hospital at all but had focused on her life as Angela. The busy sounds of the hospital were gone, however—in fact the entire building appeared to be vacant. Angel poked her head through the door to her dad's room. He was gone, but an imprint remained in the bed.

Moving quickly down the hall, she caught up with the male figure that was a younger, healthier version of her dad. Angel walked next to him and spoke to the right of him, "Dad, I remember it all now!"

Joe turned his head to the right and looked through her, yet he acted almost as if he actually saw something. Angel moved forward and to his left. "Dad, can you see me?"

Oh no. Her insides began to turn. Whatever he was experiencing, Angel wasn't a part of it. The situation was identical to her daily dealings with Teresa. Angel could see him but he couldn't see her.

While she followed her father, Angel whispered to herself, "This can't be happening."

Her dad picked up the phone at the nurses' station and then put the phone back down. He moved downstairs to the lobby and sat down in the empty waiting room. Angel sat next to him for a few moments and soon she found herself drawn to the front doors.

She moved through the exit to the hospital, and her dad followed. Angel believed her father couldn't see her, but for some reason he was following her. So at this point, she knew staying with him was important. She felt this in the core of her being—Angel must not lose her dad again.

She watched as her father encountered a man and learned this man was the General—the person they'd looked for on Skid Row. The two men went to a place called The Café, and Angel sat down at their table in an empty seat. As the man named Flavio approached the table, Angel was transported back in time—to the accident.

She sat in the front seat of the car, as Angela, her younger self—and was totally astonished at the sight of a carefree Teresa. Her sister seemed like an entirely different person, easygoing and in spite of their mother's illness, happy. The essence of this young woman was completely unlike that of the Teresa of today.

"Hand me that cassette, Ang. I want to listen to Abba. Oh never mind, I'll get it." As Teresa leaned over, the steering wheel shifted to the right and the car swerved. "Oops."

Teresa sat up and corrected the movement, pushing the steering to the left when a loud popping noise filled the air. A blowout caused the car to swerve over the line. The sound of a car

honk followed, and Angel noticed her seat belt wasn't fastened—
in fact, neither girl's seat belt was buckled.

At the moment of impact, a metal-on-metal crunch sound
filled Angel's ears. The car rolled a few times, and Angel remained
inside going through the accident as it happened. Her foot hit the
radio dial causing the volume to rise, and by the second roll, the
passenger door opened. Angela's body was thrown from the car.
She landed on the ground with a broken neck—a quick, painless
death.

Angel moved freely now, still at the scene of the accident, but
away from Angela's body. She went to the car, which had landed
in an upright position. Teresa was semiconscious in the driver's
seat when Angel approached.

"Oh, good, you're okay," Teresa said. "I think I hurt my leg."

"Don't touch anything. Help is on the way," Angel said.

Angel stepped away from the car and noticed the driver of
the other car approach her sister's vehicle. But then he suddenly
backed off at the sound of sirens. A few cars had stopped at
the side of the road, and the drivers of these vehicles were also
approaching the wrecked car. Nobody noticed the man, who was
Flavio, slip away. Angel stood at the edge of the road and watched
in silence as Flavio's car slowly backed away from the accident and
disappeared around the corner.

Angel then saw and understood the aftermath of the accident
for the first time. Everything, both spoken and unspoken, came
to her clearly now.

Within seconds, the paramedics and police were all over the
accident scene. Teresa, who'd gone in and out of consciousness,
swore to the police that her sister was up and walking around
outside her car door. The police, concerned over her injuries and
her young age, didn't want to tell her that her sister had died on

impact. And as was typical during this time in their lives, the police couldn't reach her father.

When Teresa told the police about her mother's illness and suggested they call her aunt, that's exactly what they did. And so it was Aunt Jessie who broke the news of Angela's death to Teresa the next day at the hospital. Then Aunt Jessie hunted Joe down with sheer determination and got him to *somewhat* sober up for his daughter's funeral.

Angel, watching it all, saw her father go over the deep end after the funeral, so much so, it seemed as if he'd be lost forever. She was glad she knew the end of this story, and that eventually the man would pull himself out of this downward spiral and be able to make some difference in the world.

When Angel focused on her mother, she could clearly see how Angela's death took the wind out of her mother's attempt to stay alive as long as possible—which was really the only choice with the stage of her pancreatic cancer. Her mother gave in to the disease the moment she found out about the death of her youngest daughter. Perhaps it was her desire to be with her daughter and protect her, or maybe it was simply destiny. But within days, her mother also had passed away.

Angel shook her head and found herself sitting in the vacant cafe next to her father. She stood up and moved toward the door, her father following behind. Angel knew he wasn't aware she was in front of him.

Her heart ached over the wasted time she'd stubbornly spent in the clouds. Finally, knowing fully who she was, Angela, and who she'd become, Angel—she realized it was time to leave her own personal hell of isolation and join her mother. With or without her father, she was ready. She just didn't know how.

CHAPTER 25

As MUCH AS SHE RESENTED HER father for leaving her years ago, she resented him even more for leaving her an orphan now.

"He seemed okay last night," Teresa mumbled. She stood outside her father's hospital room with JJ and her aunt.

"He seemed okay an hour ago when he was talking to me," Aunt Jessie said.

"Why don't you go in and say good-bye to him, Mom?" JJ nudged Teresa toward the door.

That was okay with Teresa, who needed someone to tell her what to do now. The whole scene felt dreamlike as her hand pushed open the door and she entered the room. A dead room without the energy of her father, whose presence—she thought—had been larger than life. The man was completely gone, and it was odd for her to feel this and then acknowledge it. Teresa rarely tuned into anything of a spiritual nature. Feelings and sensitivities were just not a part of her daily life. But for some reason she was in tune today, and now the room seemed as if the energy present the day before had simply vanished.

As quickly as she entered through the door, she exited.

"He's not here," she said.

JJ stepped in the doorway and pointed to the bed. "Mom, he's right there."

"No, that's his body and nothing more." Teresa moved toward the long hallway. "I need some air."

As she walked quickly past the other patient rooms, she could hear her son and aunt following closely behind, as well as an additional set of footsteps that seemed to walk in time with them, probably the priest. She led them down the stairs and through the back doors to the outside, where she looked up at the sky.

In her heart she hoped to see her sister and father floating along with her mother in the clouds, but she knew better. Ominous dark cumulus filled the heavens above, which seemed to enhance the depressed, sinking feeling that was taking over her body. She'd wanted to stay away from her father to avoid this effect, but now she realized it would've happened anyway. Teresa turned to her son and asked, "Where's the priest?"

JJ and Aunt Jessie looked back at the door and spoke in unison, "I thought he was behind us."

"I heard it too," Teresa said.

Goosebumps broke out over Teresa arms. *Maybe Dad was following us,* she said to herself. Then she shook off the idea, telling herself that her dad's craziness was rubbing off on her. Yet in some odd way, although she'd never have wished for her sister to be stuck someplace for years, she hoped her father's story was true. The thought of her family being around was something she could easily warm up to. Perhaps because she'd pushed away the memories for so many years, she'd almost forgotten the better moments of her youth.

"It's cold out here, Teresa. Let's go back inside," Aunt Jessie said.

Teresa allowed her aunt to lead her into the hospital and back up the stairs to a seat near the nurses' station, not far from her father's room. JJ sat with Teresa while Aunt Jessie spoke to the hospital staff on the topic of Joe's remains. Teresa settled back and let it happen. Not a normal line of reaction from her. In time, she thought, she'd have a vague recollection of the day her dad died and she'd wonder if she was actually there. Because right now she felt as if she was *not* in this moment, quietly witnessing the finality of her father's life.

"Okay." Aunt Jessie approached her. "It's already been taken care of. We don't even need to make a phone call. Joe will be moved to Fulton's Funeral Home. No autopsy because of the nature of his demise."

"So, it's done, then?" Teresa asked.

"Yes, let's go," Aunt Jessie answered.

Teresa hesitated for a few minutes, unsure of how to feel and what to do next. Then slowly she headed toward the front of the hospital with JJ and her Aunt Jessie following behind. They walked to the parking lot.

"What now?" Teresa asked. "Do we return to what we were doing before he reentered our lives? Can we ignore that he came back?"

"I'm going to call Uncle Joe and a few others when Father Benjamin calls me with the exact time and date of the viewing. Why don't you come to my house so we can figure this out?" Jessie responded.

Teresa shook her head. "Thank you, Auntie, but I've got some work to do."

Teresa and JJ left the hospital and drove in silence for a while. She drove past the exits for JJ's school, the house, and her work before JJ spoke.

"Mom, where are we going?" he asked.

"Huh? Oh, I don't know." She felt as if she'd fallen asleep. Teresa couldn't remember any inch of the route she'd just driven.

She got off the freeway and turned around with the intention of going home and crawling into bed. Her mind wandered back to a time before her mother's illness. Angela, Teresa, and her mother were in the kitchen. Teresa had just gotten home from school and was looking in the refrigerator when she overheard her mother talking to Angela.

"It's hard being young," her mother said.

"It doesn't seem hard for Teresa," Angela responded.

"Well, she's older than you, honey." Mom bent down and rubbed a spot on Angela's forehead.

"I don't like them. I'm not going back," Angela whined.

Mom spoke in a softer tone. "Do you want me to call the school? Because you're going to have to go back. You need an education, honey."

Teresa shut the refrigerator door hard and reopened it.

"Oh, dear, I didn't know you were home," Mom yelled from the living room.

"I just got here," Teresa said.

Teresa had completely forgotten about what a hard time Angela had in school and how much her parents tried to protect the girl. When it was happening, Teresa didn't care a lot; she'd been a social butterfly and didn't want the burden of her little sister. Now, as a parent she completely understood Angela's situation, and wished she'd done more to help her sister while she could've. Children tended to behave inhumanely toward each other at times.

She shook her head and realized she'd daydreamed the entire way home. Teresa was no longer surprised over the memories of her family; she found it impossible to get away from the past now, anyway—and it really wasn't so bad anymore.

"Do you want to go to school late today?" Teresa asked JJ as they parked in front of the house.

"Are you kidding? No, not if I can intentionally avoid it," JJ answered.

"Compliments of Joe. Here we are." She waved her hand toward the house.

As Teresa gathered together her business items, she noticed a few missed calls on her phone. A message from the school—the police were there looking for her and JJ. And then the police, who must have obtained her cell phone number from the school, would like a return call.

She began to realize this problem of JJ's wasn't going to go away on its own. Her body ached with her heart, and she feared JJ's situation was much worse then he'd let on. Perhaps it was this fear that had fueled her denial of any juvenile delinquency issue with her son. Teresa put her phone in her pocket and yelled to JJ.

"JJ, I've got to run an errand and I don't want you here alone. Get in the car, please." JJ was at the front door when his mother yelled to him. "Hurry."

As they headed away from home, Teresa noticed a patrol car turning onto their street. She imagined the police were on the way to her house. Where else would they be headed at this time of day in her neighborhood? Great, now she was harboring a fugitive.

"Where are we going?" JJ asked. "You're being weird, Mom."

Teresa resisted the urge to scream at her son; instead, she gripped the steering wheel tighter and decided to go to her Aunt Jessie's house. It'd give her some time to figure out what was going on with JJ, and maybe call the attorney her father had suggested.

"Well, I'm wondering why the police are so adamant about finding you. They showed up at your school. What is it you're not telling me?" she asked.

JJ shook his head. "There's nothing to tell, Mom."

Adrenalin pumped through her body and seemed to have awakened her brain. No longer dwelling on the past, Teresa maneuvered the car through traffic as she spoke. "Did you get that phone number from Joe? You know, the attorney's number ..." she asked.

"No, but I can get it at Aunt Jessie's house, on the Internet," JJ answered.

Teresa focused on the road as the two of them drove the rest of the way to Aunt Jessie's house in silence. What the hell had JJ gotten himself into? *His timing is horrid*, she thought while she pulled into her aunt's driveway. Teresa hadn't noticed the rain until it was time to get out of the car.

"Come on. Let's make a run for it." She grabbed her purse and held her jacket over her head. JJ held his backpack over his head and followed behind. They stood on the porch waiting for Teresa's aunt to answer the door.

"I can't believe this is happening," Teresa said.

"Look, I'm not a criminal. I didn't do anything wrong," JJ pleaded.

Teresa's aunt opened the door with bloodshot eyes. A smile filled her face when she saw who her visitors were. "Come in, come in. I'm glad you changed your mind."

JJ dropped his head down as he entered the house. Her Aunt Jessie eyed JJ with an eyebrow raised.

"It's a long story. Let's talk over coffee." Teresa pushed her son toward the kitchen table.

"I guess we're outlaws now," he mumbled.

"Stop being so melodramatic, JJ." Teresa was more than annoyed with JJ's behavior. It was so unlike him to get into trouble, and so unlike her to run from the police. Maybe they *were* fugitives.

"Well, then why don't we just go down to the police station?" JJ focused on the ground.

"Because, JJ, something's not right with your story," Teresa snapped at her son and then turned toward her aunt, whose eyes were wide open.

"What's going on here? When I last saw the two of you a few minutes ago you weren't on America's Most Wanted list," Aunt Jessie said.

"Auntie, the police are looking for JJ. I'm not completely sure why." Teresa sat down at the kitchen table and pulled JJ's phone out of her purse. A new message had arrived from Seth that stated something about the car being reported stolen because "M" didn't want to get in trouble. Teresa put the phone back in her purse.

"Why not call the police and find out why?" Aunt Jessie asked.

"No, we're going to let our attorney handle it, as soon as I call him," Teresa said with confidence, continuing with a mumbled, "just in case."

Teresa helped herself to a cup of coffee and then sat quietly at the table considering the best way to handle JJ. While Aunt Jessie moved around in the kitchen unloading the dishwasher, Teresa remembered the spice cake recipe that she still had in her purse.

"Do we have time to try that recipe?" Teresa asked. She then spent a few seconds digging around her purse. "If you have all the ingredients, let's try it."

"What's this?" Aunt Jessie grabbed the paper from Teresa, placed her glasses on her nose, and looked at the scrawled set of instructions.

"Oh, I haven't talked to you." Teresa tapped her forehead. "Yesterday, Joe said this is Mom's spice cake recipe. She made him memorize it."

Aunt Jessie placed her hand over her mouth in shock. "Mija, we've tried to get this right for years. Do you think it's real?"

Teresa shrugged.

"Oh, Joe would be so happy if we made this work today—this bittersweet day." Aunt Jessie dabbed at her eyes with the napkin she held. Then she set to work on the recipe, first digging through cabinets and drawers to pull out ingredients. She placed all the items on the counter.

Teresa turned her attention to JJ while her aunt puttered in the kitchen.

"So, JJ, who is 'M'?" Teresa asked.

"Do you mean Murphy?" JJ responded.

"I don't know. I'm asking you." Teresa sipped her coffee and waited for her son to respond.

JJ played with the water bottle he'd removed from the fridge. "Murphy drove us to the party. It was his idea. We call him M. But how do you know that?"

"I'm asking the questions now." Teresa heard the businesslike manner of her voice, which scared her a little—then she continued. "How come I've never heard his name before?"

"He's not somebody I usually hang with, Mom. Murphy's into some weird stuff." JJ peeled the label off of his water bottle and avoided eye contact with her.

"Weird? How weird?" She wanted the details.

"Oh, not that way. He's kind of a nerd. I'm talking Star Trekkie type nerd." JJ looked up and directly at Teresa.

Roni Teson

"How does a nerd like that get invited to a parking lot party?" She couldn't make sense of her son's story.

As they spoke, Aunt Jessie clanged around in the kitchen, pulling together the spice cake.

JJ looked down again, a sign that he wasn't telling the absolute truth. "It was a flash mob, Mom. Murphy got the text, or no, no ..." he stammered. "I think it was an e-mail. He said it would be fun to go see what it was like."

"Okay, enough already. You're not telling me everything, and you could be in some serious trouble. What's a flash mob?" Teresa eyed JJ with the most intense stare she could muster.

"It's like all these people meet in a public place and perform some sort of senseless act. These nerdy guys were trying to get a bunch of kids from school to fill up the parking lot outside of that bar. It wasn't as big a turnout as they'd expected. Even so, they took a picture and posted it on the Internet. And when the fight broke out with some of the kids from our school, we took off running. I know that Murphy left his car there because he was afraid to go back. Sometimes the piece of junk doesn't start. We had a long walk to the bus. It was stupid, but that's it."

"JJ, before we call the attorney, I need to know everything. Were you drinking or partying in any way?" Teresa asked.

"No. That's what makes this so painful. At least I should've been doing something really wrong to get in this kind of trouble." JJ's voice rose up and his cheeks turned red.

"Okay, so why are the police focused on you?" Teresa thought this was odd.

"I don't know. Maybe it has to do with my driver's permit ..." Tears welled up in JJ's eyes, and his hands shook as he lifted the bottle of water to his mouth.

"What is it, son?" Teresa pleaded with him. "Don't block me out of this—just tell me. I promise I won't make it worse."

"JJ, was a girl involved?" Aunt Jessie interrupted, flour in her hair and on the rims of her glasses that she peered over the top of. "Because this type of trouble usually involves a girl."

JJ's voice had a slight tremble as he spoke. "No." He wiped his hands on his legs and stumbled over his own words. "But I may have been the reason the whole thing happened." JJ let out a loud sigh.

Teresa shook her head, and although she was seeing red, she forced herself to stay quiet for a few seconds and then respond to her son in a calm manner. Otherwise, she knew he'd clam up again. "Okay," she said in the nicest tone she could summon. "How did you cause it?"

JJ looked up and finally made eye contact with his mother. "I'm the 'flashster.' "

Teresa told herself to lean back, nod, take a deep breath, and then speak. "What does that mean, son?"

"See, you're calling me son." JJ seemed to have panicked. "I knew you'd do that."

Breathe ... Go slow ... He's going to break ... "JJ, it's okay. Just tell me what it means."

He flicked at the single tiny crumb that remained on the table from Aunt Jessie's last meal while he hesitated with his response. His eyes reflected some type of internal conflict as if he'd held a secret he hadn't planned on sharing.

JJ's shoulders slumped in defeat as he spoke. "I've been creating these flash mobs anonymously for a while. The principal has been trying to figure out who it is, but not for the same reason as the students. In fact, the kids at school see this guy as a hero. They named me the 'flashster.' You know, like a 'mobster.' I know if they find out it's only me, all of my work ... Well, they're gonna hate me."

A tear spilled down JJ's cheek suddenly saddening Teresa's own heart.

"It's going to be okay, JJ." She moved closer and rubbed his back. "You've got to tell this attorney everything, okay? And nobody's going to hate you."

JJ gulped some air as he tried to hold back on crying. The boy then nodded his approval.

"Okay, let's call the attorney. What's his number, JJ?" Teresa asked.

"I only have his name," JJ said with a sniffle. "I can get it quick. Is it okay if I use your computer, Auntie?"

"Of course you can," Aunt Jessie answered.

JJ hugged Teresa and said, "I'm sorry, Mom. I didn't know this would happen"

Teresa patted her son's back. "Okay, go get the number. We'll see what we can do to get you out of this mess."

JJ smiled slightly as he wiped the wetness off his cheeks with the back of his hands. The chair legs made a screeching noise on the floor when he slid out from the table and left the room.

Teresa stood up and grabbed the cleaning cloth. She began to follow behind her aunt wiping down the counters.

"I knew he was up to something," Teresa said. She polished along the rim of the sink.

"Oh, he's a boy. They all do crazy things. I'm sure he'll be all right." Aunt Jessie turned the mixer on.

Teresa busied herself cleaning, not knowing how to address the topic of her father. Aunt Jessie finished mixing and went on to grease the baking pan. The two moved in sync in the small kitchen, just like old times. Teresa's heart sped up and she smiled at the thought of the several years she'd lived in this house.

"I was with your father when he took his last breath." Jessie's voice quavered, "I'm sorry about the whole thing."

"Oh, Auntie—none of this is your fault." Teresa moved to Aunt Jessie's side and squeezed her aunt's shoulders.

"I'm glad I was there." Aunt Jessie filled the baking pan with batter and sprinkled the glaze over the top.

"Okay, I've got the number," JJ interrupted, seemingly lighter, as if a load had been lifted. He handed Teresa a scrap of paper with the phone number scribbled on it next to the name, Steve Haut.

Teresa looked at the cake just before her aunt put it in the oven. "Hmm," she said.

"I know. It looks good, doesn't it?" Aunt Jessie grinned.

"What do we make of this if it does taste like Mom's? It looks awfully familiar," Teresa said. Could her father have remembered the recipe after all these years?

"It's been a while since we've tried this, hasn't it? Although this attempt is much different than all the other times ..." Jessie set the timer on the oven, poured herself a fresh cup of coffee, and sat down at the table.

Teresa dialed the attorney's number though she continued to clean the kitchen. She spent about five minutes on the phone with him after she got past his condolences for her recent loss. Apparently Los Angeles was a smaller city than she thought. Word got around. For a moment she thought it probably hadn't been such a good idea to call somebody her father had referred, but she really didn't know who else to call. By the end of the conversation, however, she believed contacting the man was the right thing to do, because now JJ definitely had an excellent attorney.

"Okay, JJ, he's going to make some calls and then get back to me. He said he's very well connected at the police station. He used to be a cop." Teresa stood in the kitchen and pulled out some more cleaning supplies. "He suggested we lay low until he gets the story—and if we don't hear back from him in two hours, I need to call him again."

"What are you going to do, scrub down my whole kitchen?" Aunt Jessie asked.

"Well ..." Teresa said coyly. "It makes me feel better. Do you mind?"

Aunt Jessie snickered. "Are you kidding? Knock yourself out, kiddo."

Teresa cleaned the kitchen, and then contacted her store and made sure her part-timers were working and handling customers. JJ played for a while on the Internet, and Aunt Jessie watched the stove and waited for the cake.

Once the timer beeped, the three of them gathered around the table, forks in hand. Then Aunt Jessie laid the cake on a hot pad in the middle of the table. Teresa bent over and spun the cake around examining the familiarity of the desert.

"This looks good, Tia," she said.

"Careful, it's hot," Aunt Jessie responded.

Teresa dug her fork into the cake and blew on the steaming hot bite that sat on the edge of the tines. Finally, she bit down on the piece of cake and smiled. "It's good, really good," she said with her mouth full.

Together, the three of them ate the cake directly from the pan and toasted Joe with their coffee cups.

"What do you think?" Aunt Jessie asked, "Could it be the right recipe?"

Teresa patted her stomach and said, "It's the closest we've ever come to getting it right. Joe did good."

CHAPTER 26

FATHER BENJAMIN CLEARED HIS CALENDAR—MEETINGS AND all—for the remainder of the week. The entire congregation, including the kitchen folks, had rallied to complete Juan's funeral preparations. In the latter years of the man's life he'd affected a lot of people, while in his death he was already missed by many.

Numerous messages had piled up on the priest's desk. As he flipped through them, he was disturbed over the fact that a call had come in from the morgue. Between Juan and Father Benjamin, they'd contacted everyone they'd known who could possibly have some knowledge of the General's whereabouts. The people from the morgue rarely phoned the father unless it was to return a call concerning a missing person he'd been looking for—and to tell him about a body that had been found.

The priest picked up his phone and dialed the morgue. He prayed for the General as the phone rang.

"Jim Brooks, LA County Morgue. How can I help you?" the abrupt voice answered.

The priest fiddled with a pen while he talked. "Jim, this is Father Benjamin. I'm returning a call from Dotty this morning."

"Hello, Father," Jim said. "Yep, we tried to reach you. Unfortunately, we've got some bad news. When the call came in early this morning, Dotty called out to the dump, and after some searching they found your missing person. Well, at least his jacket fits the description. I'm sorry. We sent a pickup out to the dump earlier today."

"I suspected this would happen," Father Benjamin said. He cleared his throat. "I'm sure you also heard about Juan?"

"Yes, I'm sorry, Father." Jim said. "It's a tough week for the good guys, isn't it?"

"That's so true." The priest felt a pressure in his chest. He'd feared this would be the outcome of the General's last journey into the streets. He let out a slight cry, biting the inside of his mouth to stop any further outbursts. And then he pulled it together to finish the conversation. "Will you need me to identify the body?"

"Most likely, yes. We'll call you back when we're ready."

"Thank you," the father replied.

And so that was the end of the General, as well as Juan. Father Benjamin resisted the urge to yell, and then he held in the tears that wanted to be let out. The priest recognized that the collar on his neck didn't make it any easier when he lost people he cared about.

He needed some fresh air, so he straightened the mess on his desk into a few neat piles, put on his jacket, and found his umbrella in his bottom desk drawer. An odd time to go for a walk, but he needed to step away from death for a little while.

Once outside, he noticed that the grounds looked exceptionally green—vibrant, almost glowing. Probably the rain now falling on them made the area look so beautiful, or maybe it was actually a testament to his friend Juan, the man who, until last week, was responsible for their landscaping.

Marcus Benjamin missed his friend. Juan would've been down at the dumpsite and all over the police to investigate the death of the General. Was it a coincidence that both Juan and the General had passed away around the same time? The priest doubted it. He'd seen too many unusual coincidences over the years. The General had probably gone first, and if it happened the way the priest hoped, the old guy was waiting for Juan.

Perhaps this thought process wasn't the norm for those in his chosen profession. But it wasn't a coincidence that the Church had assigned him to one of the least-public parishes in the US, and on the darker side of the tracks. He was not on a quick career path to the top of the most powerful religious institution in the country. In fact, his mentor at the seminary had used the word "quirky" to describe Father Benjamin.

He had, however, managed to obtain a pleasant Southern California location for his assignment. That had to do with the few connections he had within the Church, through his mother. She was disappointed in his lack of ambition within the hierarchy of the Church, but she still did what she could to help him get a position near to her.

Father Benjamin walked the grounds in the drizzle, and then he decided to go to the kitchen to be around some of his people.

Anna's voice could be heard clearly in the yard as she commanded the volunteers in the kitchen. "Come hell or high water, we'll get this meal prepared," the woman yelled.

Father Benjamin stood at the door and watched the team of workers Anna had pulled together. He smiled. She'd come a long way, and she certainly knew what she was doing in that kitchen. Her meals were always served on time, regardless of what else went on in the world.

Anna was stirring something on the stove when she spotted the priest, and she immediately dropped what she was doing. She went to him without hesitation, put her arms around him, and squeezed. Her bloodshot eyes and somber expression added to his own sense of sadness.

"Father, I'm sorry," she said in a hushed tone. "I didn't see you."

"How can I help?" he asked.

Anna wiped her hands on her apron and became all business. She put her arm through his and escorted him into the dining room. "Can you help with this area? It's a mess." Her eyes widened as she took a deep breath. "And most of the guys waiting outside don't know about Juan. Can you go tell them? And see if Ralph's out there. He's good about cleaning up the tables and straightening the chairs. Also, will you lead us in a prayer when we let them in—before we serve the food?"

Father Benjamin allowed himself to laugh for a second. Anna always had something that needed to be done, and through it all he knew she could be counted on to stay on task.

"Okay, okay," he said. And when he looked around the room he was shocked to see such disarray. "Were they in here late last night?"

"Yes, we held a prayer vigil," Anna answered.

The father turned to speak to Anna, but she was already back in the kitchen—that woman moved fast. He pushed in chairs and straightened tables on his way to the front door. From the window the priest saw various covers and umbrellas held over the heads of those lined up on the side of the building where the eave of the roof offered little shelter from the rain.

He grabbed his own umbrella and stepped through the door. Low and behold, there was Ralph—near the front of the line.

"Father, is it true what they're saying? Did they find the General dead at the dump? And did Juan die this morning?" Ralph's boisterous voice seemed to carry across the county.

What did it matter anyway? Not many secrets among the homeless. In fact, they probably knew all the details about the General before the priest did.

"Well hello to you too, Ralph," the father said.

"I'm just saying, people are talking," Ralph mumbled as Father Benjamin moved in closer.

"Anna says you'd be willing to help me set up the dining room. She said you're good at it." The priest winked.

"Sure, Father, I'll help." Ralph turned to the man in line behind him and spoke. "Hold my place, Sam. I'll be back."

The older man nodded his head under a yellow tarp that he'd wrapped around his body. Father Benjamin dismissed the thought that he looked familiar when he saw Ralph limping up the steps to the dining room.

"What'd you do to your leg, Ralph?" he asked.

"Nothing, it cramps up in the cold. Now are you gonna tell me about the General and Juan? I go to those meetings almost every day with both of them. Word's out, Father," Ralph said.

Ralph must suffer from some sort of mental illness. The priest had witnessed both Ralph's soft side and the raw angry side. The man had an irrational temper. Logic couldn't explain his behavior.

"Yes, it's true. Well, we think they found the General."

"They did," Ralph said. "That old guy, standing in line behind me said he saw the General climb into a dumpster for the night. He said the next morning the trash truck took the whole bin away. I asked him how he knew that. Sam said he saw it when the truck woke him up. But that was a few days back."

The priest abruptly turned around and ran down the stairs to the spot where the old guy, Sam, had been standing. A yellow tarp lay on the sidewalk.

"Did anyone see where Sam went?" Father Benjamin picked up the tarp and began walking down the line. "Have you guys seen Sam?"

"That's Juan's," said an old woman with missing teeth and a cigarette in her hand. She coughed and pointed. "Juan had that tarp."

"Juan's gone." A man wearing a trash bag and standing farther down the line yelled. "He died this morning."

Father Benjamin approached the trash bag man. "Who told you that?"

"I don't know. Some old guy. I think he said his name was Sam." The man spit on the priest when he spoke. "Sorry about that, Father. Hey, that's Sam's blanket. He had that yellow thing wrapped around him."

"Did you see where he went?" the priest asked.

"He's up in front somewhere. Why'd you take his blanket?" the man asked.

The priest ignored him and pulled out his cell phone, quickly dialing the morgue. Dotty answered on the first ring.

"Hello, Dotty." Father Benjamin stepped away from the folks in line as he spoke. "What can you tell me about how they found that body at the dump site?"

"I took a call this morning from the pay phone on Fourth and Washington. Some guy said he saw the General climb into a dumpster at that corner a few days ago and that we'd find the body at the dump."

"Did the guy identify himself?" Father Benjamin asked. He wondered if he was losing his mind—he was having some strange thoughts, for sure.

"No, but I think he was homeless. He refused to give his name, said he didn't have an address, and he told us to be sure to contact you. That's why I called you."

"Did the voice sound familiar?" he asked.

"God, I don't know, Father," Dorothy said. "Oh, I meant to say, 'Gosh I don't know, Father.'"

"Think about it for a second," the priest requested.

"No, it was just an anonymous guy," she answered him.

"Okay, thank you."

The priest put his phone in his pocket and approached the same toothless woman he'd talked to seconds ago. He tapped her on the shoulder, "I'm sorry, Ma'am. Did you say you saw someone in this tarp?"

She faced in the direction of the building, and the hood on her outer layer was pulled over her head. As she turned toward the priest she exhaled smoke in his face and then slurred. "Oh, I'm sorry, Father. I didn't see you there."

"Did you see someone with this?" Father Benjamin waved the smoke away while he held up the tarp.

"I did. That's Juan's rain jacket." A cigarette sat in between stained fingers that she used to point at the tarp. "Juan was wrapped in that thing."

"When did you see him?" Father Benjamin asked.

"Well, you know the answer to that. You and Ralph were talking to Juan a minute ago." She sucked on the cigarette, leaned on the wall, and then picked at her remaining teeth. "And I'm bothered by that, Father. Did you kick him out or something? He wasn't homeless last week."

The priest felt a flutter in his chest. The timber of his voice seemed to rise up in excitement. "Today, you think you saw Juan today?"

"Oh, I know it was him, Father." The woman played with the ragged hem of her hoodie. Her few remaining teeth appeared to be rotting, which could explain the smell that accompanied her words.

"How do you know that?" the priest asked.

"He had a yellow rain jacket, remember?" She pushed off of the wall and staggered a little. "Are you going to open up soon? It's wet out here."

"That old guy up there in this tarp was Sam. Do you know Sam?" the priest pushed.

"Juan had some demons, but that lady's happy now. She's not chasing him anymore." Her eyes glazed over as she stared out to some faraway place. She was probably under the influence, but for some reason the priest refused to leave it alone. Something inexplicable was happening and this woman was either playing him or she knew the answers.

"Did anyone else see Sam here earlier?" Father Benjamin yelled out.

"I'm telling you, Father, that's Juan's." The woman touched the priest's arm as she spoke now without a slur and in perfect pitch, each word enunciated as she looked Father Benjamin in the eye with an intensity that gave him a chill. For a brief moment he thought he saw a glimpse of what the woman looked like when she was younger. She stood in front of him sober and clean in a dress with makeup and a sparkle in her eye. "Father, sometimes things aren't as they seem."

The priest shook his head and blinked his eyes. As soon as the woman let go of his arm, she appeared to have morphed into her older self. She leaned on the wall again and slurred while she sang, "I'm having pancakes for dinner. One, two, three, all for me."

A little dazed, Father Benjamin left the crazy woman, jogged up the stairs to the center, and dropped his umbrella at the door. He went into the dining room where he found Ralph wiping down the tables.

"Ralph, how well did you say you know Sam?" he asked.

"I told you, I just met him tonight. He gave me a fiver and asked me to take a walk with him." Ralph stopped wiping the tables. "Why do you ask, Father?"

"How'd he end up in line with you?" The priest wiped the rain remnants off of his arms and tried to calm his rapid heart rate. He realized he was acting a bit crazed.

"I told him I was going here, and he should come along with me for nice company and a free meal." Ralph moved through the dining room scooting chairs in; the priest followed.

"How old was this guy Sam?" he asked.

Something about those eyes, the priest thought.

"I don't know. I never really got a good look at him. Say, what you doing with his tarp? He said I could have it when he was done with it, and he said it'd be soon. Did Sam leave?"

The priest hadn't noticed that he'd still held the tarp; in fact he'd been waving it while he spoke. Father Benjamin handed the thing to Ralph.

"I was trying to find him. I wanted to know how he knew about the General. If you see him again, will you tell him I'm looking for him?" the priest asked, knowing his efforts were futile.

"Sure. I can do that. But I get the fiver, okay?" Ralph folded up the wet sheet of plastic and put it in the corner. He then surprised Father Benjamin when he left the dining room to wash his hands in the sink that sat in the adjoining hallway to the kitchen.

"Cleanliness is next to Godliness, Father." Ralph smiled and dried his hands on a paper towel.

Father Benjamin hoped Ralph's mood would stay the same. "Did that old guy remind you of Juan?"

Ralph made a smacking noise with his mouth. "No, Juan's not homeless."

"You know that woman with the missing teeth? She says she saw you with Juan today." The priest didn't understand why he couldn't drop it—Juan was gone. His denial was starting to play tricks on his brain.

"Juan's dead." The smile left Ralph's face when he spoke. "I know Juan well enough to tell you that wasn't him."

"Do you know that woman out there, too?" Father Benjamin asked.

"She's nuts. Don't believe a word she says." Ralph shook his head.

The two men worked in silence completing the setup of the dining room. Father Benjamin pulled a few dollars out of his pocket and tried to give them to Ralph.

"I can't take your money, Father." Ralph waved his hands in the air.

"Why not? You took Sam's money," he responded.

"That's different—it didn't come from the church," Ralph said.

"I want you to hold it then and give it to Sam when you see him." The priest pushed the money toward Ralph.

"What's this obsession you have with Sam? He's like everyone else out there." Ralph raised his voice as he walked toward the front door. "And I think you scared him away, so I lost my place in line."

The priest followed behind Ralph. "Stay here. It's okay. In fact, you can eat in the kitchen and then you can help clean up. I'll get you a bed at the shelter for later."

"I don't want no special treatment," Ralph said. "You'll be driving me crazy following me around for weeks asking about that old guy. I know you, Father."

Ralph slammed the door as he exited the dining room. The priest watched from the window as the man found his place in line but wasn't allowed back in until a fight almost broke out. Somehow the waiting homeless worked it through.

"Are you ready, Father?" Anna yelled across the dining room as she approached the front door. "Darn, it's raining harder now."

"I know. It's weird, I saw this man in line with Ralph and now he's gone. The woman without her teeth said he was Juan." The priest ran his hand through his hair and babbled on. "I'll tell you something about him was so familiar, but I was distracted so I didn't see him completely. It was his eyes, though. I don't know. And now he's gone."

"We all miss him, Father." Anna put her hand on the priest's shoulder and patted him. "Are you okay to lead the prayer? I'm going to bring them into the dining room before we open the line and we need to tell them. Let's get them out of the rain, okay?"

"Yes, bring them in." Father Benjamin realized he sounded like the crazy one. He closed his eyes for a second and exhaled.

Anna opened the door and waved in the group. Most of the men walking past Father Benjamin mentioned they'd heard about Juan from someone else that'd been in line with them. Word had definitely gotten out.

As the bodies filled the dining room, Father Benjamin motioned for their silence.

"I know you're hungry, cold, and wet. It's unfortunate that we have some bad news to share. As expected after his recent hospitalization, Juan Torres passed away this morning. We're going to have a few minutes of silence in his honor. And then I'll lead the room in a prayer."

Normally this group of people was rowdy and ill behaved, so Father Benjamin was surprised at the somberness that descended. It was as if the crowd sobered up and became respectful for those few minutes.

CHAPTER 27

THE CAKE MELTED IN JESSIE'S MOUTH, and she let her mind escape into the sugary flavors of the topping as she savored every bite. After a few mouthfuls, she sipped her coffee and allowed herself to believe for the moment that Marion had sent the recipe from beyond the grave.

Jessie wondered what had gotten into JJ with his recent antics. She couldn't imagine what had been the cause; acting like a hoodlum wasn't at all like her nephew. JJ had always gotten good grades at school and helped around the house. He behaved better than Teresa had when she was growing up, before the tragedies.

Jessie wanted to talk to Teresa about the notebook but didn't know if this was the best time to approach the subject. Thinking about the story Joe'd concocted made Jessie chuckle. Angela in the clouds and Marion yelling at him for years?—ironically, that part was something Marion would do. Jessie laughed a little louder.

"What's so funny, Auntie?" Teresa asked.

Jessie looked up and found both JJ and Teresa staring at her. "I was thinking about your dad and something he said."

Teresa, who had found Jessie's magazine collection and was flipping through the pages of an old issue of *Cosmopolitan* while sipping her coffee, put her face back in the magazine and muttered, "He had a story to tell, that's for sure." Then she smirked and rolled her eyes.

Jessie set her hand on the magazine to interrupt Teresa's reading. "What do you make of him becoming such good friends with that priest?" she asked.

Teresa looked up, a slight smile on her face. "At first I thought it was unusual. Now, I'm glad he had a friend."

"I think you should read the notebook. If not right away, maybe some other time." Jessie wished her niece were a little more open-minded. She realized the story was impossible, but it was also something like a fable with her brother as the hero. And that thought made her feel much better than Joe simply dying. At that point though the somber feeling took over once more, and she felt sorrowful over the reality of the situation. "It's all such heartbreak. Hey, what happened to that 'family' book?"

"Oh gosh, I think I left it in the backseat of my car." Teresa returned her eyes to the magazine and then calmly added. "Why don't you hang on to Joe's journal. Don't burn it just yet."

"Okay. Do you want a brief summary?" Jessie felt pleased that Teresa would consider reading her dad's story.

"No, not right now ..." Teresa's voice trailed off.

Jessie's thoughts traced back in time as the three of them sat quietly at the kitchen table. Years ago Jessie had promised Marion she'd take care of Teresa, and as a result she'd found herself spending most of her time with Teresa, like a mother would. When Teresa married and started a family of her own, for a while Jessie felt freed of the responsibility. A guilty freedom, but freedom nonetheless.

Then Teresa's marriage had failed, and Jessie felt accountable for that because she'd quietly celebrated her own liberty. In some ways the divorce was probably a greater hardship for Jessie the protector than it was for Teresa. The whole guilt/happiness thing was crazy, though, and unnecessary, because Teresa wasn't a high-maintenance individual.

Her niece knew how to take care of herself; she really didn't need Jessie for that. But the constant worry tugged at Jessie. Mostly because she was unable to prevent Teresa from having to go through more disappointments in her life. After all these years, Jessie still couldn't let go of the worry, and she still couldn't protect Teresa from the pain.

Teresa's cell phone rang. "It's the attorney," she said jumping up and answering the phone. Then she held the phone to her ear while she paced throughout the house.

Jessie and JJ watched Teresa move back and forth, into the living room then back through the kitchen, rarely saying a word other than an occasional, "okay" or "yes."

Teresa found a notepad in the kitchen drawer and began taking some type of dictation as a result of the conversation she was having with the attorney. And then the call ended with her closing remarks. "Okay, well, I'll see you at my father's funeral then." She paused and listened. "Okay, thank you, Steve."

Teresa put her phone away and moved with a deliberate calm to the table where JJ and Jessie were still seated. She then pulled out the chair next to JJ and sat down. "After the funeral we'll need to speak to the district attorney. JJ, the police are mad."

She put her hand to her chin and scanned the notes she'd made. Then she touched JJ's arm as she spoke. "Apparently they have reason to be angry. A false police report was filed by Murphy's mom, the parking lot was trashed, underage drinking and fighting went on—disorderly conduct. Not to mention the public demonstration without a permit."

Jessie interrupted. "So the car was Murphy's?"

"I knew it. I knew he did that." JJ's eyes took on an expression of resentment, and the paleness on his face became a pink color. "I can't stand that guy."

Teresa pursed her lips and ignored JJ's comment. "Yes, Auntie. The car was Murphy's." She then referred to her notes and continued. "JJ, your attorney is actually working a deal with the district attorney that entails community service."

"What? I didn't do anything," JJ whined.

"Oh, my son, but you did." Teresa lifted JJ's chin so that she could look into his eyes. "He said they talked to your friends and they actually have enough to press charges against you and maybe send you to a juvenile detention center."

JJ bit his lip while Teresa stared him down.

"They could take away all the computers in our house and really mess up your life, you know?" She let go of his chin and looked down at her notes.

"Your good grades and the principal's reference have led them to suggest no charges, no court date—straight to community service. Clean up with a road crew, one hundred hours minimum, and this will be monitored by the district attorney's office." Teresa's face was expressionless. She looked at Jessie and gave her the quiet sign while JJ hung down his head. The two women waited in silence for the boy to respond.

Several minutes passed and then JJ asked, "What about Seth?"

"Oh, all of you boys will be participating. Murphy may have other troubles because he was the cause of the false police report," Teresa said.

Jessie noticed her niece was amazingly calm during this whole serious discussion. She thought this was good considering what they'd all been through so far this week.

"Murphy is the cause of this whole thing," JJ charged.

Teresa frowned. "No, son—you are. Mr. Flashster ..."

Red outlined JJ's eyes, and his checks were now covered with splotches of pink. But he seemed to do a good job of hiding his anger when he spoke. "Okay, I get it," JJ whispered.

"We do have a meeting with the district attorney's office—after we get through the funeral. Steve, your attorney, assures me if you finish up their program properly no formal charges will be brought against you. I believe you can get out of this if you do what they say." Teresa raised her brows. "Okay?"

JJ nodded and spoke in a hushed voice. "Okay, Mom. Thank you."

"Oh, one other thing. The principal wants to talk to you. Your friends shared your 'flashster' status with both the police and the principal." Teresa rose up, pulled her notes off the pad of paper, folded the page, and then put it in her purse.

"Just remember, the principal got all of you boys out of trouble. You will do as he asks." Her tone of voice was stern as she scolded JJ.

The pink turned into bright red across JJ's cheeks. His jaw muscles flexed, and he appeared to be grinding his teeth. "Oh, no. I'm dead at school. Everyone's going to know," he said.

"Why would you say that? You don't know how they'll react," Teresa responded.

JJ appeared to be deep in thought, and then he asked, "Can I have my phone back? I can at least find out what I'm up against at school tomorrow."

"Let me think about it," Teresa answered.

Jessie was glad the matter was almost resolved. She took another bite of cake and commented, "I can't stop eating this," with her mouth still full.

Teresa stood up and exhaled. She smiled as she put her hand on Jessie's shoulder. "Auntie, we're going to go home for a while. I've got some work to do and JJ has homework."

"Now that you're not in hiding." Jessie chuckled.

Teresa laughed. "It was touch and go for a while there."

Jessie was proud of how Teresa had handled her son's situation, and she seemed to be in a decent frame of mind over her father's demise. JJ, on the other hand, was not having a good day. He pouted his way to the front door dragging his backpack behind him and continued slowly down the sidewalk—in the rain—with his shoulders slumped.

Jessie laughed to herself. He'd get through this fine. She heard Teresa comment about the sprinkles and then she told JJ to step it up or move out of her way—she didn't want to get wet.

CHAPTER 28

JOE HESITATED OUTSIDE THE CAFE. HE didn't know which way to go. He moved to the left, then spun around and decided to go toward his right, which was when he almost ran into Angel.

"Have you been with me this whole time?" asked an elated Joe.

Angel's frown turned into a smile. "You can see me, Dad?" she wanted to know.

"Yes, where in the heck did you come from, and where have you been?" Joe was grateful to find his daughter here. He'd been worried about how this would play out, and now, for the time being, anyway, he felt some much needed relief from worry over his youngest daughter's plight.

"Finally. I've been following you." Her eyes sparkled. "I remember it all now, Dad."

Not yet, he thought. She was going to leave him again. Joe'd been warned by Marion that once Angela really knew exactly who she was, that'd be the time she'd be leaving—but it would happen before his job with Teresa was complete. And the confusing part about the communication from Marion was her claim that

Angela's departure was imperative to Teresa's own ability to move forward in her life. He didn't get that.

"I'm happy for you, baby. It's time for you to go to Mom now." Joe wiped his eyes, and then made a face—no tears, again, please.

He inhaled and quickly smiled at his young daughter, both happy for her and sad to be losing her now at the same time. "I'll take care of Teresa and your girls. You're late by several years—it's time."

He bent over to eye level and held her cheeks between his hands memorizing her face. Angel's eyes conveyed a stubbornness she'd sometimes shown even as a tiny baby. "I'm not leaving you here, Daddy."

"Oh, no. That's what happened last time. I won't let you get stuck again. You're going," he insisted.

Angel frowned. "I can't leave you here."

Marion told him this would happen, and she told him she'd help him when the time came. *Where are you, Marion?* Joe thought.

"Some things are out of our control." Joe blinked back tears that he refused to let fall. He'd thought he'd have less emotion on this side, but it seemed as if the floodgates were open, and he was being affected tenfold.

"Well, I don't know how to go." Angel spoke in a soft tone.

"I know, but it's going to happen soon." Joe hated the idea of losing his daughter again. He let go of Angel's cheeks. His daughter must have been there listening.

"Did you hear what that man, Flavio, said about your accident?" Joe asked.

"Much more than that, Dad. I had a flashback, and he was right," she said.

"All that anger I had ..."

273

"Dad, would it have changed anything if you'd known about it then?"

He wiped his hands on his pants and stood up straight. His heart pounded in his ears. "How can this be?" he whispered.

"What?" Angel asked.

"I can hear my heart beating. I can feel it."

"It's only a memory. Your heart's not beating." Angel's smile seemed to fade.

"I don't think anything would've changed the course of my life. Whatever we went through was supposed to happen the way it did. That's something I didn't know until now." Joe leaned against the wall and let his back slide down until he was in a sitting position.

"What about free will and all?" she asked.

"Some things are supposed to happen, Angel." Joe let out a sigh, and then he stood up and put his hand out toward his daughter, gesturing for her to follow him. "Come on, let's go."

"Where are we going?" She walked on after him.

"I've got a feeling we need to head out of here and find your mom." Joe turned and waited for Angel to catch up.

"Where is she?" his daughter asked. "Do you know where Mom is?"

Joe had no idea where to begin, but he didn't want to share his uncertainty with his daughter because he knew they'd somehow find Marion. Panic from Angel wouldn't help.

"Teresa's, that's where we'll find Marion. But first, I have to get word to someone on where to find the General. I can't leave his body out there to rot." Funny, he thought, how the dead had so many leftover jobs to handle.

"How are you going to do that?" Angel asked.

"I thought you'd know how I could get through to the world of the living," Joe said.

"We can try and borrow someone's body. It's not fun, though, and it can feel crowded inside."

"Crowded?" Joe asked. He was at a loss, trying to understand.

"I did this thing last night, with Teresa. I tried to get into her dreams and I ended up in her body. It's confining and difficult to stay inside. I wasn't alone in her body—her soul kept trying to push me out." She paused and thought. "Either that, or it was hugging me."

"How does it work?" he asked her.

"I think the body needs to be relaxed and then on some level willing."

He'd known a lot of relaxed drunks in his day—guys who wouldn't kick him out perhaps. "Okay, we're going down to the Row and we'll find somebody there."

Joe and Angel found their way to a street near Skid Row. The guy Joe targeted was sleeping in an alley with a yellow tarp over his body.

"Do souls leave their bodies early?" Joe asked, hesitant about sharing a body with another man's soul, and wishing they could simply find an empty body—or some other way to get this done.

"I think so." Angel nodded toward the breathing lump under the tarp. "But he's alive. Put your head into his head and take a peek before you enter."

Joe leaned down and within a second he felt as if he was being sucked into the body. And then he somehow found himself in a standing position with the tarp wrapped around his shoulders. His legs felt wobbly, and as quickly as he stood, he fell back down. The world spun around him. It'd been a while since Joe had taken a drink, but this was a feeling he recognized immediately. He pushed the body up against the building. Gasping for air, he braced himself as he stood up again.

Rain landed on the tarp over his head while cold air blew under it. The body he'd borrowed smelled like a month without a bath. He couldn't see Angel but supposed she'd follow. Although she'd tried to describe the confinement of being in a human body, he only really understood it now that he was fully restrained within the encasement of this well-weathered flesh.

Joe flipped off his right shoe and found a five-dollar bill in there. He scooped that up and put it in his pocket, where he found a quarter. He began moving one step at a time and not easily when he saw Ralph up at the corner.

"Hey, Ralph. I need some food. Can you help me?" An unrecognizable croaky voice came from his throat.

Ralph stopped for a second and looked down the street. Joe raised the five-dollar bill from his pocket. "I'll pay you, man."

"Why didn't you say so?" Ralph approached with a smile on his face. He grabbed the five-dollar bill from Joe and stuffed it in a hidden pocket in his waistband. "Do I know you?"

"Name's Sam. I need some help to the church kitchen." Joe struggled for air. This guy's lungs seemed worse than those in the body Joe had left behind. He dropped the tarp and placed his foot out to approach Ralph.

"It seems as if you do." Ralph scooped up Sam's left arm, "Bring that tarp. It's going to rain harder."

"I don't need the damn thing." Joe marveled at the croaky old sound leaving his mouth. He really had to concentrate on both moving the body and speaking—he almost felt like a puppet master.

"Bring it. You won't regret it," Ralph insisted.

"Okay, then when I'm done with it, you can have it for being so kind to me." Joe had tried to put a nice tone in the timber of the old guy's voice. The sound just came out more slowly—the harsh quality remained the same.

"Okay, I'm going to hold you to that."

Ralph was strong. He gripped the left arm and carried Sam most of the way. At the end of the block, they stopped at a pay phone Joe knew was near the area where the General had slept and died in the trash bin. Joe dialed the morgue and resisted telling Dotty who he really was, but insisted she call Father Benjamin.

"You know the father?" Ralph asked after he listened to every word Joe said into the phone.

"No, but the General did," Joe answered.

"And the General's dead?"

"Yes, he is. And so is Juan. He died this morning in the hospital. Nobody knows it yet."

"Damn, I made it longer than both of those guys?" Ralph's face scrunched up and he turned his head with a sniffle. Either the old guy's body smelled so bad Ralph couldn't stand it, or he was hiding his tears—being the tough guy he thought he was.

The walk to the church kitchen went quickly enough, and Joe realized he probably didn't need to do much more. Tell Ralph, and the world would soon know. But for selfish reasons, he wanted a last look at the kitchen and some of the folks he'd dealt with these last few years.

The witch woman he'd met up with years ago, the woman who'd told him he was haunted, was in line today. He thought this was unusual because he hadn't seen her since that time, and she looked almost the same. Her face was a face he'd never forget.

Father Benjamin came out of the kitchen and spoke to Ralph, while Joe kept his head down. Of course he didn't expect his friend would recognize him, but still—running into the priest was something he hadn't expected, and something he wasn't ready to face. Joe told Ralph he'd save his place in line, and he tried to avoid looking up at the father, but for some reason their eyes happened to meet. Joe hoped Father Benjamin wouldn't suspect something was up, yet why would he, really? The idea of this body being Joe was too farfetched.

Within minutes, the whole line of homeless folks was talking about Joe and the General. Joe couldn't see the point of sticking around. He had to go back and find Angel, anyway. He dropped his tarp so Ralph could have it later on and moved quickly down the line with his head held down, thinking nobody would notice him. But the witch woman's bony hand grabbed Joe's arm as he attempted to pass her, and with a strength he'd never thought she could muster, she spun him around and winked at him.

"Get out of here. I'll find you in a few minutes," the old woman whispered.

"Marion?" he said.

She pushed him behind her as the priest began to make his way down the line. "Go on. Wait for me there."

He moved hurriedly away from the folks in line, taking one quick peek back. The old woman looked inebriated and not at all like Marion. Had Marion stepped into someone else's body? How could it be, after all these years, that the old woman looked exactly the same?

Joe hustled into the alley around the block where he sat right down. The physical body he'd commandeered was in truly bad shape. He pushed down on the legs, and with a loud pop vacated the tight-fitting shell—which fell flat against the wall and back into its previous state of sleep. Joe looked around for Angel and panicked when he couldn't find her.

"I'm right here," she yelled from the edge of the alley.

Then he panicked again when he saw the world wrinkle slightly right beside her. "It's rippling again," he said as he sped to Angel's side in fear that something in the other dimension beyond that wavy curtain would suck her in and she'd be gone forever.

"What ..." Angel spun around and pointed. "There, I see it too."

Both Angel and Joe remained rooted to the spot at the end of the alley, transfixed by the point in the air near Angel's head that had previously melted. They waited in silence for another movement. When after several minutes of focused staring resulted in no similar occurrence, Joe let out a long exhalation of air he'd been somehow holding in his lungs. He wiggled his arms and legs, stretched his neck, turned his body, and then gave his attention to his youngest daughter.

"We're still here," he said, knowing that ripple had something to do with the next phase of their existence—or at least his daughter's coming stage.

Angel touched her stomach. "I feel lighted stars winking inside of me. This whole thing is so beyond my understanding."

Joe smiled at his little girl. "Did you see that old woman back there?" he asked. He wondered whether to mention the woman might possibly be her mother, in fact.

"I saw it all." Angel nodded while her eyes scanned the surrounding area.

"Have you seen that ripple before?" Joe wanted to know. "I was waiting for the light and somehow I think I got that part wrong."

"No, I've never seen a ripple before. But, Dad, I don't think there is a wrong." Angel reached out and put her hand in her dad's. Strangely, to him, her hand felt warm.

As he strolled with his daughter Joe felt out of breath and sore. He assumed he was still experiencing symptoms he'd picked up from the body he'd commandeered. And, indeed, gradually his being began to feel better, as if it'd healed itself in a much faster form than his physical frame ever could have.

Joe walked absentmindedly along the sidewalk and spoke to his daughter. "I've got to check on Teresa before I leave. It's okay for you to go with your mom, Angela. I'll follow you soon, I promise you."

"I'm not ready to leave you here yet." Angel stopped, crossed her arms, and stomped her feet. Her pupils dilated, she hesitated, and then she spoke. "I'm scared, that's all."

"Okay, okay. We might have some more time," Joe responded. Then he put his hand on Angel's back, as if he could touch her, and led her further along the sidewalk. After they moved slowly down the street for a while, Angel appeared to have relaxed.

"What did it feel like to be in that body?" she asked.

"It was cramped like you said." Joe experienced the viselike grip around his head as if it were happening again, and a slight tremor traveled through him. "Leaving that small space was sickening. And that loud popping noise—my ears had the physical reaction of ringing."

"Once you've been like me for this long, smelling and touching are really good things to enjoy, but the tightness was too much for me, too."

"Trust me, smelling wasn't such a good thing a few minutes ago." Joe laughed.

As quickly as the words came out of his mouth, it occurred to Joe this was a most unusual circumstance. His daughter appeared to be the same age as when she'd died, yet she'd matured in ways he couldn't fathom or explain. And now and then he'd get a glimpse of the child she had been before. How was any of this possible?

"Let's find your sister." Joe blinked and he was standing on the sidewalk in front of Teresa's home. *This can't be real*, he thought to himself. He turned as Angela appeared at his side, and it was in that instant he knew it was her time to leave, and he could handle it. He would see her again. He believed he would.

"This is her house, Dad," Angel said. "I always wanted to talk to her and never knew why I kept coming back to this place when she didn't respond. I'd have thought she would've sensed she wasn't alone."

Angel paused for a moment and seemed to be searching for the right words. "In my flashback I saw Teresa as an entirely different person. She was carefree, fun, and full of life. The woman who lives in this house isn't that way at all."

Joe thought about his wife's insistence that Teresa needed his help. He supposed his oldest daughter had more than withdrawn over the years and Marion was right about that fact. But he wasn't certain about what to do next, or if he could make an impact from his current state.

Joe remembered his older daughter during their family's "golden years." "She was outgoing, and definitely ready to take on the world. But I tend to agree with Jessie on this one thing— Teresa's had a good life, despite all she went through. I can't control how she handled the cards she was dealt. We all have choices, right?" Joe stood at his youngest daughter's side looking at Teresa's home and imagining the life she'd made for herself.

"Well, yes, but didn't you say you were going to help her?" Angel gave him a sideways glance.

"I'll do what I can, but in the end the choice is ultimately hers, just as your life is yours. Doesn't that make sense?" He wanted Angel's approval more than anything though he was at a loss as to what he could do for Teresa at this point in her life. How could he help anyone who wasn't willing to help herself?

"I'm not sure what you're getting at, Dad. Sort of sounds like a cop out." Angel furrowed her brow.

Joe stood in front of Angela and carefully chose his words. All the while, he used the softest tone he could find and drew upon some inner strength he didn't realize he had. "I know you've been out here for years, for decades. Angel, my sweet Angel, you're not responsible for anyone but yourself. Teresa is going to be okay. Right now, it finally is your time to continue on."

A quick flash of movement drew Joe's eyes to a spot about a foot over Angel's right shoulder and down the sidewalk a few yards. Angel's head turned to follow his gaze, and she left his grip. If he squinted and focused on the ripple, he could see the outline of another place right within reach.

Marion had told him that the vibration on the other side was faster, like that of a fan. If he could train his eye to grab the outline, he might have a glimpse into her world, she'd said. "It's all right here in front of you."

And now that the other world *was* right here in front of him, finally he understood what Marion meant. Angel moved to the area he'd been looking at, the largest wavelet he'd seen since his dying experience had begun.

Half of Angel's body seemed to be entering the soft tear in the sky. Joe heard her speak into the space. "Mom? Wait ..."

Angel turned back toward her father. "I should've left here the first time Mom tried to get me. I've got to go now, or I might ..."

Angel was gone, and Joe wasn't able to comprehend how it'd transpired, because it happened so fast. Then the ripple flattened out, and all appeared to be ordinary again, except for in the next moment when he heard the echo of his youngest daughter's giggle. The laughter seemed far away, but he believed she was close, really close. And he hoped that soon he'd be joining them there, wherever *there* was.

CHAPTER 29

TERESA AND JJ HAD BEEN HOME a few hours—JJ in his room studying and Teresa in the kitchen working on her laptop—when she heard the muffled laugh of a girl that seemed to come from JJ's room.

Teresa shut her computer and sighed deeply. Her son's behavior went beyond disappointing. The boy seemed to have no boundaries these days. She stood up and contemplated her feet as she walked across the house placing one foot ahead of the other, quickly moving to JJ's room. There, she pushed the door ajar without knocking to find JJ at his desk with his history book open and a highlighter in his hand. He'd been studying and looked up from his book, his expression one of shock at the sudden intrusion.

"What's up, Mom? No knock?" JJ dropped the yellow pen on his book and shook his head.

"Did you hear that noise?" Teresa demanded. If he was taken by surprise at the moment, she was doubly so.

"What noise?" He raised his eyebrows.

"The girl, laughing." Teresa's insides were spinning like the washer in her laundry room. Though she realized it'd be a while before she could trust her son again, that probably wasn't a good reason to trample all over his privacy. She looked down at her hands and mumbled. "I'm sorry, I thought ..."

"You thought I had a girl in here?" JJ laughed. "You must think I'm really bad."

"No, seriously, did you hear anything?" Teresa asked.

"It was from the sidewalk or across the street in that direction. I heard it too." JJ pointed toward the front and then picked up his book and made a few noises with his mouth.

Teresa moved closer to her son. For whatever reason, the blood raced through her veins, and she thought maybe, just maybe, she understood what it felt like to be a cop and be inches away from a bust that fell short in the end. Though it wasn't as if she wanted to catch her son doing something wrong, she couldn't help but think he was up to something, now—and all the time.

"Is it someone you know?" she asked.

"I doubt it," he answered. And then he picked up his text book and feigned interest in what he was reading.

Teresa rolled her eyes and reached for her son's hand. "Come with me. Let's check outside."

JJ resisted slightly and then shrugged and stood up, dropping his yellow pen on his book once more. He pulled a sweatshirt over his head and waved for her to leave the room in front of him.

Outside, the rain had turned into a mist that cooled the air and left a clean feel to the afternoon. Teresa heard a dog bark and crickets chirp—everything seemed perfectly normal.

"I don't hear anything, or see anything," JJ said.

Teresa held her forefinger to her mouth and whispered. "Wait, be quiet and listen. I hear the faintest noise. I think I saw something, too."

She and JJ both looked up to the same area above and to the west. "Strange, it looked like the sky just melted on the other side of that bush. Did you see that?" JJ asked as he moved down the walkway and across the sidewalk to their neighbors' yard. "But close up, it all looks ordinary here."

Teresa followed JJ and stood next to him in front of her neighbors' house. "I saw something out of the corner of my eye and I heard something. Do you feel like someone's watching us? I know it sounds strange, but ..."

"No, I feel it, too," JJ said.

"Let's go back inside. I'm a little spooked."

The two moved slowly up the walk and into the house. JJ seemed to be on Teresa's heels as he shadowed her into the kitchen. His energy level had picked up and suddenly his mood seemed to improve.

"What do you think that was?" he asked.

"I don't know." Teresa busied herself in the kitchen.

Wiping her forehead with the back of her hand, she looked through the pantry and decided to make potatoes when she found a bag of them on the shelf. She put the bag on the counter and picked out a few good looking spuds. Water flowed down her hands as she rinsed the vegetables. Then she wiped her hands and found the peeler.

Peeling potatoes in the kitchen took Teresa's mind off of everything else. She concentrated on the outside of the vegetable and in time made the brown go away. After the fourth potato, she turned on the stove and one by one plopped the potatoes in the water.

"Mom, you're making potatoes?" JJ's face contorted with the question.

"Why not?" she answered.

And then unexpectedly, and for no reason, she felt lighter, almost carefree. Maybe her sense of relief came from partially resolving JJ's issue or from the closure of her father's death—but her head seemed clearer. Or perhaps her improved state was from something as a simple as the few minutes they'd just spent outside in the air. Whatever the cause, she hadn't felt this good in a long, long time.

JJ put his head down on the table. His hand rested on his soda can. His voice was muffled as he spoke, "I'm sorry, Mom. I should've told you about all of this."

Teresa sat near him at the table and touched her son's head. Her feelings of distrust from moments ago vanished as the mother in her emerged. "You know the word has gotten out at your school."

"I'm sure it has," he said. "I'll shut it down. No more flash mobs. Now that the mystery is gone, they won't want to go anyway."

"Are they really going to be mad at you?" she asked.

"Probably. Seth was the only one who knew. So I know he told on me." JJ lifted his head from the table.

"Oh, don't blame him. You put him in that position by telling him your secret," Teresa scolded.

"I guess." JJ took a sip of his soda.

They sat in the kitchen together for a while, each engrossed in personal thoughts, until the potatoes softened in the water. Teresa emptied the water and began mashing the potatoes. Her knuckles turned white as she pushed down and twisted the masher with a sense of contentment. She added a sprinkle of cheese, a lump of sour cream, and a slab of butter, her efforts entirely targeted on the potatoes. In a minute, she pulled a spoon out of the drawer, dipped it into the mixture and brought it up to her mouth. No. The potatoes needed salt and pepper and maybe some garlic.

Reaching up, Teresa dug through the cupboard and found the spices, then added these to the mixture. She put the results in two bowls, placed the food on the table, sat down next to JJ, and said, "Eat."

As she held the spoon up to her mouth, the phone interrupted her first warm bite.

"Why do we still have that land line anyway?" JJ asked.

"Because I'm an old-fashioned gal." Teresa dropped her spoon in the bowl and ran to pick up the phone.

"At least you opted for cordless, instead of rotary dial." JJ chuckled.

Teresa was shocked to find herself glad that Father Benjamin was calling. Her heart pounded a little. This man had been the closest human being to her father in the years before Joe's death— now she seemed to be connected to him in ways she'd never have imagined. And for some bizarre reason, the idea of her relationship to the priest warmed her heart.

She chuckled slightly as a picture of the Grinch entered her mind—at the specific scene where his heart grows four inches. And for some strange reason, she hoped that silly little message was from her mother—but then it struck her the movie was one of Angela's favorites.

"Did I catch you at a bad time?" the priest asked.

"Oh, no, Father, just more strangeness ..." Her voice trailed off.

"Yes, that's why I'm calling," he said. "Although it could be my imagination, or should I say the imagination of my friends from the street."

"What happened, Father?" A friendly compassionate voice was what she heard, and then she realized it was her own. Her heart expanded another inch or two.

"It was as if Juan was there for a moment and a strange woman ... Well, never mind," he replied.

"Do you believe in ghosts, Father?" Where did that come from?

"Yes, but this was different," Father Benjamin answered.

"How was it different?" She felt at ease staying on the phone with this man, but at the same time totally surprised at her own unusual behavior.

"We seemed to have had a Juan sighting, but not quite Juan. The person in question was an old, homeless guy, and I'm not sure how his appearing at the church was related to Juan. After this old guy disappeared, an unknown woman also indicated the man outside the kitchen had been Juan, and she ..." Father Benjamin stammered. "Well, she changed for a moment. It was like something from a Stephen King novel. Very unreal, but I saw it with my own eyes."

"How did she change?" Teresa asked.

"She went from appearing to be in a drunken state to being completely clear and sober. She transformed into a nice-looking, ordinary woman, in fact. Or maybe I just need a good night's sleep." The priest dismissed his story. "Anyway, I called to check on you and JJ."

Theresa held the phone closer to her ear. "Come to think of it, we had something odd happen tonight. We both heard laughter outside the house, but no one was there. It was weird. JJ saw something in the air that he couldn't explain. At the same time, it's all easily shrugged off. We certainly could have been imagining things."

"Did you hear your dad laugh?" inquired the priest.

"No. This was a young girl." Teresa let out a nervous chuckle.

"I'm not sure what that could be, but you're right. All these strange incidents can be easily dismissed, and usually are dismissed.

It's the reason I'm trying to pay close attention." He sounded quite sincere.

Teresa took a deep breath and thought about the loss this man had suffered. She needed a moment to go beyond the priestly collar and fully understand a person inside of that uniform was now in pain. Consciously, she put more of her nice tone on as she continued, "That's unusual for a priest to be so open-minded. Do you want to talk to JJ? He mentioned he was taking notes. He's really interested in these otherworldly happenings, if that's what they are."

Father Benjamin spoke in a quiet tone. "Teresa, you're being very kind right now. Thank you, but you really don't need to patronize me."

Yesterday she would've jumped all over the accusation; today she felt nothing but calm patience arise. "Oh, Father, I'm sorry. I'm not patronizing you. I really am just trying to be nice. And my son has an interest in this type of thing. What would you call it? Supernatural ..."

"I'd say it's more spiritual." The priest spoke in a hushed manner.

"Yes, that would make sense," Teresa said. Spiritual, of course—indications of the possibility of a life beyond this one would be of spiritual interest.

"Are you up for an early morning breakfast? And can you bring JJ?" the priest asked.

No, say no, she thought to herself as the opposite words flew out of her mouth. "Okay. Is there anything open at 6:00 a.m.?"

"Yes, the railroad car that was converted to a restaurant on First. Do you know the place? The best pancakes in town," Father Benjamin answered.

"Yes, yes. We'll be there." *Where are these words coming from,* Teresa whispered to herself.

"What? I didn't catch that last comment you made."

"Nothing, Father. We'll see you tomorrow." Teresa hung up the phone and went back into the kitchen. JJ had enjoyed his share of the potatoes. He sat at the table with an empty bowl and the soda can in his hand.

"What? We're meeting the priest sometime tomorrow?" JJ asked without waiting for her explanation.

"You heard." Teresa frowned. "It was like Tourette's syndrome. I had no control over the words that came out of my mouth. I hope you feel up to it."

"Oh, yeah. I think we have some things to talk about." JJ laughed as he spoke. "I'm not sure that the padre will want to hear it all, though."

"Why's that?" Teresa asked. She'd sat down at the table again and was eating the still-warm mashed potatoes with satisfaction.

"Well it's not exactly standard, Catholic protocol."

"What is Catholic protocol?" Since her son hadn't been brought up in the Catholic Church, she wondered why JJ thought he knew all about it.

"Aren't those guys real conservative? Like ghosts and spirits don't exist?" JJ asked.

"I'd think it'd be the opposite, because of all the angels, burning bushes, and parting seas in the Bible—a lot of miracles and strange happenings. You'd think the Church would be the most open to this type of thing. But in truth, you're right. They're worse than me." Teresa chuckled.

"Yeah, why is that, Mom? Why aren't you more open to things?" JJ asked.

Teresa sighed, and rubbed her hand across her face as she spoke. "I don't know. If I were a therapist, I'd probably say it's got something to do with my mother and sister dying, as well as my father leaving. I guess I'm a little disillusioned due to all the crap that's happened to me in my life. But, in my own defense, I'm trying."

JJ squinted as he took a sip of his soda. Then he stood up and deposited the can in the recycle bin. "You're right, Mom. You are trying. You let me jot this stuff down, and you sort of helped. Maybe you're loosening up. Do you think your father is watching us, now?"

"I don't know. I get a chill sometimes, like right now." Teresa reached out, grabbed JJ's arms, and squeezed. Laughter filled the kitchen.

"Okay, okay. You're messing with me. But I like it," JJ said.

Teresa felt she had seasoned the potatoes just right and had done pretty well with her son, too.

CHAPTER 30

FATHER BENJAMIN SELECTED A PAIR OF jeans and an old polo shirt for his meeting with Teresa and JJ. He hoped the street clothes would help Teresa relax. However, she seemed to be a different person on the phone last night. She seemed to have lightened up, leaving the priest cautiously optimistic.

He paused for a moment and whispered, "What am I doing?" The priest had been close to Juan; perhaps Marcus was simply wishing something unusual was going on. Dragging Juan's family into this probably wasn't okay, but the need to investigate spurred him on, regardless.

Was this feeling that an unusual event had occurred simply because he missed his friend, and he was indulging in some wishful thinking?

The priest arrived at the restaurant early and picked a quiet corner so they could talk. Teresa and JJ arrived shortly thereafter and scanned the cafe, sitting down in the lobby when they didn't recognize the priest. Father Benjamin raised his hand and waved them over, but the two of them remained seated where they were. The priest laughed and stood as he spoke, "Teresa, I'm over here."

He watched Teresa finally recognize him and tug JJ along through the dining area to the table he'd chosen. As they settled in to coffee—JJ having an iced tea—and ordered their breakfasts, JJ pulled out his spiral notebook.

"Father, I only recently started jotting things down. But I think we've had activity for years," JJ said in a professional manner.

"Activity?" the priest asked. He was certainly surprised to hear the word.

"Well, that's what they call it in on the show 'Paranormal.' I guess you don't watch that," JJ responded, tapping his pen on his notepad.

The priest chuckled, took a sip of his coffee, and ran his hand through his hair. His heart lifted a little at the sight of Juan's grandson diligently investigating the possible paranormal. "Have either of you read the journal that Juan wrote?" he asked.

"No, Father. My Aunt Jessie has it now. I told her to keep it because I thought I'd be tempted to throw it away," Teresa said.

Father Benjamin noticed that the tight lines which had previously held her eyes in a glare seemed to have vanished. Her whole face appeared much younger, less stressed.

"I haven't seen it either, but I'm interested to read what he wrote," the priest responded.

JJ held his notepad up. "In reviewing my notes, Father, the night before last, both my mother and I had unique experiences. I woke up with my head full of stories that I believe my Aunt Angela had shared with me. She'd told me, in my dreams, I think, a whole bunch of facts that didn't make it to the notebook before I forgot most of them. My mother ..." JJ interrupted what appeared to be his best attempt at a formal speech and turned to Teresa. "Why don't you tell him about the hand."

Teresa choked on her coffee, caught her breath after a moment, and with a softer look on her face began her own part of the story. "On the same night that JJ had his incident, I woke up and my fingers were wiggling in front of my face. I had absolutely no control over my entire arm. I thought I was dreaming, but my eyes were open. The slight breeze from the movement of my fingers must've woken me up. Within moments though, it felt as if a weight was lifted from my entire body, and my arm dropped. I had control of my limb again. I didn't panic. In fact, I rolled over and went back to sleep. I would've forgotten about it, actually, if JJ hadn't brought up his incident."

Father Benjamin wasn't sure what to make of their experiences. "Did you see anything?" he asked, hoping to get additional information.

"No, I didn't," JJ answered. "But something felt different. Like the air in my room was thicker than usual. And then last night, we heard the giggling. When we went outside, I saw this melting type texture in the air, probably about three feet up or so. It seemed as if the world had become one dimensional and melted together for a moment. And then it affected the area around the bushes, sidewalks, and grass. The world sort of melted outside of our house then quickly went back to the way it was. Like an optical illusion or something."

Father Benjamin thought about the unusual stories that many of his parishioners shared with him upon the deaths of their relatives. In all of his time spent near death he'd never heard of or witnessed anything similar to what JJ had just described. "Well, I certainly don't have an explanation for any of that."

"Why the street clothes, Father?" Teresa asked, out of the blue.

"I'm not sure. It felt right." Heat rose to the priest's cheeks as he blushed.

"What is it that prompted you to call me and ask to meet? I'm curious," Teresa went on.

"We told you about the General, right?" The priest waited for both JJ and Teresa to nod. "Well, someone called in his body's location to the morgue. He had climbed into a trash bin to get warm and died in the bin, which was emptied at the dump. He would've never been found had the call not been made."

"I don't get it," JJ said. "What's odd about that? It doesn't fit in my notebook, here."

"The caller told Dotty at the morgue to tell me. I suspect it had something to do with Juan, because at the kitchen last night there was a Juan sighting. And oddly enough the whole line knew about both Juan and the General." Admittedly he felt a little silly repeating this story as if it had significance, though he somehow suspected it did.

Their omelets appeared and the three waited a minute before continuing on with their conversation. "Couldn't that be gossip? I thought word of mouth was fast on the streets," Teresa said. She picked up her fork.

"Yes, we could dismiss all of it. But something about that old guy Sam and the elderly woman who claimed she saw Juan. I know it was some type of sign from him." Yes, that was what he felt—he felt that Juan had sent him a sign from the other side.

"Father, can you get into trouble here?" Teresa asked.

"What do you mean?" The priest didn't understand what she was getting at.

"I mean, doesn't the Church frown upon this alternative, advanced type of thinking?"

"Oh, I'm just having a conversation with Joe's family." The priest nodded, "No conflict here. And it's not rocking my faith at all, if that's where you're headed." Quite the contrary, in fact.

Teresa sipped her coffee and smiled at the priest.

Father Benjamin took a deep breath and then exhaled. He wondered about this sudden transformation of Joe's daughter. She appeared to be a different person, but for some reason he wasn't ready to completely let his guard down. "Teresa, you seem different. Did something happen?"

"What do you mean?" she asked with a slight smile on her face.

"Well ... You're more relaxed. I don't know, perhaps a lot more compassionate than the angry young woman I met with a day or so ago."

"Was that only a day or two ago?" Even Teresa's voice sounded less constricted with tension. "Anyway, I don't really know what could be different. I feel bad that you lost a good friend. I've also had to deal with this business of my son's initiating these flash mobs and being caught by the police. It's been a rough week. At some point I decided to quit fighting it and to let it be. I can't fight everything, including my feelings. I think I spent enough time in the angry stage, Father. After twenty years, it's about time for me to get over my old set of emotions."

She picked up her fork again and winked at the priest.

"That's amazing." The father stared at Teresa without comment. Only when the woman put her hair behind her ears did he realize she radiated a sense of calm, an atmosphere that hadn't been present yesterday or the day before—as if she were at peace.

"What?" Teresa caught the priest staring at her.

"It's like you're a completely different person." He was baffled by this sudden transformation.

"I do notice something's different. We ate mashed potatoes yesterday instead of green things and carrots," JJ said.

The priest and Teresa laughed together as they finished their meal, and the conversation turned to everyday concerns.

CHAPTER 31

Jessie was reading the morning newspaper and sipping her coffee when the doorbell interrupted her usual routine.

"I'm coming," she called and jogged from the kitchen to the front entrance with her housecoat floating around her skinny legs. Jessie pulled open the door to find a boy on her front porch holding a dog with a rope attached to its collar.

"Hello, Mrs. Torres," the boy said.

"Well, hello. Whom do I have the pleasure of meeting with this morning?" Jessie wondered what merited a visit from this child of about twelve.

"I'm visiting my Grandma Lucy, up the road. Remember me? I'm Carlos."

"Oh, my. How you've grown. How's your grandma?" Jessie thought the boy looked familiar, but she couldn't quite place him. Where did Lucy live?

"She's fine. Grandma Lucy is using a walker now, but she's still the same." The boy looked Jessie directly in the eye.

"Good. What can I do for you today, Carlos?" Jessie asked.

"I found this puppy wandering down the block. I've gone door to door, trying to find out where she lives." He lifted the little dog up toward Jessie.

"Awww. I see. Well she's not mine." Jessie stepped back from the door and was about to say good-bye when the boy interrupted her.

"Wait!" Carlos put his hand up to stop her. "My grandma sent me here."

"Oh. What's up?" Jessie stepped forward. "Does she need some help?"

"She needs you to keep this puppy. Gram said it was time you had some company and you'll thank her later." Carlos set the dog down and stood with his arms crossed while the dog sat with perfect posture and looked on expectantly.

"I'm sorry, young man, but I'm not a dog person," Jessie protested.

"Please. Grandma's allergic, and she said I can't keep the pup another night. I'll come by and walk her for you while I'm visiting my grandma. Please?" the boy begged. "I promise to help you."

"Did you call the pound?" The last thing Jessie needed was a dog.

"No, they don't keep them very long. They put them down. Why don't you keep her for the night, and then I'll find her another home first thing tomorrow." Carlos stepped down from the porch then went and pulled a wagon up the sidewalk.

A small pet bed and some dog food sat inside the wagon. "I've been calling her Bella and Bell for short, but you can make something else up if you like. She won't be any trouble at all. Please?"

Jessie reached down and petted the small dog's shoulders. She'd read somewhere that dogs didn't like being patted on the head. "My brother's wife loved little dogs. He never let her have one when she was alive," she half-heartedly muttered to herself.

"As Gram would say, it's a sign." Carlos made a slight whistle sound with his teeth. Then he smiled at Jessie and pleaded some more with his eyes.

"How old are you, Carlos?" Jessie asked him.

"Gram says I'm beyond my years, but officially I'm thirteen this week."

"Well you are definitely wise beyond your age, young man." Jessie bent down on one knee to get another look at the small pooch. "I'll tell you what, you can leave her here. But, you've got to come back tomorrow afternoon to retrieve her. I've got a funeral to go to and I don't want this little gal tearing up the house."

"Oh, she won't tear up the house. I promise." Carlos smiled as he bent down and spoke to the dog. "Okay, Bell, this is Mrs. Torres. She's nice and she'll take care of you. I'll see you tomorrow."

"She's so quiet. Does she bark much?" Jessie asked.

Carlos ran down the sidewalk pulling his red wagon, "Only when the doorbell rings. I'll see you tomorrow, Mrs. Torres."

Jessie moved the pet bed, food, and little Bell into the house, putting the dog bed into the kitchen where she could keep an eye on the pretty little cream-colored creature. Within minutes, the puppy became Jessie's new shadow, moving about the house along with the human. When the pup needed to go outside, she stood by the door and barked just once. She seemed to be a perfect pooch.

"Oh my, Marion would've loved you," Jessie whispered.

Jessie thought for a moment about Joe's notebook. Suddenly, she remembered Angel's dogs. Was it a coincidence that Bell seemed so similar to the little girl dog, Belle, in that notebook of her brother's? Was Carlos even a real kid?

Now she was honestly thinking crazy. Oh, no, that kid couldn't have been her brother. That boy was real and so was the dog food and the bed.

Jessie began rifling through her kitchen drawers looking for a phone book. She needed to find this Grandma Lucy and validate that Lucy's grandson was visiting her as he claimed, and that somehow Joe wasn't playing games from his grave.

Bell stood at Jessie's feet, watching every move Jessie made. "Good doggy …" Jessie realized she'd been talking to the pup since she'd taken her in.

Finding the white pages, Jessie began flipping through the directory, only to be reminded that the entire book was sorted by last name. Who was Lucy?

The Internet. She could try an address search of her entire block and find out her neighbors' names. But this was a job for JJ, in fact. Was the boy back in school yet? Jessie dialed Teresa's cell phone, which Teresa answered on the first ring.

"You must be psychic, Auntie. We're going to stop by on our way to JJ's school." Teresa didn't even say hello.

"Well, hello, my niece," Jessie said.

"Oh, sorry. Hello, Aunt Jessie."

"Okay, get over here. I need your help."

"Wow, from polite to demanding. What's up?"

"I'll show you when you get here." Jessie hung up the phone and spoke to the puppy. "Come on, Bell, let's check the computer." She was already getting attached to the dog. That boy knew what he was doing, leaving Bell with Jessie.

Jessie held Bell in her lap and powered up the computer. The pup fit like a glove with her head tucked down, settling in perfectly and fitting under the desk just right.

"Oh, my, Joe. What'd you do, here?" Jessie spoke to herself as she stroked the puppy's back. She began her search of her own address to see if her neighbors would follow. "Darn." She soon grew frustrated with her search; this was definitely a job for her JJ.

"All right, Bell, let's get a fresh cup of coffee and wait for the family. You're going to like them when you meet them ..." Jessie's voice trailed off, and she shook her head. What was she doing talking to this dog?

Jessie waited for her niece in the kitchen with her cup of coffee while Bell made herself at home in her bed near the table. "Strange days, indeed," Jessie whispered.

Shortly after the two of them had found their comfortable positions in the kitchen, the doorbell rang, eliciting a firestorm of barking from that little dog. Jessie wasn't used to the racket that Bell created with her yapping and dancing around in excited circles. "Shhhhh," Jessie whispered in an attempt to quiet the cute little thing. "For such a small dog, you've got a big mouth."

Jessie opened the front door with the barking pet in her arm. "What's this?" Teresa asked, evidently surprised.

"I know. It's a bit shocking, isn't it?" Jessie responded. Then she smiled.

JJ and Teresa settled at the kitchen table with fresh cups of coffee and listened intently to the story of Carlos and the puppy's arrival.

"I don't remember anybody named Lucy on this block, Auntie. Do you?" Teresa asked.

"No. That's what I was trying to search for on my computer. JJ, can you go to my computer room and find the names of my neighbors?" Jessie asked.

"Yes, give me a few minutes. I can find it." JJ stood with his overly sweetened coffee in hand. He licked his lips, and spoke as he walked into the computer room, "This is the best coffee ever, Aunt Jessie."

"It's the percolator that your mother will one day pass down to you and your wife," Jessie yelled toward the computer room, and winked at Teresa.

"All right Aunt Jessie, what's up? Why did you send him out of the room?" Teresa spoke in a low voice.

"I've got to tell you, something strange is happening." Jessie felt perspiration pop out on her forehead.

"Since that seems to be JJ's thing these days, we should call him back in."

"No, I really need to know about who this Carlos kid is." Jessie put her hand on Teresa's wrist and continued, "Okay, this notebook that your father wrote is quite the tale. Within its pages is a crazy story about your sister and these little pups. The description and name are so similar to this tiny dog that I'm perplexed."

"What do you mean?" Teresa asked.

"I'm not so sure now that his story is made up. I thought he'd concocted the world's worse excuse for his absence over the years. Now, I think he just wanted us to know, and it's that simple." Jessie realized she'd been squeezing Teresa's wrist. "Oh, sorry," she said as she let go of her niece's arm.

"Okay, so tell me about it. Because we had breakfast with the priest and he claims he's seen some odd things, too. I think he's having a hard time with it—he came to breakfast in ordinary street clothes." Teresa twisted her mouth, looking confounded.

"He got you to go to breakfast with him? How'd he do that?" Jessie was herself somewhat stunned.

"I know—that's another thing that's really strange. I agreed. Father Benjamin asked, and I said yes." Teresa laughed.

"Come to think of it, you look good this morning, Tia." Jessie fastened her eyes on Teresa and examined her carefully. "Less stressed, almost happy. You look as though the whole world has been lifted off your shoulders, overnight."

"I feel better, somehow, some way. It's unexplainable." Teresa put her hand up to her chest.

"Well it's been a long time since I've seen you this relaxed." Jessie thought about the years of waiting, the unknown whereabouts of her brother. The toll this had put on Teresa's life was enormous.

"Where's the notebook, Auntie?" Teresa asked.

"Will you read it?" Jessie thought this was the best thing that could happen now.

"Yes, because now I'm curious." Teresa rifled through her purse.

Jessie watched her niece pull out a tube of lipstick and then layer some on without a mirror. The woman seemed better than all right; she seemed cured.

Although Jessie couldn't quite put her finger on what Teresa was cured of, Jessie did know one thing for sure—she really liked this version of her niece.

With a relaxed look on her face, Teresa dropped the lipstick into her bag and continued. "I feel ... better. Better than I've felt in a long time."

Teresa paused for a moment and ran her finger around the rim of her coffee cup. "I can't tell you why the change of heart, but I can tell you my heart isn't as heavy as it was. I kind of feel like the air around me is a whole lot lighter—almost weightless."

Jessie crossed her hands and lifted her head so as to make eye contact with Teresa. "Okay, then you might be ready for my theory."

"Your theory?" Teresa asked. She looked surprised.

"Yes, my theory." Jessie sipped at her coffee, before calmly placing her cup on the table. She took her time before speaking again—really thinking through the best way to explain her theory. "Well ..." Jessie swallowed, and then much to her chagrin, the words simply flew out of her mouth. "I believe that somehow your father, or Marion, sent this pup to me. You'll understand this better once you read Joe's journal."

Jessie then rose from the table and went to the cupboard where she'd stored the remainder of the spice cake from the day before. She placed the cake on the table along with three plates, a knife, and some forks. "Have a bite of cake while I go and get the notebook," Jessie said. She patted Teresa's back on her way out of the kitchen.

She'd placed the notebook on her nightstand the night before. Now, she smiled as she took up her brother's journal and leafed through a page or two. Would Teresa and JJ think it was all bunk? And if they did, would they later reconsider?

When she returned to the kitchen, JJ and Teresa were eating cake and looking at a piece of paper.

"This is weird, Aunt Jessie," JJ said.

"What?" Jessie asked as she handed Teresa her father's notebook.

"Well, a woman named Lucille Hutchinson owned your house years ago. This is the only thing close to a Lucy I can find on your block with the Internet search." JJ held the paper out to Jessie.

"That's got to be just a coincidence," Teresa said.

"Yes, it must be a coincidence," Jessie agreed. "This person is someone who's alive and in the neighborhood." Jessie dismissed the piece of paper from JJ and went on, "Believe me, this kid was very much alive and breathing. Maybe the house we're looking for is owned by Lucy's husband—whose name we don't know."

Bell sat in her bed near the kitchen table. She licked her paws, wiped her face with them, and acted as if she belonged right where she was. "Are you going to keep her?" Teresa asked.

Jessie walked over to the puppy and bent over. Bell licked her hand as Jessie picked her up and sat back down at the table with the dog on her lap. "I already feel that she's been here forever. Such a mystery as to where she came from though. That boy, Carlos, said he'd be back by tomorrow."

"Oh come on now. You don't believe he's coming back over, do you, Auntie?" asked Teresa with a smirk.

"Classic," JJ said. "If he does come back, you'll never give that thing up." He pointed at the dog.

"Quit pointing—that's rude." Jessie put her hand on Bell's back and gave the dog a reassuring squeeze. She got up with the puppy, walked over to the dog bed, and placed Bell gently back in the bed. She really didn't understand what had come over her and why she was so protective of this little animal.

"Oh, Auntie you're a goner. That dog is staying here." Teresa laughed.

I am a goner, she thought to herself.

JJ stood up. "Yep, I think so, too." He then turned toward his mother and said, "It's time for me to go to school." He yawned. "This early stuff is for the birds."

"Okay, look who's in charge now," Teresa told Jessie. "But I'm listening to him, and taking his orders."

JJ then shoved a large bite of the cake into his mouth, grabbed his backpack, and waved his mother toward the front door.

"Why is this one so anxious to get to school?" Jessie asked.

"Yeah, why are you? With all the ruckus over the 'flashster' I'd think you'd want to avoid school altogether. And by the way, I'm not so sure that's a good title for a guy to have. It sounds kind of like ... Oh, never mind," Teresa said.

"Yeah, I know how it sounds. But what can I do? Anyway, getting to school at the last minute will help. I can avoid the jocks, and that's the group I'm worried about." JJ walked around his mother and stood at the front door.

After looking at her watch, Teresa jumped up as if shocked at how late it was. "Oh, God. We have to go, Auntie. Bye ... Move it." Teresa got to the door and pushed JJ in front of her while Jessie rose swiftly to follow them out.

"Oh sure, now you're in a hurry," JJ mumbled.

Jessie waved from the porch as her niece's car backed out of the driveway. Once they had vanished from sight, she turned her attention toward her new housemate.

What shall I do about this little doggy? she wondered.

"What do I do about you?" she asked out loud. "You know, that boy isn't coming back. I don't know who he was, but we're never going to see him again, are we?" As if on cue, Bell barked twice in agreement.

Maybe it was Jessie's frame of mind, or perhaps it was the change in Teresa, or possibly the mannerly demeanor of little Bell—whatever the reason, Jessie decided she was keeping the dog. And retaining the name Bell. The entire sequence of events was too much of a coincidence for Jessie not to surrender to the inevitable. And if this puppy really did take care of Angela for all these years, then it was up to Jessie to see to it that the dog had a loving home.

"You're crazy," she mumbled to herself, shaking her head. "No way this happened how Joe explained it in his notebook. It's impossible."

Bell then circled around Jessie's legs and let out a few barks to communicate her own feelings on the subject.

"Okay, okay. You're home," Jessie said. She'd go to the Internet later and read up on puppy care.

CHAPTER 32

JOE LET HIS YOUNGEST DAUGHTER GO. Then he thought about it for a moment as he stood in the space she'd just vacated. Teresa and JJ came outside, probably to find out where the laughter had come from. Looking at Teresa's face at this moment, Joe knew that his wife had been absolutely right and that Angela's leaving the place she'd been stuck in for so many years was the best thing that could have happened to Teresa.

Suddenly, Teresa appeared lighthearted, relaxed, and almost cheerful. All the pressure of the world seemed to have been lifted from her being, and she was herself again—or at least how she'd been as a teenager. Even the color around her body—her "aura" he guessed people called it— had gone from a dark shade of red to a pleasant violet hue. Angel's presence had literally been weighing her sister down.

Joe watched his remaining family members for a while and then decided it was time to make his own exit if he could figure out how. After understanding the consequences for Teresa of Angel's remaining nearby, Joe had no intention of hanging around and becoming a hidden burden for his daughter. Of course, burden, probably wasn't the best word to use in referring to Angela. Or maybe the whole thing—Angela's being stuck near Teresa, as well as the weight on Teresa—could've been tied to the accident; he didn't know for sure. But he did know that Angel's leaving had affected Teresa in a way he'd never imagined—and it was wonderful.

Joe thought about the cloud, and within nanoseconds he was in the cloud with the two dogs. "Can you understand me?" he asked as he sat carefully on the fluffy lip of the thing. Both pups barked and barked.

"I take that as a yes," Joe said. "Well, I can't understand you."

What now? That was the question.

And no sooner had he wondered what he should do next than laughter from above the cloud interrupted his thoughts. The sound seemed to fill the air and with such glee that he couldn't help but grin in response. He recognized the racket as coming from Angel, though soon, her uncontrollable giggles trailed off. Yet he could still hear some muffled chuckling coming through. Oh, he was relieved at how happy she sounded.

"Angela?" Joe asked.

Out of the corner of his eye, Joe saw the sky ripple in that same way as before. When he turned his head the very air melted together like a piece of plastic left accidentally on top of the stove, and for a moment he thought his vision had blurred. He shook his head and noticed an actual rip in the sky. Shaped like a tent opening, the tear measured about two feet vertically. A substance dripped from the flap that looped down inside the atmosphere. Joe's heart fell to his toes in sudden excitement as Angel's giggles suddenly grew louder, and then a light fell upon the cloud he was on.

"Really, now, with the light?" Joe yelled toward the opening with a snicker.

"Get them all, Mama." His daughter's voice echoed through the slit in the sky.

Joe scooted his body as far back into the cloud as he could go. He was afraid of being taken directly "home" with Marion and Angel. He felt as if he had one more thing to attend to and hoped he'd be able to vacate this limbo state shortly after he finished. However, he wasn't exactly sure how he'd go about saying his final good-byes to those he'd leave behind, for now. His movement stretched the cloud, which caused pieces of the soft substance to fall away. The girls began to bark and circle around the top part of the cloud, meaning what, he didn't know. Kail jumped onto Joe's lap, licked his hand, and leaped into the hole in the sky. Belle jumped into Joe's arms, barked twice and she was gone at the moment the cloud fell away. White pieces blew by Joe while he fell at earth speed to the ground. He didn't know if Belle had made it, the bottom fell out so quickly.

At some level, however, he understood both of the girls were gone, and somehow Marion controlled the whole thing. He gave up on trying to comprehend any of it. As Father Benjamin used to say, "Sometimes you just gotta have a little faith."

After his free fall through the air, Joe landed hard, stomach-side down. His mouth hit the ground and filled with grass. *How can I feel this ...* He sat up, spat the grass out of his mouth, brushed off his face, and wiped his hands on his pants. Taking a quick look at his surroundings, he realized he'd landed in a cemetery, directly behind a crowd of people at a graveside burial.

"Oh my, this is a huge gathering, and I seem to be talking a lot to myself. Maybe I'm hoping somebody will answer. God, I don't know how Angela did this for so many years." Joe shook his head and focused on the assembled people. The folks toward the back of the group were dressed in homeless gear, and as Joe got closer, he heard Father Benjamin's voice.

My funeral ... It's my funeral. Of course, he thought.

Despite the reality of his situation, Joe couldn't help but smile at what he saw. After only a few days, he missed the people in his life. A chance to see them all again in one place put him in high spirits, at least until the gravity of the event hit him.

Maybe Teresa and JJ were attending his services. He hoped so. It would've been nice to have spent more time with them before his death. He moved easily through the crowd, totally unseen, and searched the closer graveside seats typically reserved for the family. He could hear Father Benjamin's voice quite clearly now. The priest appeared to be quoting verses from the Bible.

Joe's spiritual side wasn't so much in tune with Bible verses. He wondered why Father Benjamin would've chosen such a formal message, unless of course Jessie had insisted.

The memory of tears filled Joe's eyes as he saw his daughter, grandson, and sister in folding chairs nearest the grave. He brushed his hand across his dry cheek looking for wetness as he sniffled—all actions remembered from being in the flesh, as Angela called it. Joe's heart overflowed at the sight of his family in the front row. Jessie sat tall and proud, Teresa wiped tears from her eyes, and JJ held his mother's hand.

"Joe, they're going to be fine. They don't need you to hang around." His wife's voice seemed to come from everywhere.

"Marion? Where are you?" Joe spun around and searched the crowd.

"I'm over here," Marion said. "Where I belong."

Joe hadn't realized how much he missed the beautiful tone of Marion's voice, which resonated now from the area where his daughter sat.

Joe searched the crowd amassed behind the seated family. As if on cue, a Hollywood fade-in on the toothless woman gave a view of her standing directly behind Teresa. With her hands on

Teresa's shoulders, the crazy old woman from the homeless line—and from many years ago on the streets—suddenly morphed into Marion.

Joe laughed and said, "I only figured that out very recently."

"I know." Marion smiled. "I'm here to tell you Teresa's going to be okay. Your instincts are right."

"I've missed you, Marion. I really messed up," Joe said.

"Yes, you did, and so did I. My goodness, it's taken me quite some time to learn that all of this stuff we must go through is a part of the process." Marion shifted to appear at Joe's side. "We need to let them find their own way, Joe."

Marion then nodded toward the group of folks at the graveside. "Trust me on this—we can help in small ways where we're going, but remaining here is not okay. You and I don't belong here anymore."

Joe reached out to his wife and looped her arm through his. He examined her face and held back the tears that would never come.

"Marion, I love you. I'm sorry. It's been so long, but it seems like yesterday." Joe blinked as he spoke. "I can't put my finger on it, but something about you is different than it was."

"And you as well," Marion said. "Let's go home."

Joe and Marion walked hand in hand across the grass. "Peaceful, that's it. You're more peaceful."

"Mature. You're more mature." Her lips pursed, and she enfolded his arm. "I've been hoping you'd grow up. But I like that you're still full of enthusiasm, like a child at times. I'd say we've both grown, though in different ways."

"What about the pups? You sent them to Angela, didn't you?" Joe unwrapped his arm and grabbed his wife's hand.

"Oh yes. I was a little naive back then. I didn't know what to do about Angela. I'm still not sure if that was the best possible choice. It might've kept her more isolated, and as you've figured out—Angela's frustration and loneliness weighed Teresa down."

Joe had really missed the sideways glance and tilt of Marion's mouth when she spoke—he'd missed the familiarity and the comfort of her little mannerisms such as that. He stared at her with a grin across his face.

"What?" Marion said and waved a hand at him. "Stop it, please." She chuckled and carried on. "Anyhow, Jessie has been wonderful over the years. I arranged for Belle to stay with her for a while. She'll come home, though. They all eventually come home."

"I feel so good right now, Marion. My body was in really bad shape." Joe held on tighter to Marion's hand as they moved through the cemetery grounds. He worked hard at avoiding headstones, and then he noticed Marion walking right through them.

"Well, you've managed to do some good in the last few years," she said. "Quite a number of folks are waiting to spend time with you where we're going." Her forehead pulled tight and wrinkled together as she frowned. "You know, all the baggage doesn't go away with the crossover. It's sad sometimes. Oh gosh, that's why suicide isn't the answer to most of our problems. Joe, Juan, whatever you want to be called ... your work will continue."

In addition to not knowing if this moment would ever come to occur, Joe had believed he'd fight this transition and insist upon staying with Teresa. And he also thought the wrath of Marion would devastate him. He was relieved and thrilled to be wrong on all accounts.

"Aren't you still mad at me?" he asked.

Marion raised her left eyebrow and gave him a one-sided glance. "Well, I was. But I worked that through. In your time, I'd say that was years ago, but in my time it feels like seconds. So don't push your luck." She winked.

After they'd distanced themselves from the crowd at Joe's funeral, Marion stopped walking and pointed toward a large oak tree directly in their path.

"It's beautiful," she said. "When we reach that spot under the tree, the sky to the right of us will appear to open. It'll almost melt and possibly tear, like the ripples you've been seeing. Then the light will come through and we'll move together to a place that will overwhelm you—in a good way." Her eyes seemed to look off into another realm and gradually a soft golden light outlined her being. She obviously no longer was in a physical body, but only a spiritual, energetic one.

She then turned to Joe and gazed at him. He responded to her with eye contact and it appeared to be what she was waiting for.

In a serious tone, she continued. "It's important, Joe, that you allow the transition period to take place. Rest and decompression time are necessary. I fought this process and had a difficult period. Thus creating a difficult time for you. I ask that you now learn from my mistake."

Joe smiled at his wife, and kissed her forehead. "I'm ready," he said. He was amazed at how quickly he'd agreed to go and how ready he truly felt.

The tension seemed to leave Marion as she took Joe's arm and her expression softened. She spoke now in a playful manner with a slight smile on her face. "I'm thinking we should leave a sign. Did you like the sound of Angela's laughter? Wasn't that a beautiful sign?"

Joe nodded, feeling another unreal tear in his eye; emotions seemed to engulf his being. He couldn't believe his own good luck. Marion, the love of his life, was walking and talking here with him. They were about to cross over together, to another dimension. His stomach, or the memory of it, fluttered with delight.

"Why don't we cause a little thunder? It appears the rain cleared so that couldn't be Mother Nature, could it? I'd like to give Father Benjamin something to think about," Marion said.

Her mischievous side was a part of her personality Joe had forgotten about. He chuckled to himself and then thought over everything that he'd undergone.

"I have a question. Were you around when I went through my own personal hell—the stinky pit?" he asked.

"All things in due time," Marion answered as she pointed toward the rip in the sky.

"Hold still," she added. "This'll be fun." And then she bumped Joe's hip with her own, and a loud thunderclap filled the air at the exact time Father Benjamin stated his final good-bye to his friend, Juan—also known as, Joe.

Joe laughed.

"Shhh ..." Marion whispered in his ear. She pulled him up to the opening in the sky.

"I can't help it. I liked the way you did that." Joe chuckled as he left the world he'd known for so long.

CHAPTER 33

"DID YOU HEAR THAT?" TERESA LEANED over and whispered directly in JJ's ear.

"Yes, the thunder?" JJ asked.

"I'm telling you, I think I heard my dad say something afterward. It was faint, but something was said." Teresa stood up as the service ended and the crowd moved slowly away from the graveside. Was she going crazy, hearing voices?

Father Benjamin must've overheard the conversation. He walked toward them with a serious look on his face and commented, "I heard it too. He laughed, I'd know his laughter anywhere."

"Like the girl outside of our house." JJ snapped his fingers.

Teresa nodded, and the group left it at that—an occurrence they acknowledged but didn't speak about any further. She knew that JJ would add it to his little book and probably obsess about the incident for a few months.

Teresa was shocked at her own reaction to all that had taken place. She actually was glad that her father had reentered her life, and then sad that he'd died so soon after that.

"Aunt Jessie, do you want to go to the gathering?" Teresa asked.

"Well, yes. I'm glad you thought of it. I didn't want to have to beg you again." Aunt Jessie smirked.

"I'm ready," Teresa said as she led her family behind the large procession of people. "I'm happy that he had a good turnout. I'm not so happy about the circumstances, but I think he's finally okay now." A significant piece inside her had shifted, for lack of a better term. Every ounce of her being now believed in something more after this life as people knew it—a thought she would not have contemplated a few days ago.

And now, with limited time left in this world, as they all had, she vowed to herself to make the best of what remained—here and now.

Teresa, JJ, Jessie, and Father Benjamin walked in silence across the grass toward the cars.

"Father, please ride with us in the limousine," Aunt Jessie suggested.

"I would be honored," the priest replied.

He then positioned himself inside the car directly facing Teresa. As the limo cruised through traffic, he spoke softly to her. "What are your plans now?"

"Plans?" she asked.

"Well, I can't help but see something has changed with you, Teresa. I'm not sure what it is, but it's certainly good."

"Thank you, Father. Thank you for everything. You've been more than patient with me. As you know, I've had some kind of metamorphosis. I can't pinpoint the details, but I realize as sad as this is, it was a good thing for me."

"What about the journal, the storage area? You know, the unanswered questions," Father Benjamin asked.

"My father had a wild imagination." Teresa smiled slightly and spoke with a sparkle in her eye. "You of all people should know that we don't always get answers to everything that happens in life. Sometimes, it is what it is and nothing more."

Teresa sat quietly for the remainder of the ride. She watched her son interact with the priest, and her Aunt Jessie become involved in their conversation. And she realized she would read the notebook and see the storage area in time. She didn't want to rush through remnants of her father and her past because she didn't want the mystery of rediscovering her history to be over too soon.

In her heart she realized that she'd still clean during times of distress and just to get away from it all, but right now her desire to clean was gone. She was here in the moment, and as heartbreaking as the death of her father was—she faced it and she was moving forward.

She might not ever completely understand what he'd been trying to tell them with his cockamamie story, and that was all right. For some reason she loved the fact that he'd gone to the trouble to concoct the tale, and besides, who was she to judge— maybe his story was even true.

Hmm ... she said to herself. *Maybe time will tell.*

About the Author

As a teenager, Roni Teson picked up the book, *Life After Life* by Raymond Moody. Fascinated with the topic of near-death experiences and our existence beyond the 'flesh,' Roni began a personal journey to find out more.

In addition to being well read on the subject of near death experiences and life after death, Roni has also spent many hours with people who have personally experienced dying and in some shape or form undergone a spiritual event. These people were everyday individuals who may not ordinarily be as connected to the spiritual world as the many mediums and spiritual healers Roni has also spent time with.

The original version of Heaven or Hell was started, and shelved a few years prior to its completion due to Roni Teson's career as an executive in the accounts receivable management industry. Divine intervention had a hand, however, when she was diagnosed with stage IV cancer and made the time, during her treatment, to complete the novel.

Over the period of her amazing recovery, Roni's own journey somewhat paralleled aspects of the lives of her characters. As she responded to the medication and was potentially beating cancer, everything else in her world imploded. She went through loss on almost every level of her life: health, career, long-term relationship, homes, cars, and pets.

Today, completely disease-free, Roni is living a life transformed. She makes her home in Southern California where she is currently writing a book about that transformation—*RUN*.

Visit Roni Teson at www.roniteson.com